This is a work of fiction.
Names, characters,
places, and incidents
either are the product of
the author's imagination
or are used fictitiously.
Any resemblance to
actual persons, living or
dead, events, or locales is
entirely coincidental.



First paperback edition

ISBN 978-1-7391855-0-3 (Amazon paperback)
ISBN 978-1-7391855-1-0  (Amazon ebook)
ISBN 978-1-7391855-2-7 (Ingramspark paperback)
ISBN 978-1-7391855-3-4 (Ingramspark ebook)

Twitter: @shayninho
Instagram: @shane.helium

Dedicated to Mum, Dad and Lorraine

# Once Upon a Human Sky

# Part 1

# Chapter 1 - Somewhere in South Aunn Teer

It's 3 a.m. Can't/won't sleep. It'll be getting bright soon. Dr. Akbar wants me to start writing a diary which could be a bit of a chore, but maybe good to document things and get the negative things out onto a page, I suppose.

It's the end of Rain-season, and yes, it's raining outside, heavily. I like the tingly sound of it sometimes, it helps calm me down a bit, but it's been non-stop for the last while. It's funny how you can be in the middle of a storm but be at your most calm sometimes. Greg and a few others love giving out about it though.

I haven't swallowed my tranquiliser medication from Nurse Kelly earlier; hence the insomnia. I copied a trick that I saw in a movie where you quickly flip the pill under your tongue, and then when she asks to see your tongue, it sticks between your bottom lip and under it. Me and my friend Simon have been doing it a bit the last few weeks. I don't like the side effects. Sometimes it's nice to feel less groggy and more creative; more alert, natural.
Obviously, the anxiety gets worse and I start hearing voices from animals, which I'm told isn't healthy, but it's never really anything negative; like, the odd random word.

There's this mouse actually who I say 'Hi' to when I skip

medication. I call him Mickey. I know, original. But he visits my room most nights, and tonight, with the rain, he was in the walls again.

He popped his head out between the bars of the air vent by the desk table leg. 'Hey, Mickey,' I said, in my usual gentle tone, so as not to frighten him; also, I didn't want to wake anyone or have a nurse call.

He said 'Hi' back, in a typically mousey way (in my head, of course) and scuttled along the skirting board.

I kept a piece of biscuit from the dinner hall earlier for him and laid it down below my bed. He's nice company at night, but if one of the nurses found out about our relationship I'd probably have my medication doubled.

I know it helps but sometimes I wonder if we could go without it, or at least try.

I suppose I should outline my story and the story of this place. I've been here for as long as I can remember; since I was three or four. Diagnosed with acute, chronic anxiety, PTSD, depression. Oh, and mild OCD.

I don't strongly remember when I first arrived, just that I was crying. My parents were abusive and died of drug overdoses. I don't remember much, if anything of them either, but all my doctors over the years have told me I'm better off without them. I suppose my subconscious memories of them are what affect my mental health.

I keep thinking I'm ugly, and I don't know why I keep a small mirror next to my bed – all I do is knock myself in it – but I can't seem to throw it away.

This place is my home, of sorts. There are about fifty patients here across the two floors. I'm based on the ground floor. Haven't seen much of upstairs in years. It's divided between the younger patients in one section and the more severe patients in another up there.
We've never been off grounds either because of the way things are out there.
We're safer and better off here in Pleasant Pines Wellness Centre.

The climate of the last forty or so years has left much of Aunn Teer uninhabitable. We get two to three months max of torrential rain, as I mentioned earlier, when there's some growth, but then drought for the rest of the year and everything dies. Most of the population have moved into the cities.
Also, because of the way things are, water and food are really scarce. There are daily murders in the cities - mainly by gangs who control the food and water - and also deal drugs. It's pretty bad out there.
I think, maybe, people want to drown their sorrows when the world is falling down around them. They want to just forget the struggle for a while. I've come to believe that that was the case with my parents. I try not to hold resentment towards them.
In many ways, we're lucky to be looked after and kept safe in here. We don't really have to worry too much about food, there's a staff garden out the back. And we probably

wouldn't survive out there with our illnesses, but in the last few years, and especially now that I'm nearly 18, I've had a curious urge to leave and explore some of the world, even if it's dangerous.
Of course, I know, once I got to the gate, I'd probably have a panic attack and turn back, but it's nice to dream.

Mickey has been exploring the left hand side of my room. He sniffed his way to my piece of biscuit.

I'm starting to wonder if I should take that pill now to help me sleep. Dr. Akbar or Nurse Shane 2 won't like to hear that 'Mickey the Mouse' and I were up until four chatting.
'Thanks,' I thought I heard him say, after he turned and ran off back to his air vent with the bit of biscuit.
Ok, I'm taking it. Better check my toes. Yep, all ten, all good.
My name's Bill. Just Bill. We tried Billy for a while but it didn't feel right. Or at least, we thought it was too 'frivolous'. The 'y' was exacerbating my mood instability.
We don't do second names here in Pleasant Pines. The staff say it brings back painful memories for some of us and it's best to look forward, not back. It's a bit awkward with the Shanes though.

Everyone here is diagnosed mentally unwell with abusive pasts as young children. We have TEMT: Traumatic Event Management Therapy. Some are orphans like me. Some were put here by their parents or guardians for different reasons. There are 25 of us on the ground floor. As I said, the world out there is dangerous nowadays. Not everyone can cope, and that includes parents, I guess. We also have art therapy once a month. Our therapist is Devendra. She's a bit mad. Her hair looks like a nest. But she's fun; always trying to make us be creative. Last week we did 'free-association finger painting'. She was 'concerned' about all the black and red Ed used. It was funny, really.

Seeing Dr. Akbar tomorrow before lunch. I still haven't told him about Mickey. It doesn't really worry me when I hear animals speak, but I get how it could seem weird, unhealthy even.

Feeling a bit sleepier now. Have to beat Simon tomorrow in chess. He'll be getting a second dessert off me again if I lose. I've been thinking of a strategy to beat him with though. I actually have a chance in chess, unlike foosball, which he is unnaturally good at. It's actually impossible to beat him in that. Like the ball sticks to his players or something.

Anyway, signing off.

# Chapter 2 - The Coffee Incident

I control the ball in the middle of the pitch, stopping it dead with my right foot as it's fizzed into me from my team mate in defence. The whole team move up the pitch in unison. I swivel nimbly, holding my opponent off with my back and a strong outstretched arm. There's an energy, a fluidity to our attack. The adrenaline of the occasion is keeping my heart and breath rate fast and in sync. I push the ball forward into the new space behind the defender and open my body out before passing the ball crisply out to the winger.

He jinks past the opposing full-back with a burst of acceleration before a deft chip into the box. The ball floats over the big captain defender's head as I run in between the goal's posts, looking to attack the cross for a goal.

I stop. The ball lofts up behind me, so I can't head it.

In a moment of improvisation and space in the box, I turn my back towards goal, and just as the ball arcs over my shoulder, I launch myself upward and backwards into the air.

I make a scissors motion, swinging my right foot as I'm falling horizontally, and lash the ball with the laces of my upside down boot into the top corner of the net, rifling it past the goal keeper's splayed arms.

My team and the crowd erupt into ecstatic cheers. The pitch is swarmed. 'BILL!' I hear someone cry out but the thronged celebration is so intense that I can't make out from whom the voice is calling.

'BILL!' Again I hear it coming from somewhere in the elation as I'm bustled back and forth.

'BILL, will you wake up! I know you're trying to catch up to the rest of us but beauty sleep is over, I'm afraid.'

It was a dream, as confirmed by the insistence of Shane 1, one of the three nurses on our floor.

'Breakfast is in 30 minutes, after medication from nurse Kelly, ok?'

'Mmn,' I mumbled back.

He left.

I was enjoying that dream, but it's slightly concerning too because it's a recurring one. I have this uneasiness that I can't put my finger on about it. It feels like it's about something unfulfilled. I mean, I do like soccer – we have sport night on TV every two weeks – but I was never going to be a professional player, so it can't be that literal. I should probably tell Dr. Akbar about it.

My alarm went off. 'The Day I Tried to Live' by the band Soundgarden. They were from way back in the 1990's. It's a cool song. The drums are lively and good for helping you to wake up. It's a bit pointless though if the Nurses just barge in anyway. I like to listen with earphones at night. It helps to stop me worrying about what Greg might be saying about me in the next room.

I hummed along while rubbing and blinking my eyes.

The medication I'm on helps me sleep and calms my anxiety, but your head feels like it has cinder blocks attached to it in the mornings. Which is why coffee is also so essential.

They only allow us two cups max and only up until twelve noon because it's a stimulant and affects mental health in high doses. It also causes insomnia if you drink it later in the day, which most of us could maybe do without.

I pulled myself upright and started to dress. I could hear Nurse Shane 1 finishing his wake-up call round further down the corridor.

Time for medication.

There are a few doors to the left of mine in the corridor and then a window looking onto trees. When you get to the end of the corridor at the opposite end to the window, you find the mess hall. This is where we all spend most of our days.

The medication queue usually starts from the corridor entrance and goes to the dispensary office window on the left, and today was no different.

I saw the usual suspects; Lorraine and Ed ahead of me in the queue, Nurse Kelly's dour face behind the window. Simon would arrive soon.

Ed was usually found with his headphones on around this time. Well, at most other times too.

'Hi, Bill,' he said rather loudly as he passed me after receiving his meds, the volume of his music clearly causing him to shout a bit.

'Hey, Ed,' I said back sleepily, lifting my head. An icy draught blew on my neck and I shivered. Nurse Shane 2 must be demanding windows be opened again.

''Morning, Bill,' Nurse Kelly said robotically as I reached the top of the queue.

'Morning,' I replied, at the same time, cocking my head back to swallow the three pills I was given.

'Thanks,' I added dutifully before turning toward the array of tables in the centre of the hall alongside the breakfast buffet (it's not as exciting as it sounds). Now the formalities were over, it was time to eat and chat.

I made my way over to the food after taking a plate from the stack and a cup of coffee.

'ASS-HEAD!'

It was Eugene, who has Tourette's syndrome. He was always particularly active on the shouting swear-words front with coffee on board and faced with the morning routine.

Simon appeared and wheeled himself into the queue as I stood indecisive at the usual breakfast items:

Very rubbery scrambled '*egg*'. Fungus sausages. Soggy toast. Beans and cereal. Plant-milk.

I decided to give Simon the thumbs up while I decided.

He's probably my best friend. We have great craic. He's always coming up with mad ideas, like when we built him a ramp in the garden, or the latest one, a plan to escape and explore the world like 'tourists'- what's left of it at least.

Apparently, years ago, loads of people used to go visiting different parts of the world every year, for enjoyment, and they were called 'tourists'.

Simon is paraplegic and uses a wheelchair. It never stopped him from being more adventurous and outgoing than most of us.

It *would* be cool to break out of here and be 'tourists', as mad as that sounds. Ten murders on average per day in the nearest city, along with drought, when the flooding stops, sandstorms, food scarcity, water piracy. Oh, and high cancer rates from the Sun. Not the most enticing, I know, but when you're cooped up for so long, you do get curious. Sometimes, maybe it's healthy to experience some bad things, like how a bit of dirt is supposed to be good for your immune system.

It was nearly eight. The news would be coming on soon and we'd no doubt be reminded of how safe and secure we were in here.

After finally deciding that I wanted beans, two fungus sausages and some of the very rubbery, very 'real' scrambled egg, I ambled over to the nearest table where Lorraine and Ed were sitting.

Lorraine was munching heartily on Maize Flakes.

She's mute. Hasn't ever spoken a word to any of us, but she tags along all the same. Although, Simon and I are convinced she did say 'Hi' to us a couple of times in the last few years; Dr. Akbar said it's impossible and in our heads.

Ed still had his headphones on as he pulled a piece of toast in half with his teeth. Listening to something melancholic, like The Smiths, no doubt, to match his mood. He loves them. Also this guy, Leonard Cohen. Sometimes I think he enjoys wallowing.

'What's up fellow looney-bins?' Simon chirped as he joined the table with a plate of breakfast.

''Morning, Si,' I replied. Ed forced a dough-cheeked grin in Simon's direction. Lorraine lifted her shoulders a little, with her eyebrows, and smiled without making eye-contact.

Simon has delusions. His main one being that the government has engineered the climate and food crisis across Aunn Teer, and that they are secretly controlling us all. Also, he believes himself to have telekinetic powers, that he can move stuff with his mind, basically.

I just see it as him being imaginative but obviously the doctors don't, and he has to take strong tranquilisers. Stronger than mine. I think he's on something for ADHD too.

Some days he gets down about having these sort of 'magical' thoughts, and Dr. Akbar doesn't let him forget how sick he is, but most days he's positive. He's the most positive of the four of us.

We all have our down days, and annoyingly, you get used to the staff's concern. Ed more than most, of course, with the down days.

I remember one day though, when Ed got really angry because Nurse Shane 2 kept nagging him to take off his headphones, and he lifted one of the big metal tables we're sitting on now over his head. Luckily nobody was hurt. But it was almost superhuman. We were finding fungus sausages in the plant pots weeks later.

He's been diagnosed with an intense emotional personality disorder and mild depression.

'So, since you're too scared to play me in foosball, will we stick to our usual wager in chess?' Simon asked me, talk-chewing a sausage. Lorraine smirked, looking up from her bowl of now mostly fake-milk. Filk.

'I'm actually feeling lucky today,' I said confidently in reply. 'How about we make it a week's worth of desserts?

'Ooh, I like those odds!' Simon responded with a coolly raised eyebrow. And so, the gauntlet was thrown down.

I got up and went to the end of the mess hall, past the foosball table to the game cupboard by the garden windows, and grabbed the chess board.

When I got back, Simon was leaning backwards with his hands clasped behind his head, looking intentionally confident, and calm as usual.

My new strategy would work though, I was certain.

Lorraine started reading a book and Ed was staring at the ceiling with his music on. The other tables were settling into their own post-breakfast activities. As we started setting up the pieces, big Kweeveen shuffled over to watch from the side. He has autism and struggles with words but still loves networking. He calls his friends 'sources'.

We started the game with our standard routine of moving certain pawns tentatively forward a few spaces. In his running commentary, Simon calls the pawns 'the working classes'.

After a few moves each, I went to my strategy and used my

Queen to take out some of his back line.

All of a sudden, he wasn't as slouched and started squinting, and said, 'What's this?' in a funny accent. But he was rattled. It was working. He rubbed his chin in thought.

'Come on, Simon,' I taunted, thinking I could win this and trying to increase the rattling. 'I'm growing old here!'

Then, strangely, as he concentrated harder, staring at the board, one of his Knights moved half a centimetre to the edge of its square. His hands were off the table, nowhere near the chess pieces. Had it moved on its own?

I rubbed my eyes and took a sip of coffee in disbelief, perhaps still dreaming, but then I realised the path that this Knight could take, which was into check-mate on my King.

I jerked up straight in my seat as his hand began to move towards the Knight,

'Wait!' I blurted, before he had the chance to move the piece.

'I want to change my last mo-'

Flailing my arms in panic, I knocked my half-empty coffee cup off the table to the floor.

Or, at least, I thought I did.

No sooner had the cup left the table top, it stopped in mid-air for a split second and then flew back into its spot next to the chess board, the brown coffee sloshing around in it.

Simon's gaze was now firmly fixed on it. But his hands, again, were nowhere near it.

'Did you…see that?' I asked, my eyes fixed on the cup too.

He nodded but said nothing. I looked down and saw some spilled coffee on the floor and blinked. Ed and Lorraine noticed our little panic.

We all glanced at each other and then over at nurse Kelly by the office.

Kweeveen pointed and said, 'm-m-m-mmmagic.'

I took the other's silence to mean that we'd forget about it for now and not mention it to anyone, but it definitely happened, I think. It *was* like magic. Can you have a group delusion? I suppose Dawhee and Nadine do.

'Will we call this game...stalemate?' I offered to Simon, breaking the silence.

Stuttering a bit and glancing at his palms, he said, 'Yeah...let's.

# Chapter 3 - Roll Call

8 A.M.

'Quiet everyone, please! It's time for the morning news. Please respect those who want to listen,' Nurse Kelly announced in the usual tinny, slightly muffled tone of the tannoy. Kweeveen had shuffled back to his favourite spot near the corner.

We all fell silent – not that we had said much since the incident, or had a choice. The familiar jingle of 'Aware FM' played and the deep, anonymous voice introduced,

"This is 100 to 1-0-3, Aware (Aware, Aware)...FM!" There was a drum roll in the dramatic music. "And now, for your morning news update, turning a close eye across Aunn Teer, here's news anchor, Thomas Dentridge."

"Good morning, I'm Thomas Dentridge…"

Ed still had his headphones on but was glancing at each of us intermittently. Simon was still slightly in shock and looking down at his palms every few seconds. Lorraine was sipping her coffee but also glancing over the table at me and Simon nervously, for an explanation that we didn't have.

None of us four are ever particularly fond of hearing the same harrowing news stories several times a day – once in the evening is enough, I think – but some, especially the older residents on our floor, take it very seriously. It's almost like they're addicted.

I think it might be something to do with our survival instinct gone obsessive; a bit like anxiety, I suppose, so maybe I shouldn't judge.

Greg is in his 50s, with depression, I think. He's the oldest on our floor. I don't think he likes me very much. He's always raving about how the news reminds him of how lucky we are to be protected and looked after here when the world is falling apart out there. The news seems almost like a religion to him.

I suppose he's right in some ways. We *are* well looked after, in the main, here.

Thomas Dentridge started the script in his loud, slightly monotone voice that he undulated at the start and end of every sentence.

"Two people have died today in Ember City following what is thought to be another gang killing." There were a few tuts from other tables.

"The couple, Mia and Eric Kromsky, were thought to have been apprehended and mercilessly killed while seeking bean and bread rations in the Dyad Gang's territory. The Dyad Gang control over 60% of the territory in Ember City." The odd head shook slowly upon hearing the news, but most just listened passively. It wasn't something we hadn't heard before, and what could we do about it from in here.

"In other news, fires and looting have broken out over night on the Main Central street of Tymblia City, in what is believed to have been a looting raid carried out by a group of Xantho-leaf addicts who sought items to barter with. The individuals are not believed to be gang members.

The drug, controlled in large part by the Remo Gang of the South-East of Aunn Teer, has been directly linked to over one million deaths in the past decade alone, either due to health side-effects or related criminal activity."

The news went on for another few minutes in a similar tone: The effects of the extreme weather, the gangs, and food or water rationing. Finally, Dentridge usually ended on a piece of positive news.

This time, he mentioned how scientists have confirmed that spending time each day next to a plant increases life span.

We have a few plants on each of the four window sills in the mess hall. I noticed Greg's gang at a table near one window acknowledging these and smiling and nodding to each other.

After the news on the radio, one of the Nurses flicks on the TV. 'C.O. News' plays where they have a more in depth run down of all the 'Aware FM' stories, plus a few more exclusives.

It can be interesting when they do good interviews with people on the city streets but a lot of it is just as grim as the radio.

But, as I said, some of the residents are addicted to it, and they're the same with the TV broadcasts, like their day revolves around it. It seems like they get a buzz from each update of that yellow banner that scrolls along the bottom of the screen; from the headlines, the developing story, the buzz words – I guess that's *why* they're called that.

The four of us try not to get too sucked in. We've enough worries caused by our illnesses to add more on top, but sometimes you can't help it.

Luckily, the news isn't on all the time. As I said, we have 'sport night', and old movies and music from before the start of the climate emergency get played between four and six twice a week and after seven before bed every day. A lot get repeated, but they're still fun. And we have the library.

Simon had calmed down a bit after zoning out for a while, enough to talk at least.
'What the hell was that?' he said, grinning nervously.
'What, the news?' I replied.
'No, ya dope, the thing with the coffee. Are we going collectively mad or what? Apart from the usual, like?'
'I dunno. Look, I'm sure it was just tiredness. We hadn't finished our coffee. Forget about it.' I tried to reassure him without confidence. It definitely wasn't something we would forget about in a hurry.
'Fancy a game of something on the Z-Cube before I go to Dr. Akbar?' I offered to Simon, to get his mind off any lingering worries about delusions and his own illness, that he might have had.
We had an old, retro video games console in the far corner of the mess hall that had a few games with it.
'Yeah, cool,' Simon answered, finally back in the moment.
Padder always sits next to it in a big armchair. He has narcolepsy, which means he can't help falling asleep at random times during the day and night. He also thinks he *is*

the armchair and tells anyone who will listen to sit on him when he's awake.

We were only allowed to play the Z-Cube for an hour at a time but it broke up the morning nicely some days.
We left Ed and Lorraine at the table and went over to the corner towards Kweeveen and Padder.
I get anxious walking past Greg and his gang's table; about what they might say about me. They never really do, I still think they might. But anyway, as we left, Ed's eyes shot up to us from his soft focus on the headphone music.
'Do you want another coffee, Bill?' he asked me, sort of shouting again. 'I'm getting another myself?'
'Yeah, actually I do, thanks.' I had only had a few sips left of my half-spilled cup from earlier.
By the time we got our game, 'Radical Kart Wars', up and running, Ed had returned from the silver coffee machine to give me my fresh cup.
'Thanks a million, Ed,' I said, taking my eyes off the screen for a second.
'No bother,' he replied, his headphones around his neck now. 'I'm going to
hang with Lorraine for a bit before we get called to the Docs.'
He turned and lifted his headphones back up over his ears as he trudged back to Lorraine at the table.
I took a sip of my new coffee but found that it was freezing cold. I nearly spit it out at the sensation.
I looked at the cup, bemused, and then over at Ed as he sat down again. It didn't seem like he was joking because he

didn't look back at me, and he wasn't really one for practical jokes. He was nice enough to get me it, so I decided I wouldn't bother saying anything and just drink a bit anyway. 'Weird,' I thought. Why didn't he mention that the machine might be broken?

I refocused on the game. Simon had now lapped me in our race and had also set me on fire. Kweeveen was wheezing with laughter from the sideline and Padder was asleep.

Dr. Akbar would poke his head out of his office soon to start the roll call of meetings.

We all visit his office for a check-up once a month.

Right as I thought it, a voice bellowed from over my shoulder, 'Morning all!' His head of dark hair caught the edge of my vision from his office door next to the dispensary office.

'Could…' he looked down at his clipboard. '*Lorraine* please pop into my office?'

Lorraine was first up. There was always a combination of relief and nervousness about visiting Dr. Akbar; relief because you could get things off your chest, but also nervousness at what he might impose to help.

I often wondered what he would be saying to Lorraine. I know she nods and smiles or shakes her head sometimes but he can't be doing much of a check-up with her. Handy in some ways for her.

She's never that long in with him of course.

I caught up a few places in the race with Simon but he was still miles ahead. I was waiting to shoot a rocket launcher at the next unwitting kart I got close to.

After several minutes, Dr. Akbar appeared again.
'Could Bill please come into me now?' he shouted, looking down at his clipboard as Lorraine squeezed past his big frame obstructing most of the doorway.

I stood up while still playing the video game with outstretched arms holding the controller and just in time to finish the race respectably in 5th place. Kweeveen clapped and Padder was snoring, almost in congratulation. He woke up for a second though and said, 'Tally-ho' before dropping off again.
'See you in a bit,' I said to Simon before dropping the controller on the chair and turning towards Dr. Akbar's office. He was already fixated on starting the next race, whether I was involved or not, and seemed fine now.
I wondered, as I marched to the office, whether I should mention anything about the weird coffee cup occurrence or just stay diplomatic.

# Chapter 4 - The Red Dot 

Dr. Akbar's office was familiar to me now after years of visits. He took over from Dr. Frick – who I miss – when I was 10. Things were less regimental back then, or at least, it feels that way.

The walls are dazzling white, never dirty and his dark oak desk sits in the middle about ten feet from the walls on either side.

He always has the blinds pulled closed and has the two fluorescent tube lights on at all times giving the room even more of a glare. He says it's because he doesn't like looking at the grey sky.

The only decoration he has on the walls is a black and white cat clock who's eyes and tail tick from side to side, and his degree. On the right, as you enter the office, is one shelving unit containing various medical books including, 'Delusions and How to Manage Them: A Practitioner's Guide' and 'The Roots of Hysteria' (I often imagine what might be in those books of his; people in strait-jackets screaming and the like, I guess), and next to that, a filing cabinet. That's it.

'Take a seat, Bill, please,' he instructed me, as normal.

As I sat down, his eyes flicked up from his clipboard notes about me and he gave me a quick scan over the rims of his glasses sitting halfway down his nose. 'So, Bill, how are you feeling?' he asked, his eyes back to being glued to the clipboard.

'I'm ok, Dr.,' I replied, trying to think of something interesting to say. 'I've been having some racing thoughts about the future, I supp-' He cut me off a little before I finished my sentence.

'No, Bill,' he started, a hint of frustration in his voice. 'I asked, "how are you *feeling?*" Remember we spoke before about differentiating between our thoughts and our feelings?'

'Oh yeah, sorry Dr., I suppose I was just starting off with a general overview of things?'

He said nothing for a few seconds, picking up the small, square timer clock from the window sill behind him and placing it to my left on the desk, in view of us both.

The tiny red light in the corner of the clock always bothered me, and there it was again. I never mentioned it though.

'Go on,' he said, still nudging the timer into the perfect position. I never found him to be the warmest of the staff, especially compared to old Dr. Frick, but he does usually give me good advice.

I continued my report.

'Well, I have been thinking a lot about what it would be like to spend a few days outside of Pleasant Pines,' I said quickly, and then, louder, 'and I haven't been sleeping too well.'

'Right,' he responded, sounding slightly concerned but also interested at last. He made a note. 'You know, racing thoughts, as you have described, especially about the future, are a symptom of your anxiety, Bill?'

I nodded even though it was a bit obvious.

'Try to be mindful when your thoughts start leading you curiously into anxious zones. You're an AC. An anxious and creative mind like yours is often trying to draw on anxiety because it's the path of least resistance when creativity isn't being employed constructively.'

My gaze dropped down to the desk-top for a few seconds in thought, but also for a break in eye-contact. I decided to be assertive.

'But what if I genuinely *am* curious about seeing the city, and they aren't just racing thoughts. I know I find groups of people challenging but I feel, since I'm going to be 18 soon, I would like to see a new environment.'

Dr. Akbar looked up at me again as I finished my mini-protest. 'I'm sorry, Bill, and watch the "feeling-thinking" again, but it's out of the question. You know this, everyone in Pleasant Pines knows it. You watch the news. It's too dangerous out there and your illness means you're too vulnerable to function in that environment.

You really have to watch who you speak to in the cities, all over Aunn Teer, really, and what you say, at the best of times.'

The reality of things dawned on me again as he spoke.

'Don't take the security of Pleasant Pines for granted, please,' he finished firmly.

There was a brief pause and another nod from me.

'Trust me, we have your best interests at heart here.'

He looked directly, unblinking at me.

My eyes dwindled on the red dot in the timer again, and for a second, I thought maybe I *should* ask him what it is, but again, decided not to. I didn't want to arouse concern about any more paranoia that would go in my file.

'What else had you said was wrong again?' he asked. I thought
for a second. There were more than a few things on my mind
now.
'Oh, my sleep has been off, Dr.,' I prompted, avoiding voicing
a bigger issue for now.
'Oh yes, ok. Well, we can certainly increase your night time
medication?'
Not really what I wanted to hear.

Dr. Akbar can be tricky to gauge. He does seem genuinely
interested mostly, but sometimes I get the sense that he might
just be ticking boxes or that he isn't always being totally
honest. I'd love to see what he writes down about me.
(Paranoia again?)

'I'm not sure I want to take more medication as the side effects
are bad enough already,' I said firmly.
'Ok...well, the journaling is important. And you can certainly
also exercise more during the day and practice meditation before
bed,' he offered. I nodded, still slightly unsatisfied and confused.
'Ok, I will try that.'
'Do you want me to explain how to meditate again?'
'No, it's fine, thanks.'

Another quiet pause. I was thinking of what had happened at
breakfast with Simon again. Was it a good idea to mention it?
'Is there something else, Bill?' He asked, analysing my body
language as I worked out what to do.
I decided to seek his view on it.
'Yes,' I said, hesitantly. 'Well, just earlier, at breakfast, Simon and

I were playing our usual game of chess.'

'Right, go on,' he encouraged, furiously taking notes again.

'And I knocked my cup of coffee. Except, I didn't…'

'I don't understand.'

'Well, the cup kind of stopped in mid air and hovered for a second before…floating back down onto the table.' I squinted a bit as I said it because it sounded bonkers saying it out loud. Dr. Akbar stopped writing as I finished and looked up, concerned again.

'Visual hallucinations aren't a common occurrence with anxiety disorders, Bill, as you know, but they're not unheard of. It may be part of your depressive symptoms. You did say you had racing thoughts too…'

I tried to interject but couldn't get a word in.

'We may need to put you on another anti-psychotic,' he continued, again intensely taking notes and ticking things.

'But we all saw it happen, Dr.,' I replied, now slightly regretting my decision to tell him.

He took a few seconds to respond.

'Have you been thinking a lot about your parents again, Bill?' He folded his hands on top of his clipboard as he asked me that. I started to feel a bit frustrated.

'No, I haven't,' I replied strongly.

'It may be that there is something causing you stress at the moment, subconsciously even. Is everything ok between you and your friend Simon? You do struggle socially.'

'Look, forget about it Dr., it was probably nothing, just tiredness due to my medication.'

I mentioned the medication side effects again and that I didn't want to have to take more.

It took another few minutes to convince Dr.Akbar that the coffee cup incident wasn't of concern any more to me, that it was off my chest now. He nodded and confirmed that I would keep an eye on it in my journaling.

Every couple of minutes, he checked the timer clock in front of us. He asked me a bit about any instances of anxiety I experienced over the last few weeks but quickly brought up the "outside" again.
'Bill, Aunn Teer is an extremely dangerous place now. There really isn't much worth seeing out there, unfortunately. There isn't any green any more due to the climate scorching the soils and finding food and water in the cities can cost you your life, as you know. Not to mention the various people trying to sell you Xantho-leaf or opiates.' His tone became more reassuring then. 'And that's for people in the full of their health, Bill. Your fears are still quite stubborn.

He was probably right. Maybe I *should* be thankful for what we have here, not take it for granted, that the staff are looking after us well and not to underestimate my condition.
I agreed that it would be pointless putting myself or my friends in needless danger in the likes of Ember City, remembering the news this morning and most other mornings.
'Your curiosity could be a degree of high mood also, Bill, as I touched on. That's why I asked had thoughts of your

parents, or anything, been causing you to feel low for any periods recently.'
I looked up from the desk to meet his gaze again.
'No, I haven't. I've been feeling pretty good actually, so that's why it's a bit weird.' He still looked a little unsatisfied. 'I'll keep an eye on it Dr. but happy to leave and forget it now.'
On that we both agreed.

He took another note and glanced again at the timer before putting his clipboard down.
'Let's leave it at that so, Bill,' he said decisively. 'Keep going with the diary, good to create space in the mind. I will ask you to read me something from it next time.'
I swallowed and stared at him in surprise for a second after he said that, thinking it a bit odd to have to tell him what I was writing in a diary. And I thought he said it would be private?
This *is* therapy I suppose, but I'd have to be careful not to read out any of the non-therapeutic bits.
'Eh...ok, Doc.'

He stood up while flicking onto the next page in the clipboard and ushered me to the door.
'Thanks...' I said, as he was already shouting over me for the next patient to come in, and I squeezed past.

# Chapter 5 - The Garden 

It was a relief of sorts to get my meeting with Dr.Akbar out
of the way. Sometimes he can just talk *at* you without much
empathy; according to a book, or something.

I marched over to the corner again where Simon was still
playing the Z-Cube. Ed and Lorraine had joined him on the
scattered surrounding chairs. Kweeveen was still standing to
the side. Lorraine watched the screen quietly while Ed tapped
a finger on his lap to his tunes, not paying much attention.
As I sat down with them, Nurse Shane 2 came bounding across
the mess hall towards us. Simon was distracted by the oncoming
arm-waving march and then realised the time. He raised his
hands quickly, with the controller in one and his other held up
in surrender.
'Sorry, Nurse, I lost track of time,' he said hurriedly, not wanting
to cause a freak-out. Kweeveen shuffled away from the scene.
'Come on, Simon, rules are rules. I want the four of ye out in
the garden after the next news bulletin, so turn that off.'
I noticed Lorraine roll her eyes up to heaven as Shane 2 was
giving out. Her expression made me think she said, 'oh, feck
off, we know' but obviously her lips remained closed.

After the Nurse finished his rant about rules, that the four of
us had heard before a lot more than others on our floor,
Simon looked at me and asked, 'Well, how did that go?'
I paused for a moment, unsure about whether to mention

that I asked Dr. Akbar about the coffee incident.

'It was grand,' I said, acting nonchalant. 'Ya know, the usual, asked me about my journalling, anxiety attacks...and mentioned increasing my meds to help with sleep, which I refused, kind of.'

'What is with them and increasing meds?!' Simon retorted 'They've already done it, what, twice in the last year?'

Ed just let out a tut and an 'ugh'. His headphones were hanging around his neck now.

'Did you tell him about your pet mouse Mickey who talks to you?' Simon asked, mouth half-smiling, half-agape.

'Eh, no,' I said, chuckling.

Sweeping the floor near us, Nurse Shane 1 butted in,
'Hey guys, sorry to interrupt. Hope the day's going ok for ye and the meetings with Dr.Akbar too. Just thought I'd let ye know, the news is coming on in...' he stopped to look at his watch while propping the sweeping brush against his stomach. 'Oh, about thirty seconds, ok?'

'Yeah. Thanks, Nurse Shane 1,' we all said at the same time, but also slightly separately.

It can be a bit odd, and annoying, how the Nurses are all so concerned about the news, especially when it only really changes once every three hours or so. I guess it's part of the nurturing way of thinking that they're supposed to have.

After the 'Aware FM' jingle played and Thomas Dentridge gave his usual self-introduction after the other introduction, he went on to say the exact same news bulletin as before, as expected. He added a few exciting words in parts to make it a bit different to the last hour, but it was more or less the same.

No one is allowed to move during the news, which is fine for the catatonics, but it's mental how Greg's gang and a few others enjoy it so much *every* time. It wouldn't be fair or easy to object though. Democracy and all that. And I'd be worried that Greg would use it as an excuse to gang up on me with the others.

'Prickball!' Eugene shouted from the other side of the hall as a politician spoke on the radio. Simon laughed but stopped when Shane 2 shot him a scowl.

Eugene's heckles lighten the mood with the news, and the staff can't do much but ignore him.

After we did our required listening, the four of us decided to go to the garden for a walk before we had another coffee.
The garden *was* nice, but going there also kept the Nurses happy.
The hardcore resident news fans stayed sitting around the TV with their second cups of coffee drinking in the news, but they would be prodded outside for a bit too at some point.
Us and a handful of others trickled outside.

The fresh air was nice. Ollie – who's my room-neighbour on the opposite side to Greg – remarked in his typically manic-Tuesday manner on the way out of the double-doors,

'Granddayforthebirdsbrilliantdayaltogetherforitlovelythingsthe
yareuptheretheskygranddayforthebirdsbirdsbirdies...birds'
'Yes, Ollie,' I answered. 'Good man, see you out there.'
He's particularly hyper and hard to understand on Tuesdays.

There are, of course, no birds around. Well, I haven't seen a bird
in the garden for years. Which is a bit sad. Ollie is convinced
they're around the place though.

The heat hit me as we walked further into the garden.
Rain-season was definitely over.
We walked along the path surrounding the two huge green
areas with shrubbery along it, in silence, for a while. Dawhee
and Nadine were throwing a ball to each other on the grass.
They never drop it. It's as if they know exactly how each
others' throws will fly. Kweeveen had found a new spot and
was standing near them now, watching like a fan again.
Simon refused our offering to push him. He was always
happier to do it himself, but we still asked sometimes.
On the outside of the paths are hundreds of yew trees side
by side along the walls.

After a few minutes of walking in silence, Simon decided to
break it,
'So, I *told* ye I had super-powers.'
We all burst into relieved laughter, after everything being a bit
serious over the last couple of hours. Well, Lorraine just
smiled and Ed let out more of an amused grumble, but the
tension was gone.
'Ah, shut up, Simon,' I said, finishing giggling, albeit still a bit

unsure given Dr. Akbar's response. 'We imagined it, or something'

'Really?' Simon replied. 'We collectively imagined it? You saw it, didn't you, Ed?'

Ed didn't look up from the path but said,

'Yup, certainly did.'

'Lorraine?' Simon continued. 'You saw it too, right?'

Lorraine looked at both me and Simon and shrugged, raising her palms upwards.

'See,' I said. 'Two against two. Inconclusive.'

'Ah, ye're no fun,' Simon concluded before pushing himself faster and further ahead of us along the path, his natural energy fully returned.

As we walked, with the wall of trees on our right, for a second, I thought I heard a low cry for help from behind one of the yew trees. I stopped for a moment to listen. The others carried on oblivious. Simon was still powering on, up further still.

The sound stopped, but I decided to investigate. I crept over to the nearest two trees – around where the sound had seemingly come from – and parted them with a small effort. I could feel my anxiety building a little but I wasn't sure why.

Behind the foliage was a tall chicken-wire fence, about seven or eight feet high, and that was a few inches in front of a slightly smaller grey wall.

No person in need of help to be seen, just the pipes for the irrigation system at the base of the wall.

Then, several feet to my left, a whispering sound and a rustling. The fence shook a little.
I let go of the trees I was holding apart and moved to the next pair, quickly parting them.
To my surprise, a small bird was caught at the top of the fence by its wing.
'Bill?' I heard Simon shout from up along the path. He had rejoined the others and all three were now stopped, looking back at me half in the bushes.
'Two minutes!' I replied, struggling to free the bird's wing and hold the trees apart at the same time.
I pulled the chicken-wire gently away from it while cupping its body with my other hand, and it was freed.
I opened my palm up towards the sky and it flew off out over the wall. The gang hurried towards me in surprise having glimpsed the departure. 'That was a bird!' Simon exclaimed, as they reached me at the trees.
I was about to congratulate him on his zoology skills but just as I opened my mouth, I heard what sounded like a faint 'thank you' from the piece of sky above the trees behind me.
I spun to look, but the bird was gone.
The three were now looking at me with raised eyebrows and possibly slight concern given the randomness.
'Yup,' I eventually replied after gathering myself. 'Haven't seen one since I was around 12 I'd say…'
We all stared at the top of the trees for a moment.
'It must be pretty dead out there,' Ed commented.

An oddly chilled breeze swept past us at that moment and Simon said, 'Let's go back in. It's...chilly out here all of a sudden.' He was still looking up at the tree tops, 'the Shanes will be wanting to do GT soon anyway.'

As we walked back to the main building on a connecting path, I looked back over my shoulder at the wall of trees again. I thought of the fence, and wall behind that - I had never seen them before - and the bird, and for a moment, my usual anxiety subsided a little. Instead, I felt a longing, and a bit of anger. We're all like trapped birds here, in a way.

We spent the rest of the hour inside, sipping our second coffees and talking about the bird; what species it might have been, of the ones we knew, and why we never really see them. Lorraine brought a book back from the library about animals and studied a page about bird species.
We concluded that it was possibly a robin and that the climate situation had killed off most of them. Everything dies in the drought, although we were still confused as to why birds didn't fly in here more often with the irrigation and trees for refuge.

The news played again on the hour. This time a new headline story had been included. Police had arrested four gang members shuttling twelve kilos of Xantho-leaf across Rua City after a gun-fight. One police officer was killed and two of the gang members.

The Aunn Teer police force is too thin. They're completely outnumbered and have little effect. It wouldn't surprise me if there were retaliation attacks on police in the next few hours.

As the news finished, with Thomas Dentridge describing how birth rates were up for the first time in five years, the two Shane Nurses walked into the centre of the mess hall and started their round up for GT.

'Right, everyone,' Nurse Shane 2 shouted, while Shane 1 arranged the seating into the normal circle. 'Take your seats and let's discuss your week!'

10:15 A.M.

# Chapter 6 - GT

After years of doing it, Group Therapy had become fairly boring most of the time. It used to be more interesting but we all tend to say the same things which I suppose is like in here in general; if we didn't, we'd probably be cured.

Sometimes, me or Simon exaggerate things just for a kick, or chime in with totally extreme suggestions for others in the group. One time, we suggested filling a wheelie-bin with holy-water and using it as a sensory deprivation tank, with the added bonus of being baptised.

Another time, after hearing one of Greg's gang, Patrick – a patient with a chronic fear of breakfast – speak for most of a meeting, Simon and I suggested that taking a bath of eggs might help, with a therapist present, of course, to talk him through it with CBT, even though we still didn't know exactly what CBT was.

Nurse Shane 2 was *not* happy with our contribution, but Patrick smiled about it actually.

Sometimes, you have to just laugh about things, if you can, because mostly we're supposed to be serious or sad about our issues.

Shane 2 usually led the interrogations, which today was the case again. Ollie was asked to speak first, about his week and anything on his mind. Unsurprisingly, he was eager to discuss the bird situation.

'Well, Nurse,' he said, and then took a big breath. 'I'mveryconcernedaboutthebirdsyellowbrownblueonesuptherei ntheskytherelove lydayforitwingsallovertheplaces,' he blurted, in almost one massive word.

Nurse Shane 2 made a note and, in his deadpan tone that only disappears when he's angry, said,

'Now, Ollie, you know that the bird population of Teer is at almost zero, like we discussed before?' 'Ohyesofcourserightyesofcoursenoworriesatallatall,' he replied in fast-motion again, nodding profusely, but also adding, 'lovelybirds' in at the end under his breath.

'Isn't that right, everyone? Due to the climate crisis, birds are as good as extinct?' Nurse Shane 2 asked the group in a typically patronising way.

A few grumbled in agreement. Eugene blurted, 'Smarmy hashbird!' The Nurse glanced at him and took a breath before returning to Ollie,

'And you're sticking to your medication as prescribed, Ollie, yes?' Ollie said he was with three rapid 'yes'es.

The interrogation continued for a few minutes despite not really going anywhere, Ollie having to be corrected another couple times about his belief in bird activity. Simon, Ed, Lorraine and I all exchanged nervous, surprised glances at the dialogue, given what had happened about forty five minutes ago in the garden.

'Seriously, Ollie,' the Nurse pressed. 'These birds you see, or hear, are part of your illness, ok?'

And it went around in circles like that until Nurse Shane 1 used a brief pause in Shane 2's directing and Ollie's babbling to change the topic.
'So, Edgar,' he said eagerly. 'How has *your* week been?'
Nurse Shane 2 looked slightly peeved at being interrupted in his therapeutic methods but took another breath instead of arguing and changed his sitting position.

The two Shanes jotted notes once again, this time with Ed as the header.

Ed's eyes were on the floor as he likes to do. He was slow to answer, which was particularly contrasted by him following Ollie.
'Em...ok, I suppose,' he answered glumly. 'Some days I feel kind of...heavy, but since the weather has brightened a bit, I've improved.'
Shane 1 replied without taking a note first and kept eye-contact with Ed's forehead.
'Well done, Ed. I know it's not the easiest to speak here, and especially if you don't have a lot of energy. And we know the weather drags you down a bit. Try to be mindful of NATs, ok? That goes for everyone; Negative Automatic Thoughts.'
Just as Ed went to reply, Nurse Shane 2 took charge again by interrupting. 'Edgar, how many times do I have to mention, remove the headphones during GT, whatever about general floor policy...'
Ed bolted upright at that and went a bit red while now intensely staring at Nurse Shane 2. He was gripping the plastic

sides of his chair by his thighs. The plastic even seemed to bend slightly under his grip.

'Now, Edgar,' the Nurse said calmly with his palm raised at Ed. 'Remember what we said before about your anger. Deep breaths, please.'

He breathed deeply in and out through his flared nostrils before muttering several expletives and then removing his headphones from around his neck.

Nurse Shane 1 changed the subject again, 'Does anyone have any comments or suggestions for Edgar on his feelings of heaviness?'

A few of us shuffled in our seats without saying anything. It was a bit of an awkward silence apart from Kweeveen belching in the corner, outside of our circle, but then Lauren, who was sitting next to Nurse Shane 2 cleared her throat,

'Ahem! Whaw 'boo ayxercise?'

Lauren has a condition where her accent changes every day, sometimes every few hours. It sounded like she was speaking in a Northern one today.

'Few roonds awf the garden. Dinna fash yersel,' she nodded at Ed.

'Thanks, Lauren,' Shane 1 added. 'Yes, good suggestion, exercise helps to get us focused on the body and out of our heads, as well as producing nice endorphins.'

Nurse Shane 2 changed the subject again, 'Lauren, is that a Northern accent you have today?'

'Aye,' she replied, nodding again.

'Does anyone have any insights on Lauren's problems with accents?'

Silence and shuffling again as the Nurses scribbled a new header. I never saw how it could be that much of a 'problem' but pretended to be thinking of an answer anyway.
Ed raised his hand a few inches off his lap and stuck up his index finger slightly. He had calmed down again.
'Yes, Edgar,' the Nurse acknowledged and took a note.
'Actually, I read that it could be to do with subconscious memories of previous lives.'
'Oh, like reincarnation or something,' Simon commented.
Ignoring Simon, Nurse Shane 2 looked at Ed for a second and blinked.
'No, Edgar, it's likely to do with a misfiring of neurons in the language part of her brain.'
He turned back to Lauren.
'I would recommend *thinking* in a neutral accent, and repeating several words in that accent in your head, Lauren.'
He turned back to Ed.
'Where did you read that, Edgar?'
'Em, it was in a book about philosophy and religion from the library,' he replied, eyes still on the floor.
Nurse Shane 2 turned to Nurse Shane 1 and whispered something.

The session went on for another twenty minutes, with two more of us speaking, Nurse Shane 2 interrupting any good advice that Shane 1 would start to mention.

Nurse Shane 1 announced at the end that Dr.Akbar would be seeing another lot of us over the next few hours.
Probably wanting to have the last words, Shane 2 then orated,

'Today's session has concerned me I must say.'

Lorraine rolled her eyes up to the sky.

'I may have to consider limiting privileges, as focus on treatment practice seems to have waned. Medication alteration might also be an option, with the Dr.'s approval.'

Most of the group collectively groaned and scoffed at this.

'Baxterd!' Eugene yelled, and then, 'Malpractice-actress!'

'We don't want an increase in medication, Nurse Shane 2,' I said in protest, a little surprised at myself that I had so impulsively, but I guess Eugene had encouraged me. 'The side effects don't agree with a lot of us, we'd prefer the minimum…please,' I added, backing down a little.

The majority nodded or mumbled 'yeah' or shuffled in their seat.

Kweeveen shuffled over just behind Patrick's seat and belched again. Patrick jumped a bit.

'S-s-s-saig affeckssss,' Kweeveen added.

Nurse Shane 2 looked around at the group before responding, 'Alright.'

A few of the others looked at me and then at the Nurse uncertainly, slightly surprised at his reciprocation. We settled again.

'I will agree not to recommend an increase in medication to Dr. Akbar, but starting tomorrow, I am restricting the use of the game console and it will be the news channels only on the television for the next two weeks.'

I sat back in my chair and the group agreed to the outcome somewhat reluctantly by mumbling 'ok's and shuffling again.

Not being allowed to watch a film in the evenings would be

no fun.

Simon and I looked at each other with concern but also slight relief that it could have been worse.

The chairs' steel legs ground against the hard mess hall floor as we moved them back to where they had been before GT. It had been such a weird start to the day.

The following few hours passed uneventfully, though Dr.Akbar continued calling patients. Lorraine and Ed played 'Laser Duke' on the Z-Cube while Simon and I watched, which was allowed, for an hour, until tomorrow at least. We ate lunch in the mess hall and the news played exactly on the hour again. Seven people had been taken hostage in the lower east side of Ember City over drug debt was the main story of the afternoon bulletin, along with further updates on the couple who were murdered.

Nurse Shane 2 finished his shift for the day at 2 p.m. and we all relaxed a bit more when he left. Within half an hour we managed to convince Shane 1 to let us watch a movie.
It was called 'Short Circuit'. A film from the 1980s about a deadly military robot who got electrocuted and then wanted to be everyone's friend and read books.
It was nice to get a break from the serious news and just watch a bit of escapism.

The residents who prefer the 'news fix' spent most of the

movie asleep in the armchairs. Padder woke up for half an hour at around 4:20 and wouldn't stop talking out loud to himself about 'space horse's hair' being 'good armchair material' and that it 'smells miraculous'.

For dinner, at 6, we moved next door, from the mess hall to, well, the dinner hall.
Seems a slightly pointless use of energies, I know, but the Doctor and Nurses say it's important to have a change of environment and to make the main meal of the day a bit more significant, especially for some of the patients who struggle with food, which is fair.

The walls in the dinner hall are a light purple colour and there's definitely a different atmosphere in there.

As the sky darkened outside in the windows, I started to think about Mickey and what he had gotten up to during the day. It's amazing how well he has done to survive around here for the year or so I've known him.

Mashed potato, peas and fungus sausages were served.

We eat *a lot* of vegetables and fungus here, from the staff garden and farm on the opposite side of the building to our garden. We're not allowed in there, but it's another reason why we should feel grateful and lucky to live here, I suppose. People are dying in the cities for food and water but the government, what's left of it, still provides funding for the Wellness Institutions like ours.

The sick and vulnerable are still looked after, at least. The general population, not so much.

# Chapter 7 - The Experiment 

After dinner, we can go back to the serving table and request a biscuit for dessert. Just one, as per the rules. I did, and tucked half of it into my white pants pocket for my mousey friend.

The four of us spent the couple of hours after dinner casually (others less casually) watching the news and chatting. Simon brought up the weird incidents from earlier again, in the hour before Nurse Kelly's bed-time call. It felt like forever ago since they had happened.

'So, we saw proof today that life still exists out there, and evidence that I have super-powers,' he checked off on his fingers. 'Anything else? What shall we do with this information?'

Lorraine looked over at me and shook her head slightly, as if to say, 'don't humour him.'

I decided to test the subject and disprove it before Simon got any more carried away. Although, a part of me was a little hopeful that maybe he did have some kind of hidden power, some magic.

'Show me again so,' I said, with the same confidence I had had before chess that morning.

I put a plastic cup of water I had on a small table in front of our chairs for the experiment, and made sure our backs covered the set-up from the Nurse sitting at the other end of the hall by the office.

'Move it,' I said, looking Simon in the eye with the challenge.

'O...K.' he replied, becoming hesitant again.

He hovered his hand over the cup, squinting down at it. Nothing.
We all sat in silence, hunched slightly over the cup. Was this a bit mad? It was, wasn't it?
Simon clenched his jaw and his shoulders trembled a bit with the second effort, his open palm five or six inches above the cup.
The water rippled.
'Right, everyone, time to start gathering yourselves for bed,' Nurse Kelly announced abruptly from the middle of the hall.
The four of us jumped.

She noticed and chuckled, 'Don't be so jumpy. Dr.Akbar has left the building, remember? All going well, he won't be back for a month. Only us Nurses here now. We're not so bad, are we?'
We all responded politely with unnatural chuckles at Nurse Kelly's joke. She hadn't seen the experiment at least. We quickly looked back down at the cup as the Nurse continued tidying.
Still as a statue. Inconclusive. Maybe the Dr. and Nurses were right about us needing increases in meds.
This 'experiment' was a bit crazy, really. Simon had just started saying 'but' to us, when Nurse Kelly shouted again, 'Come on. Form a line at the kiosk for medication, please.'
Everyone shuffled over to the window, behind which Nurse Kelly now sat arranging the little paper receptacles.

I wasn't going to give up that easily though. I winked at Simon on our way over to the queue, in acknowledgement of the ripples we *might* have seen in the water, but also about the intention to do our skipping-meds trick.
Something told me we needed to keep experimenting.

With our yellow and red night pill under our tongues, we split ways at the corridor to the bedrooms, making the thumb-and-pinky-up wobbly sign that surfers do at each other, even though we've never surfed in our lives, and I doubt anyone has for forty or fifty years now. We saw it in a movie. Tubular!

# Chapter 8 - Rendezvous 

Calm and silence, after the click of my bedroom door. It's nice to get back to my room after a long day. Today was particularly long and plain odd though.

I do find groups of people and formal meetings, like with Dr.Akbar, difficult due to my illness. There are always niggling little worries and a self-critical commentary going on in my head.

Even though we're all patients and have a mutual understanding to some extent, there are still social hoops you have to jump through and triggers for me in groups.

I get on better in one to one interactions. It's partly why I'm so close with Simon.

But we've always clicked.

Slipping off my white canvas shoes and the rest of my clothes down to my underwear, I pulled the bed clothes back and climbed in. I popped the pill out from under my tongue and placed it under the white light of my lamp. I left out a sigh as I settled.

No sign of Mickey yet, but he wouldn't be along for another few minutes; most likely, he needed to pick up my scent (or the biscuit's) first.

I reached over to the nightstand on my left and took my headphones from inside the little compartment in it.

I think I mentioned it before, we have a small library off the mess hall here, with books and CDs. It's great. All stuff from

the end of the 1900s to the early 2000s. And the nurses give us little MP3 players to transfer the music onto.
The Beetles, Nirvana and Prince would be some of my favourites. After the early 2000s I think music got worse.
Or maybe the better stuff went more underground, but we don't have much good stuff from then on.
Then, of course, newly recorded music disappeared almost altogether after that because of the climate crisis and much of the media shutting down.
Non-essential media they called it, apparently.
We just have the news channels, one old movie channel, one sports channel, the odd talk show and a retro-music radio show now which are partly state funded.

I decided to put on 'Strawberry Fields Forever' by The Beetles before I started ruminating on what Greg might be plotting next door. It's a real dreamy song and makes me imagine a world not so ruined or dangerous, but also a bit magical.

As the opening bars of the song played, down at the bottom of my desk, Mickey's head appeared from behind it.
'Hey, Mick,' I said, quietly, under the music playing in my headphones.
I sat up and reached for my pants on the bedside chair for the halved cookie. Mickey scuttled out in front of the desk and moved slightly closer to my bed. He stood up on his hind legs and twitched his nose, smelling my usual offering in the air.

I placed it down in front of the nightstand and then clasped my hands on my stomach.

He didn't hesitate and went to the biscuit.

'Strawberry Fields' was fading out with its psychedelic-orchestra ending and I heard a voice that I had never heard before in the song.

'How was your day, Bill?'

It wasn't coming from the music.

I ripped the headphones off my head, a little worried now, and looked around the room.

Empty. Silent, for a moment.

'It's ok,' the disembodied voice said, this time spoken with a mouthful of something. 'Down here.'

I looked down to where Mickey had been. He was waving at me tinily. I was now truly questioning my sanity again, after making a lot of progress in recent years.

I jumped up onto my knees in the bed, looking with disbelief at the mouse. 'Yes, it's me speaking to you,' he said calmly, before nibbling another bit of biscuit. 'It's really ok, you can relax. Let's not attract any attention,' he continued.

I stuttered, worrying that, by replying, I was stepping wholeheartedly into mad-world.

'H-h-how the hell are you...talking?' I managed to ask.

'It's those,' he replied, pointing up at the top of my nightstand. I turned my head slowly towards where his mini finger was pointing, finding it difficult to avert my eyes from the mouse I thought I knew.

I pulled my gaze away and refocused, I saw the bright yellow and red, slightly dissolved pill under my lamp, and things started to dawn on me.

Maybe it wasn't so crazy that Mickey was speaking. I *thought* he had said things to me before, but I always put the odd word from him down to being just my imagination or part of my illness.

'You shouldn't take those,' he said, kindly, now having finished his meal, licking his hands.

I stared at him again for a few seconds – a little more assured now than before – and then picked up the pill from my nightstand.

'These?' I said, showing him it, certain now that I wasn't dreaming with the physical sensation of the pill between my thumb and index finger.

'Yes,' he said matter-of-factly. 'They're not good for you. They cloud your mind.'

I placed the pill back down by the lamp.

'Ok...but I've been taking them my whole life. I need them to sleep. I need them to control my condition. I wouldn't be able to function without them.'

'But have you ever tried to go without them? Maybe you're not as sick as you think?'

I absorbed Mickey's words and thought deeply for a moment.

'I suppose I haven't...' I replied.

'My name's not Mickey, by the way,' he said with a chuckle. 'It's Mynos.' 'Mynos…' I replied, sounding the name. 'Not too far away though, I suppose.' We both grinned, Mynos, again, in a mousey way.

'Nice to properly meet you, Mynos,' I replied.

'And you, Bill.'

'How do you know-'

'I have good ears. You have a good soul, Bill, and talents that they don't want you to express.'

I sat listening, intensely upright in the bed, as the mouse continued to talk. 'Don't let them get a hold of you like the others. There's more going on out there than you know,' he said, pausing before continuing. 'I saw you freeing the bird outside. They don't want anything getting in, disrupting things.'

'What's out there? How do you mean "disrupting things"?' I asked the mouse both with eagerness and concern.

'It's not my place to tell you but-' Mynos suddenly stopped talking, his ears pricking up. 'Someone's coming. I must go,' he said, now panicked. 'Talk to your friends, but keep this to yourselves. Try not to take their medicine.' Mynos finished his advice hurriedly while half-turned on return to the wall vent for cover.

'Thanks,' I whispered after him. 'I will.'

The door handle clicked downwards and the door opened. Nurse Kelly stuck her head into my room.

'Bill?' she inquired lowly. 'Who were you talking to? Are you feeling ok?'

I thought of an excuse quickly, things were faster in my head too without the meds.

'I was just listening to rap music,' I said while clutching my headphones. 'And was singing along.'

'Right,' Nurse Kelly replied gruffly. 'Can you keep it down please? There are other residents who would like to get some rest.'

'Sorry, Nurse Kelly,' I replied and sunk down a little into the bed. 'I will be off to sleep myself soon but will be quiet 'til then.'

'No slacking in the morning, alright?' she added.

I smiled with my mouth closed in agreement. Her head disappeared and she closed the door. That was close.

What the hell just happened? I reran and processed my conversation with Mickey/Mynos for at least an hour in the dark.

The possibility that I had gone completely mad still lingered, but it felt like it really did happen, and it felt plausible that there was some kind of cover up going on. The medication, the bird, everything about today. I would have to tell Simon first thing tomorrow.

Definitely would be keeping all this from Dr. Akbar, of course.

I switched positions restlessly before sleep. But for the first night in a long time, for whatever reason, I hadn't felt the need to check my mirror or count my toes. This was not how things normally go in here.

# Chapter 9 - Fully Psycho? 

I woke early, determined.
I only took half the tranq pill last night; just enough so I could sleep. Dressing quickly into my usual white clothes, the conversation I had with Mickey/Mynos came vividly back into my head, along with the questions.
What did it mean?
What could we do? Or, was I going psycho?
I lay back down in the bed and pulled the covers up to my chest waiting for a Nurse to knock. I think it was Shane 1 on duty. My bed didn't feel as comforting any more.
After a minute or so, the expected thudded knock came. I closed my eyes as the door clicked open.

'Good morning, Bill,' he announced; it was Shane 1. 'Get yourself organised for breakfast and medication, please.'
I squinted my eyes and pretended to only be able to mumble my standard 'mhmm' in reply to the wake-up call.

The door clicked closed again. I jumped up straight after to sit at the edge of my bed and re-tell myself the plan once more.
I was to hold my door ajar and wait for the Nurse to hold Simon's door open for him, so I could catch him before the medication queue.
I eased the door open. A face jumped in front of mine and shouted,
'Handsome scuttler!' I nearly choked on the sharp inhale I

took from the fright; it was Eugene. He pointed behind me into my room and then ran off towards the mess hall. What did he mean by that?

I recomposed myself, checked that the coast was definitely clear, and stood at the gap in my door. I tapped it with my index finger, anxiously watching Simon's door for movement. After a few moments it opened. I made my open door-gap narrower. Nurse Shane 1 asked Simon if he was sure he didn't need any more help, as he backed out of the room, handing the door-holding over to him. Simon said, 'no, really it's grand.' and the Nurse moved on.
I waited for Simon to get into the corridor and turn towards the mess hall before bolting after him.
'Simon!' I shout-whispered as I power-walked at him. 'Something mental has happened,' I said, breathing heavily, still in a scratchy whisper
'Well, we are in a mental institution, Bill,' he replied dryly.
'No, seriously. Just trust me on this, please.'
He stopped pushing himself and looked at me.
'Don't take your med today if you can,' I continued. 'Hide it under your tongue again, like at nighttime, ok?'
'What, why? What's up?'
'Just trust me. I'll tell you properly over breakfast.'
He nodded slowly and raised an eyebrow. We continued on into the mess hall to join the queue for meds.
Nurse Kelly was playing her favourite nondescript, soothing piano music over the tannoy.
I scanned the queue and hall quickly for Ed and Lorraine

before joining it but realised I was too late to warn them too. They had already sat down with bowls of *Maize Flakes*, so had received their meds before we arrived.

The queue trudged along. I flexed my tongue in anticipation of the technique required. Simon kept glancing up at the back of my head as we moved towards the window.

My turn.

Looking down at the small cup Nurse Kelly placed in front of me at the kiosk counter, I noticed that there were now four pills there instead of my usual three. 'I think this is wrong, Nurse Kelly,' I said, recounting the pills with a finger.

'No, that's correct, Bill,' she responded.

'What? Why?' I asked.

They lied. This was unfair.

'Dr. Akbar felt that, after yesterday's meetings, it would be beneficial to increase medication for all patients.'

'But I thought it was agreed upon that it would stay the same? Nurse Shane 2 agreed in GT?'

This would complicate things. It was difficult enough to hide one under my tongue at night.

Nurse Kelly again responded unflinchingly, 'I'm sorry, Bill, but after discussing the outcomes of yesterday's sessions with the Nurses, the Doctor decided it best to alter treatments. It's out of my hands. Please take them now, they *will* help any worrying or unhelpful thoughts in general.'

I did what I was told and cocked my head back to dump the pills into my mouth. I shook the cup a bit, as if one had gotten stuck, so as to buy a couple seconds while my tongue maneuvered.

It was too much of a mouthful to hide them all but I managed to tuck two of them under my tongue.
'Open please, Bill,' Nurse Kelly asked. I swallowed the other two pills with a cup of water and opened wide as requested. All clear. She nodded and said, 'Good man' while looking over my shoulder to Simon. The next guinea pig.
I turned and left the queue and frowned with concern at Simon, trying to warn him in some way about the increase.
I looked at the others behind him as well, shuffling forward. They most likely would be fairly passive about the development, some, maybe, even happy to have more numbness.

I didn't take long at the breakfast buffet table. I automatically shoveled a couple fungus sausages and some fake scrambled egg onto a plate and hurried to the table Lorraine and Ed were sitting at.
I spat the leftover meds into my hand and pocketed them. Ed had his headphones on of course, so I tapped my ear to signal him to take them off. He did, seeing the concern in my eyes.
'Ye had extra meds today as well, yeah?' I asked them discreetly. They nodded.
'Well, do ye not think it's out of order?'
Lorraine looked at Ed, perhaps with a little guilt. Ed sighed.
'I dunno...it's up to them, I suppose. Not much we can do.'
'I know, fair enough,' I agreed. 'But it's wrong that they just

went back on their word, or at least what Dr.Akbar told me.'

Ed sipped some coffee in thought,

'Yeah, he told me there weren't any plans for an increase too. But he kept asking me if I find them helpful...and they do help my mood, I think.'

I hunched over my elbows on the table, edging closer to them both.

'Look, Lorraine, Ed, me and Simon do this thing where we hold a pill or two under our tongues without swallowing, and then flush them, or throw them in a bin,' I explained. 'Don't take the meds if you can. I know we could get into trouble if we're caught but trust me, they're *not* good for us.'

Simon arrived at the table with a casual mouthful of his usual beans on toast.

I was alarmed then, that he mightn't have gone along with the plan.

'Did you take them all?' I questioned.

He moved his right hand from the wheel of his chair and displayed his palm.

'Relax,' he said; two yellow pills and some saliva.

He put them into a tissue on his tray while asking, 'What's the issue so, Norman Bates?' (The guy from the movie 'Psycho' we had watched last Halloween.)

I had been chewing a nail anxiously. Maybe I *had* gone fully psycho. It was too late to retreat now though, so it was best to tell them.

'Ok, well, you know the way the mouse, Mickey, gets into my room at night and I feed him and speak to him?'

Simon looked at me expressionless, just chewing open-mouthed.

Ed had one ear of his head-phones on and Lorraine was now looking around nervously thinking that someone was listening.

I pressed, 'You know the way we didn't take our sleep meds last night, Si?'

'Yeeees?' Simon drawled, through a doughy mouthful.

'Well, the mouse spoke *back* to me. His real name is Mynos and he warned me, us, to stop taking the medication, that it's inhibiting us or something, and there's more going on outside of here than we know…'

Lorraine looked, again, nervously, at the other two, while they looked at me.

The beginning of a smile formed on Simon's mouth.

'Well, it was nice knowing you, sane-Bil-'

'Seriously,' I insisted. 'I know it sounds like I'm just being more insane than usual, but honestly, this really happened. He said he saw me freeing the bird yesterday too.' The end of my sentence trailed off into a whisper as Nurse Shane 1 walked past us, inquiring politely, were we alright, as he normally did to most tables.

We smiled and nodded, and he kept going. I huddled closer again, focusing on Simon.

'You know the way you think you have, like, super-powers or something, Si, and that we should break out?' Simon's ears pricked a bit at this.

'I think you could be right. I think the coffee incident yesterday was real.'

After some more initial dubiousness and questions, the three came around to my story. I convinced Simon that I wasn't in a state of delirium or high anxiety, I wasn't twitching or shaking, and they began to see the possible importance of not taking our meds.

'See, I told you I was right. I'm not going mad. We're pawns in a grand scheme and we should bust out of here guns-ablazing,' Simon declared, holding a plastic butter knife upwards. Ed patted his arm back down and looked over towards the office. The Nurse was reading.
Lorraine giggled silently with her shoulders, her nervousness had eased

We discussed the logistics of the four of us doing the med-trick – whenever possible from now on – for twenty minutes before Nurse Kelly shouted for quiet and the Aware FM jingle played loudly through the tannoy.

# Chapter 10 - Anarchy in the City

'Nine dead today in what police have described as "a massacre". Unconfirmed reports suggest that an armed looting raid occurred in a residential tower block on the outskirts of Rua City. It took place in the early hours of this morning. Up to four gallons of water and months of food rations were stolen. The tragedy has led to further calls for funding towards improving public indoor farming infrastructure to aid the disc-wide food crisis of Aunn Teer.
A woman living on the fifth floor was woken from her sleep after hearing the gun shots…
"It's completely out of control now! Everyone is living in fear for their lives, knowing that any food or water, whatever you have in the cupboard can make you a target."
The grim details and speculation as to what gang carried out the attacks continued. We listened while slowly eating.

The world fifty years ago sounds like paradise. Our Wellness Centre is in a fairly remote location, and we have security, but how is it that we're never raided for the food we have? It does make you appreciate each meal when you hear these stories, I guess.

Thomas Dentridge continued in his tone that sounds a bit like he fancies himself,
'Temperatures soared to 60 degrees Celsius in parts of the South East yesterday. Rain-season officially came to an end

today, with Sun-season beginning.'

We don't notice the heat so much here with the air conditioning on 24/7 during Sun-season. The solar panels are put to good use. And between the tree shade and sprinklers, the garden is normally bearable for the forty five minutes or so we spend there most days.

The mess hall buzzed with quiet conversation again after the news came to an end with a coincidental story about the population of robins. Apparently it had increased in the last year to over three hundred.
I noticed myself glancing over at Greg's table wondering if any of them were looking at me. They weren't, thankfully.

Alot of the residents talk about the news here after it finishes – the people who are *able* to listen and talk, at least. I think in the face of bad news and shock, people like to talk to other people and friends to help digest the information; share the worry. It's what we're told in here, 'A problem shared is a problem halved.'
It's kind of an important part of our day, both the news and the conversations around it.

For the rest of the morning, when the Nurses were busy, we watched Simon try to move his coffee, with an open palm facing it. He looked a bit like a kung-fu master in an old movie.
In between sips of coffee and watching Simon straining to

perform without luck, the guys asked me more about Mynos; What his voice sounded like, details about the outside and things like that.

I obviously wasn't able to give them much detail but we all realised that we were already looking at Ollie and others a bit differently now. He was over by the double doors.

Maybe he wasn't just babbling randomly after all. Who knows what we all have going on deep down inside and the different ways we process the world. Maybe he was just tuned to a different wavelength. As I thought that, Kweeveen belched loudly from his corner and smiled.

When we went to the garden, I asked Ollie how he knew there were birds around. He just replied with his usual hyperactive speak,

'lovelydayforallthebirdstodaysthedayfabgreatlookatthemalltw eettweetbrilliantda yforthemexcellent…' while staring off wide-eyed and nodding at the greyish sky over the trees.

Simon tried moving some of the stones in a rockery, but again, no luck.

I was looking forward to speaking to Mynos again that evening. I had a lot of questions for him obviously, even though he seemed to not want to explain too much.

Simon gave up his efforts in the afternoon without managing to move anything with his mind. I felt a little embarrassment and self-doubt because he couldn't; that they might start thinking my warning-story was just pure madness again.

But they're my friends, the only family I have, so I have to believe they trust me.

One thing I knew for sure was that, as well as Dr. Akbar, we wouldn't be mentioning a crumb of this to the Nurses. We'd probably end up lobotomised or something.

After the intense morning - dodging, hiding, explaining - and after Simon gave up attempting magic, the day passed uneventfully.
At dinner, I was sure to break off a bit of biscuit again for later. Afterwards, we watched a film (Nurse Shane 2 was off again) called 'Falling Down' from the 1990s starring Michael Douglas. He goes on a vengeful rampage because people have annoyed him. Moral of the story: Count to ten. Simon kept nudging Ed during it while snort-laughing.

Nurse Shane 2 was on evening duty, unfortunately, and soon after he arrived, he began the round-up after the nine o' clock news. 'Ok, everyone,' he bellowed, even though the hall was fairly quiet, 'Finish up what you're doing and form a line please at the kiosk.'
Lorraine, Ed, Simon and I exchanged knowing looks and nods as we began to move.
This was our first chance to act on the plan as a group. Maybe tomorrow, with even less medication in our system, we *would* see Simon move something.
The orderly queue formed and moved like a conveyor belt.

As I reached the window, I found two night-pills in the receptacle instead of one. It was as expected though, after the morning increase.

Picking up the small paper cup, I again exaggerated my actions in swallowing the meds, to create a bit of time for my tongue to adjust its and the pills' positions in my mouth.

The Nurse examined my open mouth with a typical squinty frown and waved me on.

It worked. I exhaled a deep breath through my nose as I left the window. Simon was next.

I didn't nod to him, or wink, as I made my way to the room-corridor, I didn't want to distract him or alert the Nurse, I just walked with my head down, hands pleated and the pills tucked under my tongue.

Then I jumped as Nurse Shane 2 shouted, 'Simon! WHAT ARE YOU DOING?'

Turning quickly, I saw that one of his meds had fallen out of his mouth and onto his chest, with the Nurse now standing and glaring down at him from the dispensary window.

Simon grasped the pill and clenched his fist around it, as if to hide it in hope that it might be forgotten about once it was concealed.

Obviously, to no avail. The Nurse stomped out of the dispensary office to confront him.

'Open your hand, Simon,' he ordered, eyes wide.

'Relax,' Simon offered, while opening his palm.

Nurse Shane 2 grabbed the bright yellow pill and held it in front of Simon's nose.

'You're to *take* this now, and show me the whole of your

mouth.' He then addressed the queue behind, louder, 'And that goes for everyone. These medications are to help you all. You might take them for granted but a day or two without the correct dose and the negative symptoms that ye all find too difficult to cope with will return.'
Scolded, Simon took the pill from the Nurse's grip and glanced over at me before popping it into his mouth again. There was nothing he could do but swallow it now, and he did.

He was about to push himself off towards me when the Nurse cut him off by grabbing the push handles roughly at the back of his chair.
Simon looked around incredulously. No one had ever done that before without asking his permission.
The Nurse pushed Simon furiously towards the bedroom corridor. Lorraine, Ed and the other residents still in the queue shuffled a little and took nervous steps backwards at the scene.
'Stop pushing me, now!' Simon shouted, looking straight ahead while he was being man-handled. Nurse Shane 2 ignored him and kept going at speed.
Everyone just watched, unable to take action out of fear.
Some of the patients might even have been happy that Simon's disorderly behaviour was being corrected.
Then, as they barreled past me and the Nurse was about to push him into the bedroom corridor, Simon bunched his fists, closed his eyes and screamed 'STOP!'
The rubber on his chair's wheels screeched on the shiny floor and it came to a sudden halt.

SLAP!

Nurse Shane 2 was flung into the back of Simon's chair and shoulder before falling flat on his stomach onto the hard floor in front of him with the momentum.
Simon opened his eyes. He looked down to his right at the Nurse on the floor and then at his chair and his hands.
He had stopped it with his mind. I saw it. We all did.
Simon then looked up at me to his left, his mouth slightly agape. Our eyes met knowingly again.
The Nurse got up slowly and brushed off his pants.
'Go to bed, Simon…' he muttered, partly subdued, partly in shock, processing what had happened.
He was surely thinking there was no way Simon could have stopped the speeding chair with his hands.
Although I was thinking the same thing, I was instead using that as evidence to confirm that Simon really did use some kind of mind power to stop his chair, like my ability to speak to Mynos. This wasn't crazy, I was sure of it.
Simon then pushed himself gingerly towards his room. I joined him stealthily. 'Everyone,' the Nurse, now having regained his composure and turning back towards the queue, declared. 'I will be administering your medication in *front* of the window, face to face, from now on, and will be doing a thorough inspection of your mouth. These are for your own and your fellow patients' benefit and safety.'

So much for our plan. We would have to wait until things calmed down again before trying the med-trick, or, maybe when

Nurse Shane 2 wasn't on. But if the others get strict, it could be weeks or months before we have a chance again.

Simon and I continued down the corridor to our rooms without saying anything. We stopped and looked at each other when we reached his door.

'That was crazy,' Simon said, almost embarrassed, and shaken.

'Well, we *are* in a mental hospital, Si,' I replied, offering a grin.

Simon's door clicked shut as I reached mine. I stood and leant my back against the door after getting in, like from a storm, thinking for a moment about what had happened. Then I remembered – Mynos.

I ran over to my bed and knelt on it, searching my pockets for the piece of biscuit. I whipped it out and placed it down at the bottom of my nightstand as always.

Bouncing off my knees, I leapt onto the floor and crouched down by the air vent.

'Mynos,' I whispered as loudly as possible into the vent. 'It's me, Bill.'

And then I waited.

I got into bed and flicked through a magazine impatiently, looking down at the piece of biscuit every thirty seconds. I had so many questions for him that I hoped he would answer. He would normally be here by now, I thought.

After another few minutes, I decided to put on my headphones. 'Anarchy in The City' by the Sex Pistols, a punk band from the 1970s.

But still no sign of the mouse.

After listening to the entirety of the 'Nevermind' album by Nirvana, I took off my headphones again, scanned the floor around the nightstand and then all around the left hand wall. Where *was* he?

I waited up for another hour before taking half of one of the night pills I had tongue-smuggled and drifting eventually to sleep.

He never showed. For the first time in months…

# Chapter 11 – A Silent Tree-horizon to A Rage-quit

It's been a while since anything much has happened. We've been keeping our heads down.

Dr. Akbar came and gave a speech the day after Simon was caught withholding his medication. He mentioned how we've all been making real progress over recent years and that it would be a shame to disrupt that now.

He brought a girl – Ellen – forward from upstairs, who had stopped self-harming, to sit next to him as he spoke at the top of the mess hall.

Unfortunately, he didn't listen to the few of us who requested to go back to the doses from before last week, and the Nurses have been double-checking everyone at the dispensary.

I've been feeling a bit more dulled as expected, but also, oddly content. But maybe I should have expected that too.

In the news, there've been reports of a new type of cancer caused by the Sun. A lot of people have died from it in the last few weeks. It's called ultra-melanoma, U.M.. It can start happening in the skin only after an hour of exposure and it kills people much faster than other cancers. It's scary.

The Nurses have said we should be safe enough here but our garden time in

Sun-season has been cut to 20 minutes per day and they've been giving us really strong Sun cream to put on. It's really thick and quite tough to spread on your skin.

A new Nurse joined the staff yesterday. His name is Godfrey and he seems alright but he's been staring at me all morning from a chair next to the office, which is a bit weird, but not to the point where I've felt anxious, yet.

Mynos has disappeared.
He hasn't shown up since we spoke to each other that night and I'm worried that something has happened to him.
I've been putting the usual bits of biscuits down in the spot every night, but nothing. I hope Nurse Kelly didn't somehow find out about him – when she came to my room to check – and put traps down.

Simon hasn't been in great form since the incident with Nurse Shane 2. He's being treated like a gang member, by Shane 2 and Kelly especially.

It's wrong what they're doing in general, I think. We don't have any say in how our treatment goes. It would be nice if I could just stop taking all the pills and get out of here, even for a couple of days to see if I could manage, at least then I'd know either way. But they don't even let us try.
I've seen the same walls and people for too long, and that's probably as much the cause of my insanity, if you could call it that, than anything. Sometimes you have to push yourself to try things to get out of a rut, I think.
The world *is* in a strange place though, I know, and we're all under the same roof. And the staff are professionals, so maybe I'm just moaning. I *am* a teenager.

Mynos disappearing hasn't helped either; all the questions I have, and then he's just gone.

If I was able to explore a bit of the outside world, maybe I could find more birds and would be able to talk with them too.

With the increase in medication Simon hasn't been able to do anything with his 'telekinesis' power either. I looked up what it was called in the library, in a book called 'Carrie' by Stephen King. It's one of the only fantasy-type ones we have. All the books we have are old, from way before the climate crisis.

All of these things don't help with the self-doubt.

I don't know if Simon's ability is anything like the girl Carrie's but we might never know with all the chemicals in his system. Whether that means the medication actually helps and stops us imagining things, or that it blocks the truth, is hard to tell now. And as I said, I've just been feeling content and less motivated to go against things in the last few days anyway.

I've been looking around at the other residents, wondering whether they had hidden abilities too.

Some might even have lost them, maybe, after all the years in here. I thought about Padder and his dreams and how he thinks he's a chair. Could he be able to visit different dimensions or something? I wonder?

After lunch, and the latest update on the UM cancer in the news, I decided to go and sit on a bench just outside the double doors on the patio to the garden, in the shade with Ollie.

We were birdwatching, of course. Ollie, again, in his hyper way, was convinced the sky was full of them.
I couldn't see anything, apart from the same grey and some tiny, wispy clouds. It would have been handy though, to have had binoculars, to really be sure.

But still it was nice to just sit there with hope, and imagination even, and look at the sky. The heat wasn't too bad at all in the shade and Ollie's energy was fun to be around sometimes.

After a few moments of scanning our tree-horizon without talking, I glanced back over my shoulder through the double doors. The new Nurse, Godfrey, was there at the table nearest to the doors collecting cups and eyeing us at the same time. When I caught his eye, he looked down at the table, and then hurried off to another table. Odd.

'Thanks for the help, Ollie,' I said, while getting up to go back inside.
'Absolutelybrilliantlydonebirdsupandaboutclassfantasticsupe rdayforthemsoundalluptherelookingbeautifulloadsandloadsa ndloads' he excitedly replied and trailed off as I left. I half-guessed he meant something like 'bye' and a thumbs up.
There wasn't necessarily anything wrong with Ollie, really.
He was harmless and super positive, but, of course, a little different and incoherent. But maybe he has some kind of other sense on a slightly different wavelength too.
I hope he gets to see a few birds up close at some point.

As I got inside, I saw Simon, Lorraine and Ed at the Z-Cube and headed over to them. No Nurse Shane 2 around to uphold the ban.

Ed, who rarely joins in against anyone but Lorraine, was racing Simon in

'Radical Kart Wars' and looked flustered.

'Hey, Billo!' Simon exclaimed, looking at me while still navigating sharp turns and leading the race, 'Eddo here is about to lose his dessert later.'

'It isn't over yet, Simon,' Ed grumbled.

He was now mashing all the buttons simultaneously, frowning and his tongue was sticking out a little.

Lorraine looked at me and made a slanty-mouth face while raising her eyebrows.

'You're going to become obese, Si, if you keep winning people's desserts,' I added.

It looked as though Simon was about to lap Ed for the second time in the race. They were now neck and neck. Ed inched forward on his seat and tried to push Simon's Kart off to the right of the track.

Instead, Simon accelerated, dropped a grenade and blew Ed's Kart off the track behind him.

Ed completely lost it, swore creatively several times out loud - which Eugene would have been proud of - and jumped up from his chair, which grated backwards along the floor with the sudden movement.

A few of the others at tables near us turned to look at the commotion.

'I'm not giving you my food,' he said sharply as he marched over to the screen to set his controller down and quit. 'This is rigged.' As he put it down, it fell apart into pieces. It was completely smashed even though he had been holding it in one hand - his right - just as he stood up. Simon didn't argue; Ed's face was red and his frown now looked like it might break a mirror.

We all just stared at the controller in pieces as he stormed off.

'How the hell did he manage that?' I said, after a moment.

'He's not very good at the game, I suppose,' Simon replied.

'No, you dope, not the game, how did he break the controller? Those things are rock solid, I couldn't do that if I tried.'

We sat in silence for a few seconds, looking at the controller pieces, perplexed, when Nurse Godfrey appeared and walked into our semi-circle at the Z-Cube.

'I saw your friend's rage-quit,' he said with a chuckle while picking up the controller pieces.

We all sat upright a bit, unsure of what to do with the stranger-danger.

'Take it easier on him next time, eh? He has powerful emotions. Simon, is it?'

'Eh...yeah, sure,' Simon replied obediently, still rattled by the other Nurses' treatment of him in the last few days.

All this Nurse Godfrey had done so far was sort of small talk and staring, so we were all a little suspicious.

'Don't worry,' he said, pointing at the demolished controller bits in his hand with the other. 'I'll hide this and get a replacement when I finish my shift this afternoon. I won't mention it.'

Simon and I looked at each other and then back at him before saying 'thanks'. Lorraine smiled, she usually has good judgement of character. He did seem genuine, but who knows, we've only just met him and the staff have lied before.

I wasn't quite sure what to think of him yet.

The rest of the day passed ordinarily enough.
Another story broke in the news after dinner that the Dyad gang had kidnapped ten children in Tymblia City and four people had died in the gunfight, including two policemen. They weren't sure of the motive behind it.
A lot of the residents – Greg's gang being the loudest – discussed/ranted about the dire need for more control over guns in the law after the news had finished. One of the many things that needed to be fixed, but the country was barely holding together in other ways as it was, so it would be unlikely that much could be done.
*We* definitely wouldn't be affecting it.

I went to bed with my piece of biscuit again. Mynos was a no-show again.
I hope he's alright. I worry.

Dreams haven't really been there in the last few nights either. Another effect from the extra medication, no doubt.
We can't do anything about it with the Nurses being so strict but it's been almost a week now, so maybe things will ease off again soon. There's a chance with Nurse Shane 1, or Kelly even, on a good day. Shane 2 will always be grumpy though.

Before I turned off my light and closed my eyes, I checked, as always, once more for Mynos, but still no sign of my little friend.

# Chapter 12 - Safe 

The Nurses have started coming in wearing special reflective
suits due to the
UM cancer from the Sun. It's scary.
Apparently, it has a 95% mortality rate. The news has been
covering it alot. But there have also been lots of child
kidnappings in the news and the two things are related.
Apparently, people under the age of 20, produce a special
hormone in their bone marrow that can protect against the
disease or fight it off. They haven't said exactly how they
extract the hormone but it doesn't sound good.

We have a group meeting today with Nurse Godfrey getting
involved. Could be interesting having a different face
coordinating.

None of us have really experienced anything 'supernatural' since
the increase in meds, so I guess, either way, they're working.

Simon has tried (unsuccessfully) to move his coffee cup
without touching it every day at breakfast. He has also been
talking about trying to tunnel out of his room into the
garden, to which I advised that he would need something
better than his dessert spoon to do it. He said it worked in
a film though.

After we had a small salad for lunch and took in the news

headlines, Nurse Shane 1 called for attention and the GT group of a dozen gathered around the middle of the mess hall where the two Nurses' chairs were as usual. There was a more relaxed atmosphere, of course, with Shane 2 absent.
I was expecting to be asked about things today because I hadn't spoken in a while.

As the chairs scraped and banged off the hard, glossy floor while we found our spots, I noticed Godfrey staring at me again from his seat. Shane 1 was flicking through a clipboard. Godfrey had been watching me at breakfast too today. I felt like sticking my tongue out at him but held it in. It was starting to make me feel uncomfortable. I've been thinking that maybe he was a spy sent in by Dr. Akbar. A plant, and not the good kind.

Nurse Shane 1 cleared his throat theatrically to get our attention again even though everyone was sitting silently, apart from Ollie who was muttering to himself.
'Welcome everyone. Good to see you all looking well. (Greg's hair was sticking up like a cockatoo's which made me giggle slightly) I suppose we will get straight into it.'
He paused and looked down again at the clipboard, running his index finger down it.
'Could we start with Nadine and Dawhee, please?'
It was a rhetorical question.
Dawhee and Nadine shuffled around in their seats a bit, preparing for the questioning.
They were a little older than me, around mid twenties.

They've both been diagnosed with schizophrenia and can't communicate properly with people unless they're together. It's kind of like their minds are linked or something. 'So, Nadine, Dawhee, whoever wants to go first, how have ye been coping?' Shane 1 asked, switching his eyes back and forth between the two, a bit like he was watching a tennis match.

Without hesitation, Nadine spoke assuredly, 'We've had communication again,' Dawhee then automatically continued. 'From people in the city.'

Seamlessly, Nadine added, 'They're in trouble, we think.'

'But less so in recent days,' Dawhee added.

Finally, Nadine nodded and ended with, 'We're worried about them and want to help.'

Dawhee's eyes twitched a bit as they spoke and they both looked around the hall above their heads at nothing in particular after they finished. Nurse Shane 1 took a note and put it to the group, 'Does anyone have an opinion on Nadine and Dawhee's thoughts and worries?'

There wasn't an immediate response. A few coughs. Then Greg raised his hand.

'Gregory, you have something to add?'

'What I've learned after years of good therapy, is when you have hallucinations, try to ground yourself in the moment by focusing on the physical sensations in your body.'

'Excellent Greg,' Shane 1 chimed. 'Go on.'

'And with experience and keeping a diary, you will get more used to knowing how to recognise them.'

Shane 1 continued on with Greg's suggestions, asking the two about their journaling and deep breathing practice, and of course, medication effectiveness.

I couldn't stop looking at his hair though. You'd think the Nurses would let him know.

Shane 1 had moved on to suggesting exercise when Nurse Godfrey interjected, 'And Dawhee, Nadine, what if these voices you heard weren't hallucinations, what would you do?'

The pair adjusted themselves again, stiffened and looked at each other as if to confirm go-ahead. This time, Dawhee spoke first, with another twitch.

'It had crossed our mind because-'

'We can see where they live when they speak,'

Again, Nadine finished Dawhee's sentence instantly. She was staring at the floor now.

'They all wear black clothes and-' Dawhee started again. 'They live in one room dwellings in the city,' Nadine finished. The pair then spoke together simultaneously,

'It's like they're praying.'

Nurse Shane 1 interrupted with a shrill tone in his voice and a concerned look. 'Now, hang on there, ok. I want you both to take a deep breath and stop getting carried away. You're allowing these 'magical' thoughts, that we spoke about before, to take hold in reality by following them.'

Dawhee and Nadine nodded and muttered, 'ok', together.

'It's certainly an interesting question Nurse Godfrey, thanks for your contribution, and no harm to think for a moment about, but let's not hamper-' 'Of course,' Nurse Godfrey replied, nodding.

Shane 1 continued the discussion with Nadine and Dawhee but it became more of a pleasantly worded lecture, as all they did was nod at instructions for a few minutes.

Eugene shouted his latest tick, 'DRIZZLEBAG' as the Nurses took notes.

Then it was my turn.

I liked Shane 1, most of us did – despite Eugene's heckle – but he started with a difficult question, after flipping over a page on his clipboard.

'Bill, we haven't spoken like this in a while. Your 18th birthday is coming up, how have you been feeling with regards to thoughts of your parents?'

It took me by surprise a bit. It was actually the first time I had thought of them in weeks, between Mynos and med-tricks and everything else, my mind had been occupied.

I dwelled on the few vague memories I had of them with that question. Then I felt a lump in my throat, thinking about the things I might have missed out on with them. I wondered whether I would have spent my whole life sick in here if they *had* been around, if they weren't sick themselves. My anxiety started growing as I felt the eyes of the group on me waiting for my answer.

The silence dragged until Nurse Godfrey interrupted, again with a question of his own,

'Bill, could I also ask, what would you do if you were better?'

His question triggered a bit of hope in me and I snapped out of the sadness. 'Em, I suppose I would look for their graves, find out more about them and maybe explore the world as much as I could-'

Nurse Shane 1 countered again,

'It's a very harsh world out there now, Bill, even worse than when your parents were alive. There isn't much to explore I'm afraid, it's too dangerous for tourism.

Like your parents experienced, many people barely have enough food or water to survive each week. You can't go out in public much at all, for fear of your life. Is it any wonder people look for an escape using xantho-leaf and get addicted.'

I nodded; they were fair points.

'Your birthday will be difficult as it's a big one, but know that we all are like family here, even if our other Shane can be grumpy.' Some of the group chuckled. 'And know that their deaths weren't your fault.'

It did feel like a family in here, a bit of an odd one, but apparently real families can be like that anyway. Simon, Lorraine and Ed are good friends, and I get on with mostly all of the other residents in different ways.

Nurse Godfrey spoke again as I smiled slightly and glanced around at the group. 'It's true that you're all safe in here. Safer in lots of ways than out in today's world.'

Nurse Shane 1 nodded vigorously in approval at this.

'Don't underestimate your medicine's significance,' Godfrey's eye's locked onto mine as he said that. 'It will keep you stable in turbulent moments. I have had to take medication too for periods in my life, so I understand,' he emphasised that last word and looked straight at me again.

He paused. Shane 1 was almost beaming at his little speech.

'I would like to ask the senior Nurse, Shane 1, if I could take charge of the dispensary job this evening, as I understand the importance from both a staff and patient point of view?'

Nurse Shane 1 was sort of suprised by the question. He had been grinning proudly around at the group before jolting back into concentration on Godfrey.

'Oh...eh, yes, of course, that's a good idea, Nurse Godfrey. I'm sure the patients will respect your empathy and authority on the value of chemical treatments.' The new Nurse had once again fixed his gaze on me. As I met it again, he winked. My eyes widened a bit and I looked at Simon next to me but he was twiddling his thumbs.

I don't think anyone else noticed.

After a couple more of us spoke, satisfied with the outcome of the group meeting, Nurse Shane 1 exclaimed,

'Right,' while throwing his arms upward, the clipboard now on his lap. 'I suppose that concludes this week's GT session. Well done all. Enjoy the rest of today; with what we discussed in mind, get your 20 minutes of fresh air and keep up the journal work 'til next time.'

I watched Nurse Godfrey clearing the chairs as everyone dispersed. What did his wink mean?

Something was up.

I guessed we would find out later at the dole.

# Chapter 13 - Judge of Character

'BREAKING NEWS, ON THE HOUR, JUST IN! The Mayor of Rua City has put the region on "Red Alert" as the death toll rises from UM. Two thousand people have died across the continent in the last seven days alone. The police and government officials expect to see tensions rising between gangs in the region as they fight to tighten their grip on resources. Instances of child kidnappings have continued to rise also, and in response to this, several civilian vigilante groups have formed, resulting in separate violent street clashes...'

'It's chaos...' Simon philosophised over the 9 'o clock news. Dentridge seemed to be particularly energised by the current update because his voice was oscillating like mad; probably thinking of the ratings.

The yellow banner scrolled across the bottom of the muted TV screen on the wall too, with bits of information about UM and that bone-marrow hormone called 'antheochrome', and other stories. The usual news-junky heads were silhouetted in front of it, like they were at the cinema (old movie houses).

'It's the natural way of the universe...chaos,' Simon continued even though Lorraine, Ed and I didn't really have much more interest in his theory than the news.

You can only take so much bad news in before it becomes a bit like banging your head against a wall, and it was worse than usual.

'It's impossible to predict the *weather* further than a few days, and even then, it can change. The universe is chaotic and random and we're lucky a big asteroid hasn't hit the planet in the last couple million years, but it's coming…'

Ed said, 'cheery…' and popped his headphones back on to listen to The Smiths. I told him to shut up, that people were dying, steering the focus onto the main morbidity. At least Simon's was a bit eccentric, but I wasn't going to encourage him. Also, I was pretty sure it would be Sunny again tomorrow.

I told Simon after dinner about Godfrey's staring and wink. Godfrey had actually been staring at Si too a bit, and he suggested that he could be a government spy, or that he fancied us. There was definitely something weird going on with him.

Or else we needed to double our meds again…

That was a joke.

'Police raided a xantho-leaf grow factory controlled by the Remo Gang today, seizing over two million ingots worth of the drug. Local communities have been ravaged by the highly addictive substance in recent years which is often used in bartering exchanges…'

Thomas Dentridge continued his oration as I watched the entrance of the mess hall for Nurse Godfrey to appear and assume his new dole role. Greg and the news-gang stayed glued to the TV.

The last story was about a school having been completed in

the suburbs of Tymblia City, which was nice. Dentridge seemed to lose a bit of vigour reading that and it only lasted two sentences.

There he was. As the ads played after the news, Nurse Godfrey marched in through the entrance past the dinner hall and library and went straight to the dispensary office.
I nudged Simon and nodded upwards towards the Nurse.
Keys rattled as he opened the door and stepped inside. He looked assured, like he really did have experience in it.
I remember the first time Shane 1 got the job, he looked a little bit nervous; couldn't find the right key or where things were.
I noticed everyone was staring over at him now, gawking actually. Novelty is big in here.
The tannoy crackled and whined a little with feedback as he called for our already-there attention.
'Ok, everyone. Good evening,' he announced. 'If you don't know me yet, I'm Nurse Godfrey, and I will be providing ye all with tonight's medication.' Simon had already started pushing himself out of our gathering and towards the dispensary window. He looked at me wittingly and shrugged. Let's see what happens with him, I suppose he meant.

'Simon, wait!' I suddenly realised, formulating a mini plan on the fly. Simon stopped. 'Let's leave a few people to go first.'
We did just that and watched, without being too obvious.
We didn't want to stand out by going first or leave ourselves open to something Nurse Godfrey might spring.

Everything seemed normal. People were just getting their meds, taking them and leaving.

Ed and Lorraine shuffled past us to join the queue. I thought about telling them that there might be something up with the new Nurse, but didn't. It was probably nothing, so no need to put them on edge.

I went next in the queue. It seemed to take forever and I got a bit anxious shuffling along.

Simon was humming that song, 'Two Tickets to Paradise' behind me. You'd be right in thinking he and Ed don't share mp3 players.

Nurse Godfrey's voice got louder, calling out names from behind the window, as we got closer. He seemed chirpy.

'Bill,' he smiled a little as I arrived at the sill.

'Hi, Nurse Godfrey,' I replied, still suspicious.

He rummaged in the cabinet below the window for my medication and set the small cup down in front of me after he found the right one.

I peeked into it warily. It seemed normal.

I went to pick it up but the Nurse's hand was still gripping it.

I looked up at him, a bit startled, and he winked at me again, both of our hands now gripping the cup. Then he glanced down at the pills. And then he let go.

I looked down at the meds again for a second and it dawned on me. Now was as good a time as any to hide them under my tongue again. He was trying to tell me that, and I'm not sure why, but something in general about the new Nurse was making me want to trust him.

I knocked back my head and emptied the two night-pills out into my mouth while immediately shuffling them under my tongue, like I had done before.

'Let me see, Bill,' the Nurse said as my head rocked forward again.

I opened my mouth and extended my tongue out a bit. He smiled with his eyes and a closed mouth, and nodded. He didn't check under my tongue.

Adrenaline bubbled in my chest. I turned to leave, making sure I caught Simon's gaze on my way as he moved forwards in the queue behind me.

I winked at him, hoping he would get the message and walked down the corridor to bed, with the usual piece of biscuit-hope in my pocket.

# Chapter 14 - Jump-scare 

I dribbled.

The terracotta ball bounced off the squeaky hard-wood court with twanging thuds. The crowd was buzzing, in a fever.

I advanced towards the other team's net with purpose. Determination coursed through my body. This was light years away from the cracked tarmac half-court – with a rusty hoop – that we used to play on sometimes back in Pleasant Pines when the weather permitted. Indoor, new, professional. There was more pressure here though with the crowd.
I still can't dunk.
It's all in the jump. Planting both your feet solidly together, balanced, before pushing off, hard.
I kept the ball protected and moving. Defenders reached in aggressively whenever there was an opening in my stance or control.
Ten seconds on the clock.
Dribbling, with my body between defender and ball, I searched for a teammate in space. Everyone was marked. Bodies moved like clockwork in coached patterns. The flurry of rubber soles on the floor, squeaking like flocked bird-calls, was almost constant. I decided to drive inside into the paint, dribbling aggressively, body squat to take advantage of gravity. The white noise of the crowd swelled like a wave around me. A big defender blocked my path within a few feet of the hoop – dead end.

I faked to take a shot. Just as I did, the defender jumped to block. I saw a teammate free just outside the three-point line at the edge of the court. I whipped a pass to him. With nobody marking him, he was free to shoot, and the crowd urged him to.

He steadied himself instinctively, with the ball held in line with his forehead, and jumped to shoot. The squeaking stopped for a second as the ball left his hands. Everybody watched its quiet ark.

A few gasps in the crowd, the ball flying through the tense-air din. I wandered into space again, watching the spinning ball come down. The neon shot-clock was at 3 seconds.

It hit the rim.

A collective, 'Oh!' erupted from the teased fans. It rebounded elastically off the metal hoop and looped straight into my ready hands.

Somehow, no-one was within three feet of me and I saw a clear path between the bodies to the net. I burst forward to take my chance, bouncing the ball twice, then hopping into that set position.

This was it. I was going to try it. Everything felt right.

A split second to bend my knees and push hard, upwards, against the pull of once-friendly gravity, pressure and self-doubt. I was in the air.

I could feel the extra 10% in my leap this time.

Again, the clamour of squeaks and opposing desires paused for a second. Again, a collective gasp, as I propelled myself up to the hoop, the ball gripped tightly in my outstretched hands. A clarity of both hope and dread together at once. Could I finish?

SLAM DUNK!
I did it.

After all these years of trying, I pulled it off, now. Here, where it mattered most. That extra 10% was mental.
I felt like I could take on the world.
The arena exploded. The opponent's heads dropped; one second on the clock. No time to claw back.
My teammates and the crowd swarmed me on the court.
A million miles away from the cracked tarmac half-court in Pleasant Pines…

'BILL!'
I jolted awake with a gasp.
A black figure stood over me, gripping my shoulders roughly. I looked around, disorientated, my eyes were still adjusting. The room was dark.
'It's me, Godfrey, wake up. This is serious.'
He put his index finger to his lips.
'What? What's happening?' I mumbled sleepily, but heeded his instruction and whispered,
'I...was dreaming...what time is it?'
'Good. It's 2 a.m.'
I rubbed my eyes, definitely awake now.
'I know your friend,' he continued, softly.
'Who? Simon?' I was a little startled now, the anxiety was waking up too as usual, questions started to flood into my brain.

'No, the mouse, Mynos. He told me about you.'

My eyes widened another few increments and I sat up rigid.

I couldn't think of any *one* question. I just stuttered.

'Look, we don't have much time,' he looked utterly serious and focused, in the half-light coming through my small window from an outside lamp. 'The security guard, Carl, at the front entrance, will start wondering if I stay too long, so I must be quick.'

We weren't allowed out past the first door before the main entrance, so never really saw the security guards.

'You want to get out of here, right?'

I snapped out of the initial bewilderment at the question and thought about it for a second.

'Eh...I suppose I *had* been thinking about it.' But the reality of actually doing it - fear - made me hesitate.

'I'm here to get you out of here,' Nurse Godfrey cut in decisively. He wasn't really waiting for an answer.

I gulped and said, 'OK.'

He moved closer again, looking straight into my eyes, sensing my uncertainty.

'Bill, you will have to trust me.'

He touched my arm.

'I can speak to animals, just like you. I can get you out of here. Off this medication. It's numbing you all. Your friends have gifts too.

This place is made to control you, not look after you. You have to start believing in yourselves. I can help you and your friends escape; tomorrow night, but you have to trust me.'

Realisation was really kicking in now. More questions

swarmed in my head. I looked around at the darkened room, processing.

'What about the Sun? Everything else. It isn't safe out there.'

'There is no Ultra Melanoma, Bill.' His words were startling and sobering. 'The news, it's a lie.'

'All of it?' I asked eagerly but shocked.

'Yes,' he replied, a kind sternness in his voice. I knew I could trust him for some reason.

This, somehow, felt like the truth all at once.

'Everything about this facility is a lie, designed to control you, brainwash you, keep you sick.'

Along with shock, I felt a tinge of anger, and then strongly, the desire, again, to get out of here.

My reduced night medication now felt even more noticeable. I wondered if he knew Mynos was alive. I started to ask but he cut me off.

'Tell your three friends. You have tomorrow. We have to make our move tomorrow night before they grow suspicious. They agreed to roster me on for tomorrow evening again. So, it has to be then.'

I nodded and gulped again, eyes fixed on the Nurse, waiting for his directions. 'I will come back to your room at 3 a.m. tomorrow night when Carl will be doing a patrol, so won't be watching the monitors. We will have a five minute window to get to the garden and we will escape over a certain point in the fence and wall behind the trees.'

This was really happening.

'What about Simon?' I asked..

'We will have to lift him, together.'

'But how will we get over the fence and wall? What if the cameras see us before we get out?'
Nurse Godfrey looked over at the door.
'I don't have time to go over everything. You'll just have to trust me that I will get you out, if you follow my lead.'
He paused and put his hand on my shoulder.
'I know this will be scary, given everything they've had you believe, but it's a chance not many get. The truth. Freedom. I will explain everything when we get to my safe house. Tell your friends, and I will be back here tomorrow exactly at 3 a.m.'

I fell into thought for a second, thinking about *everything*. My entire life spent in Pleasant Pines. Who I am. Did it matter any more?
The lies. The constant feed of news, medication, our disabilities, fear. Some of us are even happy here now and wouldn't want to leave anyway. I lifted my unfocused gaze from the floor and looked at him again; his as relentless as before. Then I took a deep breath and said, 'Thanks, Nurse Godfrey,' sincerely.
It would take time to fully absorb all of this and I wouldn't sleep unless I took that left-over tranq pill I had, but there was no way I was going to do that now, with what I knew.

'It's Godfrey Taylor,' he added. 'I have a second name, like you. But call me Godfrey.'

With that, he stood up from sitting at the edge of my bed and pointed to the door, and then at his watch, '3 a.m. tomorrow.'
I nodded and watched him leave. It was going to be a long night.

# Chapter 15 - Team Phoenix 

As expected, I didn't sleep.

Even though Godfrey had only been with me for five minutes or so, it felt like it would take years to manage accepting this new reality.

Questions and thoughts about the past and the future swam around my head until morning. Everything about my room – the room I had spent the last seven or so years in after moving down from the 2nd floor – was now different.

Pleasant Pines was different. What *was* my home, of sorts, before, was now more like a prison.

The small windows became smaller. The beige walls in between the few drawings and posters I had up became insipid.

The red dot in Dr. Akbar's office came to mind.

I went through a combination of wonder, anger, confusion and sadness at the thoughts of the life I had spent in here. What had I missed out on? What was the extent of my unexplored gift?

As I lay there in the almost-dark, my curiosity and desire to get out of here grew more than ever. I felt cheated, lied to. Some of the staff were always friendly and in many ways, the care and safety we had received felt comforting, but it was insincere. To trick us. And why us?

We were brainwashed and it would take a long time to break free from that, even after we physically got out, and that could still go wrong. But we had to.

My (fostered) anxiety built in my chest in the hours before 'wake-up' - about the task to come. None of us had ever been outside of Pleasant Pines, nor had anyone tried to escape. The four of us had talked a bit about it in the last couple years but never truly felt the motivation to leave or explore such a dangerous world. We were always told that we weren't built for it.
But it wasn't that dangerous. Godfrey said the news was a trick too.
And now it felt more personal. Now, the motivation was there to see exactly what we had been deprived of, in the truth about ourselves and our own bodies, and the world. We were going to stand up for ourselves.

I hoped Ed and Lorraine would feel the same. I knew Simon would. We all would have a little fear about getting caught, or the possible dangers of outside,  but every time we felt that fear we would now think of how Pleasant Pines, and whoever else, created it in us.
There is no UM cancer, he said. How much of the rest of it isn't real? Even though the news could be addictive and interesting sometimes (it could be the highlight of your day even), I always had a feeling of uneasiness with it, deep down. Who decided what way to deliver it and why? Where was the information coming from?
That's why I tried to distance myself from it in the last while; not to get sucked in.

The wake-up call came.

On the way to the mess-hall I saw Simon being escorted by Nurse Shane 2, who hadn't let up with him since the week before. I met him with a serious, unblinking stare at the end of the corridor as the Nurse moved on to the office

'What's up?' he asked, as we joined the queue. 'Is the mouse back?'

'No,' I said, preparing myself to deliver the news. I took a breath. 'We're getting out of here. Tonight.'

'What?' he blurted, but in a way that sounded like he almost expected it. I continued, 'Nurse Godfrey visited my room last night. He spoke with Mynos…on the outside.'

Simon then looked both a little shocked and excited.

'We have to tell Ed and Lorraine after this,' I added.

We shuffled along in the line as always but inside, I now felt like an actor in a play, carrying out a role, for one more day – *if* Godfrey's plan worked…It would work.

With Nurse Shane 2 dispensing, there was no chance we could avoid swallowing the pills this morning. We would have to take our so-called medicine once more.

I took it dutifully and opened wide for the Nurse to see every corner of my mouth. This was a means to an end, I kept thinking, while looking the Nurse in the eye, wondering how much *they* knew.

As soon as we all were sitting in our usual spot with whatever dodgy breakfast we had, I started talking. Simon listened but kept checking to make sure Shane 2 was still in the office.

I told the three of them everything that Godfrey had told me. I brought up Simon's coffee incident and the other odd things that had been happening; Mynos, the news, the medication, all of it, to help them see the picture. It took a while to convince them that we could trust Godfrey.

They believed me.

The surprising thing after that was, although they were all shaken and emotional about the information, they also seemed vindicated about themselves, energised a bit. We all now had confirmation that we weren't insane, whatever that meant anyway. We could express our natural selves; know about and believe in our abilities, even though we didn't fully know what they were yet.

But we weren't free yet. We *had* to accomplish the plan.

We discussed it over coffee until lunch. I wondered whether the coffee was real for a few sips. I also noticed that Ollie was missing from the hall.

Simon drew a diagram on a napkin of the escape-route we might take and how we would meet. Lorraine even added some notes to it and Ed left his headphones around his neck.

I told them that Godfrey was going to be in the dispensary office tonight again, and that we would all be able to do the med-hiding trick.

There was lots of nodding as we huddled on our elbows, with purpose, over the metal table.

Nurse Shane 2 had been placing Sun-block dispensers

throughout the mess-hall, as the similarly themed news was pumped in as usual. Death, terror, caution, worry, paranoia. Why had they gone to so much trouble?

It *was* convincing. The interviews with actors posing as people on the streets were hard not to believe. All lies?

I watched the other residents transfixed again. Greg, shushing people with each new bulletin. It was sad and wrong. We have had a life of choice taken from us without even knowing it. Padder, in the corner, and a few others, were lucky in some ways to be away in another world.

The last 'good news' story was about a team of scientists having reached the edge of Aunn Teer by boat and had successfully mapped over half of the disc.

Still no sign of Ollie.

We were supposed to have a GT session today but Nurse Shane 2 cancelled it according to orders from Dr. Akbar. It was to raise awareness around 'double layering' of Sun-block; one of the measures imposed on society in the cities to reduce the risk of the imaginary UM. They gave out leaflets to us with diagrams of people putting it on.

That goal of theirs, to induce fear, was becoming more apparent here by the hour.

The lengths they were going to, to paralyze us, were incredible. Who and why were the biggest questions the four of us had now.

Unexpectedly, Dr. Akbar appeared at the entrance of the mess hall.

He strode to the bedrooms, followed by Nurse Shane 2 looking stressed, with a gurney. There were concerned murmurs and turning heads at the other tables. The energy changed.

They went into Ollie's room. We were starting to worry about him now. The importance of the plan faded as we waited for the Dr. to reappear from the corridor.

A tense few minutes passed. There was a clunk as Ollie's door opened again. A few of the other residents had gotten up and were standing nearer to the office for a better look. And then the gurney reappeared, with a white sheet, covering what must have been Ollie.

Dr. Akbar immediately followed and walked in front of it, partially hiding it from view as it was pushed by the Nurse out to the entrance hall.

Their faces were somber.

The shock began to set in for us.

'Everyone,' he addressed the mess-hall after returning from the entrance. 'I'm very sorry to have to report that your fellow resident, Oliver, has passed away overnight.'

There was a staggering of sighs and heads dropping and people looking at each other in reaction.

'What happened?' one of Greg's gang, Andrew, asked angrily. 'He seemed fine…'

Dr. Akbar took a breath before replying, 'It seems that Ollie took his own life.

We will have a memorial service for him here tomorrow evening.'

With that, the Doctor left to follow Nurse Shane 2 and Ollie's body.

It was a kick in the stomach. The reality of this place weighed heavier than ever at that moment. The poor guy. He always seemed so positive in his own eccentric, hyper way. I felt like crying and going back to bed.

But we couldn't give up now. This place was evil.

I told the others that we couldn't let this distract us. In one way or another, the people running Pleasant Pines wanted us to stay stuck and indifferent, not fight. If we wanted to honour Ollie, we would have to get out of here for good.

The day moved slowly after that and my anxiety bubbled upwards in my body as we got closer to the planned escape. My stomach and chest tightened by the hour.

I tried not to dwell on Ollie's death, we couldn't afford to now, but it was hard.

We all put in our headphones when the news came on in the afternoon. Our own little secret protest.

The first song I put on was by a band called R.E.M. It was called, 'It's the End of the World As We Know It'. I smiled a bit to myself at the lyrics which had taken on a whole new meaning.

It was a relief to just zone out for a bit with music and take my mind off what had happened, or what could go wrong later. Again, I reminded myself that that's what they wanted - for us to doubt ourselves.

Before dinner, the four of us went into the garden to suss out the possible escape route. We took care to not arouse suspicion from Nurse Kelly, who had taken over at lunch time.
We spelled Ollie's name out in stones from the rockery on the grass, then walked down the garden path to the back row of yew trees. We parted them in a few spots, trying to gauge how we might climb the fence and wall behind it.
Simon was totally committed as expected, but I was surprised how eager Lorraine and Ed still seemed about doing this too. Maybe more of the residents have an itch to get out of here than it would seem. And maybe Ollie's suicide would send a message, that not everything was perfect on the inside.
Ed tried lifting Simon's chair with him in it; we would have to lift him and the chair separately.

On the way back inside, we looked up at the building we had spent our lives in. The sky above it was grey, cloudless, hot, like always in Sun-season.

We noticed more cameras than we had ever before, and, up above the 2nd floor windows, a small out-building in the roof garden with the radio and satellite receivers attached.
We would just have to trust Godfrey, like he asked, that the security guard wouldn't check the cameras for those five minutes.

After dinner, I threw on 'Nighttrain' by the band Guns n' Roses in my ears, to try to keep myself focused and motivated while the news played on cue. I found myself going for glasses of water a lot to keep myself moving.

I watched the reporter mouthing the latest story on the TV screen. Images of people crying, boxes of vacuum-packed food and drugs, and guns flashed along. The recurring yellow information banner scrolled along the bottom. It was all sort of hypnotic; perversely seductive, like it was made to almost feed an addiction to new information and obsessing and reacting. The music in my headphones took the effectiveness away from it though. I tried some of the band The Cure on Ed's recommendation.

I took a piece of biscuit and put it in my pocket for Mynos again. I knew that he probably wouldn't be in my room but did it out of ritual, hope, and also, maybe a tribute now.

Without him, we mightn't be in this position tonight, with this chance, with a whole new life and world ahead of us outside of here. Without him, the medication, staff and news might have slowly taken hold and we might have ended up like Greg or some of the others, wanting to stay here for life; safe and secure in engineered ignorance.

It was getting close to bedtime. We all kept glancing at the clock, unable to concentrate on the film, 'The Titanic'.

I don't think any of us were concentrating, really, because Ollie not being there was sad and odd.

I looked at the other residents I liked as they watched: Dawhee and Nadine, Eugene, Kweeveen, standing as usual, Padder in his armchair.

I would miss them and, if we got out, might never see them again. But if we failed, we might never have the chance to get out again, or worse.

The Titanic was beginning to sink and was in chaos as Godfrey arrived for his shift, which didn't help my nerves. I fought the negative thoughts. It helped when he caught my eye and sent me his wink again.

The credits played. Godfrey was pottering in the dispensary office now. We waited for him to call for the medication queue, and, as a few people got up from their seats, he did.

This was it.

# Chapter 16 - Escape 

I spat my two pills into the bin as soon as I got into my bedroom.

Sleep was never happening, so I decided to listen to the album 'Dookie' by the band Grín Day. The album was from way back in 1994. The song, 'Basket Case' was on, it's a bit of an anthem for me and the lyrics are ideal.

I don't know why they let us listen to punk music here.

I won't complain though.

It was actually the second album ever I downloaded onto my mp3 player from the library here. The first was Boyzone's first album, 'Said and Done', for some reason.

This was my second night in a row without sleep and I was tired but filled with adrenaline.

I flicked off my lamp and waited, checking my clock after every few songs. My leg was bouncing up and down in the bed, half with the music and half with the nerves; a mixture of anxiety and determined excitement.

I went over the plan a few times in my head. What would the outside be like? Would it be too hot? At least at night it wouldn't be scorching.

For the first time, I had to worry about food. When would we next eat? Then I thought about the last few weeks in general, how surreal they were.

I checked the time again: 1:30 a.m..

I put on some songs by an old guy called Dunovan and a young guy called Geoff Buckley and fidgeted in between clock checks, growing more and more nervous.
And then it was time.

Just as I turned away from the clock hitting 3 a.m., while ripping my headphones off, the door clicked open. Godfrey's silhouette stooped in. He closed the door smoothly behind him and stepped towards me.
'Are you ready?' he said calmly, barely above a whisper.
I nodded unconvincingly but whipped my legs out from under the white sheets before hesitation could set in.
This was really happening. I feel like I've said that a lot to myself recently.

I grabbed a small bag that I had packed with an extra change of clothes, some drawing materials, a nature magazine – and popped in the mp3 player – as I started to follow Godfrey out. He turned to me before we got to the door, 'Stay in the corridor while I get the others. We have a few minutes now, like I said, while the security guard checks the front. Trust me, and do as I say.'

I focused on the quiet clicks of the door opening and closing as we stepped out of my room, hopefully for one last time. The corridor light was a little dazzling and the anxiety spiked because I felt exposed.
I was terrified one of the staff would come bounding down

the corridor towards us from the mess hall any second, or Greg would burst out of his room, and this would be stamped out before it even began.

Godfrey glided across to Lorraine's room and entered. It felt like an hour before they both came out but it probably was only a minute. I nodded and grinned solemnly at Lorraine, she smiled back but with more confidence, and we moved to Simon's room door.
I peered in as Godfrey entered. Simon was ready and waiting in his chair. We fist bumped as they came out.
Now to get Ed. His room was at the bottom of the corridor and in view of some of the mess hall, so, more risky. My heart beat was rapid now.
I thought to myself, 'Please don't be seen,' repeatedly as we waited for Godfrey to again reappear with Ed. Lorraine put her hand on my shoulder.
Ed's door handle angled downwards and I breathed a bit again; Godfrey, followed by Ed with a bag like the rest of us and his 'Edphones' around his neck as always.
He looked pale, almost see through. More nervous than me. Godfrey hunched over Simon and Lorraine and pointed two fingers at his eyes, and then his index finger at himself.
We all looked at each other for a second in acknowledgement and started following Godfrey as he beckoned us to follow him into the mess hall.

A paranoid thought hit me then, of the huge risk we were taking by trusting Godfrey. What if he *was* really just like the

other staff? What if he was leading us into a trap?
But it was too late to worry about that now. I couldn't. It
was time to trust, like he asked. We were in the middle of the
leap of faith.

The lights were off in the mess-hall except for a few pilot
lights and a soft blue glow from the garden.
Godfrey stopped us at the edge of the hard floor and
pointed at the aisle along the side of the tables, to the
garden doors. We followed him briskly that way, stooped
over, in a single file; Simon first, then Ed, me and Lorraine.
Ed and Simon reached the doors ahead of us a few seconds
after Godfrey. I took it slower and crept along between the
tables and wall cabinets to catch up.
Suddenly, I heard a voice, 'BILL! Get down.'
I shot down to my knees without thinking, under the cover of
the tables. The adrenaline helped my reflexes, at least, but my
mouth quickly went dry.
It was a girl's voice. I craned my neck around as I crouched, and
saw Lorraine crouched too at the first table behind.
Who said that?
As I looked at her, bewildered, she pointed up above the
tables, towards the front entrance of the hall. Then I saw
the flicker of a torch-light between the gaps of the table
and chairs Lorraine was behind.
I glanced over my shoulder at Godfrey, Simon and Ed. They
were crouched now too, as low as possible at the garden
doors, glancing from us to the entrance. I peeped cautiously
over the table.

The torch-beam scanned the part of the mess-hall near the dispensary office but
I couldn't see who was holding it as they hadn't come all the way in.
The light dropped to the floor and disappeared, followed by whistling in that front corridor.
We all exhaled in relief. The threat of being seen had passed for now. Carl was on patrol alright.

I could have sworn Lorraine had spoken.

We didn't dawdle and scurried to join the others at the double doors. Godfrey made the 'ssh' signal, gently twisted the latch and opened them. We were at the garden. Only another small bit to go.

Adrenaline had definitely taken over from anxiety by now and I felt more in the flow of the moment. The garden was dark apart from the few dim blue solar lamps set along the paths. Our legs crisscrossed in front of them as we hurried along. I remembered the cameras, and felt them watching us a bit.

We made it to the wall of yew trees at the back of the garden. I worried for a second about whether Carl was back yet; it was hard to tell how much time had passed.
Godfrey went straight to the two trees that were thinner and had more of a gap between them than the others.
Just this obstacle now, and we were out.
'Ok,' Godfrey said to us, quietly in command. 'I will go first. Watch my technique. Stay as quiet as possible. Simon next. I

will be on the other side.' We watched anxiously, in the almost-dark, as he grabbed the pole joining one part of the fence to the other and used it to climb up onto the wall. He did it without making much noise at all.

Ed and I lifted Simon up out of his chair. As high as we could towards the top of the fence. Godfrey was sitting on the wall with outstretched arms and pulled him up.

Simon whispered to Godfrey, who nodded and then dropped down to the outside.

Lorraine went next; Simon helped her at the top, he was now perched on the wall.

She joined Godfrey on the other side.

Ed and I were just about to hoist Simon's chair up to him over the fence when we heard a 'psst' from above.

We stopped still and our heads jerked upwards at Simon. He was pointing towards the back patio.

That feeling of dread came over me again.

It was the torch-light, flickering on the grass.

We all hunched over again for cover as we heard the double doors opening. Carl stood on the patio and scanned the garden with his torch.

Godfrey had chosen the perfect spot. A yew tree and some shrubs stood directly in between where we were at the fence, and the patio doors, blocking the torch-light's path to us.

We would have to move quickly now, in case Carl walked into the garden where we *would* be in view.

Simon beckoned silently, for us to hurry with his chair. We grabbed and thrusted it up to Simon's eager grasp at the top of the wall.

But in our haste, he hadn't clutched the wheel properly. The chair slipped out of his hands as we stepped back. I winced and put my hands on my head in anticipation of the loud metallic crash that would ruin our cover. Ed lunged forward desperately to try and cushion the clatter.

But there was none. I opened my eyes; confused, surprised, relieved - my hands still on my head. There was no way Ed could have caught it.
Simon's chair was floating a foot above the ground in front of us. We looked at each other, eyes wide in amazement.
Simon's hand was outstretched and trembling, above his floating chair. He had stopped it with his mind.
Then, from behind us, across the garden at the patio, we heard the clunk of the doors closing. The flicker of the torch had disappeared. Carl had gone back inside.
Ed put his head in his left hand and bent over in relief. My shoulders dropped an inch.

'Come on, lads!' Simon rasped, still straining to hold the chair invisibly and half-holding his breath. 'It's not over yet.'
We snapped out of the relief and astonishment and grabbed Ed's chair from its levitation. It didn't feel any different from picking it up off the ground except for a tiny bob as we gripped.
No time to worry or dwell or hesitate, Carl would be back at the monitors soon. This time we made sure Simon had his chair firmly in his hands. He bundled it over the wall to

Lorraine and Godfrey.

'Go, Si,' I whispered strongly. 'We'll be fine.'

Simon dropped down to the other side, at my insistence, with the help of the others.

Ed still looked terrified but ushered me to go before him.

'Are you sure?' I asked.

'Yes. Go on,' he replied, not making eye-contact.

We didn't have time to argue over niceties either, so I pulled myself up onto the fence between the trees, like the others. Gripping the pole and fencing, I levered my body up to the top and propped my torso against it before catching the wall behind it. I dragged my legs up after.

I was up on the wall. We *were* getting out of here.

Our world was going to be so much bigger outside of this wall. I looked back at the mess hall windows again for the last time and jumped down to the other side.

'Come on, Ed!' I shout-whispered back over the wall. I hadn't looked outward yet at all.

We heard the faint clink and rattle of the fence as Ed grabbed it and hauled himself up to the top of the wall.

Just as he did, there was a flash of light from the sky. A big spotlight had burst on from the roof of Pleasant Pines. That outbuilding with the antennae. We could just about see it through the tops of the trees.

The powerful beam of light moved quickly across the garden towards Ed on the wall. He was exposed now and would be right in the line of sight of the beam from the roof.

With no time to avoid it, having one leg on either side of the wall, he braced himself and put one hand over his face in a last, vain attempt to hide.

The beam was about to land right on him - we ducked - but when it did, Ed disappeared.

My mouth dropped. I fell backwards onto my hands, looking to either side of where he had been on the wall. Lorraine had her hand up to her mouth and Simon was transfixed to the spot where the search-light was zeroed.

Godfrey was unmoved.

'Edgar!' he directed, still composed, not shouting. 'They haven't seen you. Keep moving!'

The search light remained trained on the top of the wall for a few seconds. There was a rustling from where Ed had been. Then, a thud at the base of the wall in front of us. Ed reappeared. He had somehow turned himself invisible for a moment.

He turned around in a circle trying to process what had happened and looked back up at the wall. The searchlight moved, slightly to the left, then right, and on, back into the garden. We hadn't been caught.

'Well done, Edgar,' Godfrey reassured him, putting a hand on his shoulder, next to the headphones. 'You used your gift to hide yourself. We will talk about it and explore it more when we're safe, but now, we have to go.'

He turned to address us all, 'He didn't see us, there would have been an alarm. But we can't be too careful, it's only a matter of time before one is raised.'

'Since when did we have an alarm and a searchlight?' Ed muttered to himself, shaken.

Godfrey walked though our shell-shocked group and into the pre-dawn that was growing behind us.

Realising where I was, I turned and looked around at this new environment and staggered forward. And then I looked back again.
The outside of Pleasant Pines, from here, looked more like a fortress, in the dim grey light.
There were big metal pylon things at the four corners of the huge compound.
I began walking, more purposefully, to follow Godfrey's lead but felt a crunch under my shoes and stopped. The sound repeated as the others stepped forward after me.
They stopped too.
I looked down to see what debris we had stepped on and saw a disjointed line, that went completely along the stretch of wall, of dead birds.

There were hundreds of them. The four of us turned while stepping backwards away from the wall-graveyard, avoiding more bird carcasses, looking from the ground to the pylons and back at Pleasant Pines in shock, fear, exhaustion, relief all at once.
The pylons were projecting, what must have been, some kind of invisible electric fence above the wall around it, killing the birds before they could fly in. I felt completely daunted by the place at that realisation-moment, but swallowed it.
We turned again, and left.

# Part 2

# Chapter 17 - Hide and seek 

We walked, following Godfrey, quickly and without saying anything for what must have been an hour at least without a break.

Then we stopped. It wasn't that dark anymore, there was a slight greyness growing.

I couldn't help but look around at the landscape. This new world. It was so open. But it *was* mostly dead.

The few scattered trees were naked, barely alive. We passed two small abandoned buildings with the windows boarded up and the walls cracked. The ground was cracked too, and yellowish. The odd boulder had some dried-out moss stuff on it; probably left over from the end of the rains a few weeks back.

We crossed some old roads that cars must have driven on, but not for a long time as there were no tracks in the layer of dusty sand on them. And we passed a disused petrol station.

Apart from that, it was empty and quiet. I kept checking the sky for birds but there weren't any so far.

We all bent over, panting. Godfrey took bottles of water from his bag and passed them to us.

'It will be dawn soon,' he stated. 'Catch your breath and drink; you'll need it in the heat. It's an eight hour walk from here to The Haven.'

I gulped some water as he spoke.

'We have done well, but you must stay close to me and

remain alert. There will be surveillance drones in the sky as we get closer to the city, and they won't be friendly.'

Not exactly what we wanted to hear.

We moved off again after a few minutes. The air was almost cool, surprisingly. No UM cancer, I reminded myself. There were lots of hills with wiry scrub dotted on them.

'So, ye all saw that right, what I did with my chair?' Simon decided to make conversation after another stretch of trekking and taking in the brightening alien terrain.

'Well done on dropping it in the first place, Si,' I replied.

'Now, Ed turning invisible *was* impressive.' Ed and I grinned at each other. 'And where was Mickey Mouse, Bill, you fungus sausage? I thought you would have called in the big guns?'

We all chuckled, to calm the tension of the escape still in our minds as much as anything. Simon was good at lightening the mood sometimes.

I did hope that I would see Mynos again. Godfrey hadn't answered me before. I decided to try again,

'Godfrey?' I started, as we came to a ridge with scattered tufts of waxy-looking, barely green, grass on it. 'Is Mynos still alive?'

'Yes, Bill,' he replied, still marching. I inhaled with relief. 'He came to The Haven on Max.'

'Who's Max?'

'My dog. He patrols the land around the safe house, and, quite fortunately, came upon your little friend.'

I was about to question further but, just as we walked over the ridge, I was stunned by the view.

We were at the top of a height overlooking a valley. It sloped right down to a low horizon, between two small mountains, that met the low, dawn Sun. A Sun that I had never seen before this low; it was incredible.

The sky around the Sunrise, and the orb itself, was tinted with a glow of purple and green that was in complete contrast with the grey everywhere else. I had never seen a real Sunrise in Pleasant Pines, but this was better than I had ever imagined in my head or seen on TV.

The green and purple light highlighted big, motionless wind turbines spread out around the hills on either side of the valley. Godfrey noticed that the four of us were paused in awe at the new view and doubled back.

'It's pretty isn't it?' he said.

'Wow,' Ed commented under his breath, and I added, 'It's amazing.'

'The colours come from the polluting gases we put up there over the years. It's why the daytime sky is grey always. Many years ago, it was actually blue. But Sunrises and sets are nice at least.'

His explanation flattened the mood. Pollution, death and destruction behind that beauty.

We continued on down into and across the valley, passing several more long-empty, Sun-scorched buildings while taking in the Sunrise again as we moved with it.

It was starting to get hot.

In and around the abandoned buildings, there were a few hardy weeds. Their existence was probably helped by the

added shade, but in lots of ways, the land was very much like how the news would describe.
I thought about what Godfrey had told me; that the news was *all* a lie. I considered pointing that out but left it go. Priority now was to get to this place he called 'The Haven'.

When we eventually reached the other side of the valley, we were struggling again, and more than before. The Sun was out in the open now, glaring down. Sweat was dripping from my brow. I took another gulp of water.
'Don't drink too much,' Godfrey advised loudly, a few metres ahead and stoic, as seemed to be his way. 'We need it to last another few hours.'
Lorraine tilted her head abruptly forwards with her bottle on her lips at his words. She only had about a fifth of her water left and was now looking at it with concern.
'It's ok, Lorraine,' I reacted. 'You can have some of mine'
She nodded and unconfidently smiled. We kept going. Simon was stubbornly refusing help to push him up the slope.
'Only another small bit now. We can rest at the top,' Godfrey reassured us. This was tough. Our bodies weren't used to it at all. But at the same time, it felt oddly good; our lungs, legs and hearts working hard. It was liberating to have this vast openness around us and a new, real challenge.

My mind wandered back to Pleasant Pines and a little anxiety. The Nurses would be discovering that we were missing about now. Would they go searching for us? If they left in cars soon they could find us.

I thought about Ollie too. He was never far from my thoughts. Could I have done more to help him? If we had had more time to plan things, maybe we could have saved him and gotten him to come with us.
I know it was hard for him to communicate, but awful that he felt he had no other way out.

Godfrey reached the top of the rise ahead of us. We strained a few more uphill strides to join him.
'Can someone help me here so, please?' Simon asked, finally finding the effort of navigating the rocky incline too much on his arms.

Ed hurried back a few steps and grabbed the back of his chair. I pulled myself up onto the ridge and the next landmark hit my view: An abandoned factory.
Two giant grey chimneys stuck out from the middle of it and it was surrounded by rusted fencing; outside that, several disused, dusty cars and more skeletons of trees.
About a kilometre to the left, and behind the factory, were more motionless wind-turbines poking up into the horizon. I wondered about how everything became so dead and still - turned off.

'Sit,' Godfrey directed. We gratefully obliged. The Sun was getting really strong now.
'That was an old power station, used to generate electricity many years back,' he continued, pointing at it as we sat. 'The

governments were too slow in shutting them all down and using alternatives to fuel burning. They would pump thousands of tonnes of chemicals and gases into the atmosphere every day.

Greed and denial. Comfiness. Politics. It was too late when they built the wind power generators that you see there behind.'

We all surveyed the desert with its story in mind. I felt my anxiety swelling again, about nothing (or everything) in particular. This was the longest I had ever gone without medication and I could feel it.

'The irony of it is that, now, with the Sun so prevalent, Solar energy has become big business.'

As Godfrey spoke and we listened with interest at the parts of history the news never told us, I heard a low buzzing sound and what sounded like a distant voice coming from beyond the power station to the right.

Godfrey's head swiveled.

'We need to hide,' he hissed, already on his feet. Panic hit me instantly. We darted after him as he ran - staying low - to cover behind one of the cars.

'Is that one of the drones?' I whispered, forcing it over the oncoming buzz. We all crouched down together, knee to knee behind the dusty car. Godfrey replied, 'yes' sharply, then covered his mouth with an index finger. The buzzing got louder, but where did the voice come from? Ed was turning pale again.

The drone was in front of the power station now, only about fifty meters from us.

Echoing off the structure, the voice boomed again, much

louder.

It was coming *from* the drone.

'People of Aunn Teer, if you can hear this, I urge you to present yourself and avail of our GPS guidance to the city, where – after processing – shelter, food and welcome are available. We, of course, all need to work together to maintain a harmonious and recovering society in the ongoing Global Crisis Management Strategy.'

This was nuts. I had to see it and peaked through the car windows. I could just about see it through the dust.

It had a metallic sheen and four fan engines, but on top of it, there was what must have been a hologram, of a man, about a metre in height, hovering along with it. He was wearing a black uniform with gold details and a black beret with what looked like wings on either side of it above his ears. There was a bluish outline to the hologram.

Godfrey jammed my head back down underneath the car window with a glare. The hologram continued announcing, 'If you have, or someone you know has, or knows someone to have SP traits, we would like to hear from you. As you may be aware, SPs are vulnerable and/or may pose dangers to themselves and others, and so, will need to spend time in a Wellness Centre for support and adaptive treatment towards the long term GCMS goal.

Yours faithfully and sincerely, Elron Hawking Goode.'

There was only the buzzing again for a moment before a triumphant piece of music played. There were trumpets and synthesizers in it. It kind of sounded like one of those dodgy ancient pop songs from the 1980s.

We exchanged looks of disbelief from our crouched hiding place. Simon shook his head.

The buzzing grew louder still, closer.

We all glanced at Godfrey for the next move, fear growing. He looked a bit unsettled for once; I felt my breathing get even more shallow.

He whipped his rucksack from his shoulder and quickly dug out a silvery square.

The drone was right on the other side of the car now.

Godfrey placed the square on the dry ground and pulled a chord from it.

In less than a second, the square sprang open and expanded into a kind of small, open-ended tent.

He ushered us into it and pulled it over our desperate huddle. It became hard to breathe in the squeeze and panic.

The drone was now in front of our side of the car, in the air a few metres from the tent; the buzzing now menacingly close.

It sounded like it was adjusting its height, trying to deduce what the tent was.

I was verging on a panic attack, my eyes flicking from side to side, head on my knees as I clutched them to my chest, hoping that it would move on; but it inched closer.

'Si, can you stop it with your mind?' I whispered in Simon's ear without moving. He shook his head.

There was no escape, we were caught. My thoughts raced into what it – they – would do to us. What else were they capable of?

The sound of a robotic arm extending whirred above the

buzzing and the tent fabric was pinched from outside, inches above my head.

Out of nowhere: a thud on the car, a bark and a crashing sound on the ground just next to us. Then, thrashing, growling, sparking and sputtering.

The drone-fans stuttered and cut out.

Godfrey leapt upwards, yanking the tent with him.

'Max!' he exclaimed at our unseen saviour. 'Well timed, my boy!'

We lifted our heads gingerly from the tight huddle, it was safe to move now. The drone was shattered on the ground. The hologram was gone, and stood over the debris with his tongue heaving, a huge, tan-coloured dog.

# Chapter 18 - Placebo 

Godfrey slapped the dog's side – hard enough to injure a jack-russell but to its enjoyment. And then it spoke.

'I smelled you coming,' he said to Godfrey.

Amazingly, I could hear the dog's voice, in my language, like with Mynos. He sounded young but assured. I suppose dogs could be both young and old in a way, now that I thought about them.

'Well, it's a good thing you did, the thermal shield didn't seem to put it off this time.'

The others looked at Godfrey a bit confused. They couldn't hear the dog like me. I decided to test this ability.

'Hi...eh, Max is it?' I said to him. 'Thanks...for helping us.'

The huge dog bowed its head and sniffed the ground next to me.

'So, you're the mouse's friend?' he huffed as his head lifted again.

'Yes, that's me. I put out pieces of biscuit for him at night and, I guess, we became friends.' It still felt totally weird and amazing to be fully conversing with an animal. He kept sniffing at me.

'Bill, everyone, this is Max, my dog,' Godfrey interjected, and then told Max our names. 'Bill and I share the same hyper-ability of communication with non-humans, in case you're a bit flummoxed.'

Everyone uncertainly said 'hi' and 'nice to meet you' and 'thanks' to Max. 'Nice to meet you and your friends too, Bill. Yours is a rare gift,' he replied. While checking his watch,

Godfrey again cut in.

'Right, let's not get too deep. That was close to being troublesome, it's hot and we still have some way to go.'

He pulled another chord from the wall of the silver tent and it instantly folded in on itself and back down to the small square.

Max leapt up onto the bonnet of the car and sniffed the air warily. We quickly sipped more water and brushed ourselves down, ready to move again.

'The drones use heat signature vision to spot us. The tent blocks it, but it didn't stop it making a closer inspection this time,' Godfrey continued, fixing his rucksack in place on his shoulders again.

'Drones?!' Simon remarked to no one in particular. 'That's mental. But I suppose everything's gone a bit that way now altogether... Sorry I couldn't help stop it, I tried.'

'There's time for you all with your gifts. But for now, we must stay focused on getting to safety,' Godfrey added, before making a clicking noise towards Max and starting to walk again.

As we restarted the march, I looked ahead at Max trotting along loyally next to Godfrey. He was lean but massive. His head came up to Godfrey's chest almost, definitely mine.

I noticed the anxiety was still quite bad in my chest and stomach, even though the danger had passed.

Sweat started to build above my eyes again. This world certainly wasn't inviting so far.

I just hoped that this Haven place was secure and cooler, and that I don't start feeling much worse mentally.

At least Max could help us detect a drone further off now, I thought, trying to stay positive.

Our heavy breathing was syncopated with our shoes kicking along the arid ground.

'You should know, the temperatures reported in the news are false,' Godfrey said after a particularly hot period of walking. 'They say 50 degrees but in fact, it's actually in the high 30s, in most parts.'

We all reacted in surprise again, slowing our strides. I was panting and sweating, but as I digested that new fact, I noticed it *did* feel a tiny bit cooler, less oppressive.

For another hour or so, we trudged in silence, the novelty of the desert landscape, like from another planet compared to the Pleasant Pines garden, wearing off with each step.

Max would occasionally trot to the back of our group and twitch his nose and ears at the trail behind us.

It was around noon. The sun was roasting the tops of our heads. If there was a search party, it would be well under way by now. And that thought started to weigh on me as much as the heat.

# Chapter 19 - Inner Strength 

My chest felt tight and I had started clenching my jaw. I kept thinking Dr. Akbar or Shane 2 were behind us, or that another drone would come zooming down on us, and there would be nowhere to hide this time. Maybe even that we *deserved* to be caught. NATs I suppose.

'Don't worry, Bill,' Max said, scanning the horizon from which we had travelled. 'I can sense you're afraid. You're safe now. Godfrey and I haven't gotten this far without knowing a trick or two.'

I tried to believe him. Push my brain back to the positives again. It *was* cool, I suppose, to think that none of the others could hear him, even though Ed wouldn't, even if he could, with the headphones back on.

This was my gift and I should be proud of it.

I lifted my cheeks into a smile at Max' reassurance and he padded back ahead next to Godfrey. Apparently, it takes less muscles in your face to smile than frown, but sometimes, it doesn't feel that way.

'What are you listening to, Ed?' I said, turning my attention and nudging his arm.

'Hmn? Oh, Nine Inch Nails, and the dark trilogy Cure.'

'Ah, cheery as usual,' I chuckled. 'I do like that one, 'Friday, I'm in Love'.'

'Mmn, it's a bit twee though,' he replied.

Then something caught my attention in the distance above some withered tree trunks. I straightened up with fear again.

It was a flock of birds. My hand was on my chest.
'Calm down, Bill,' I said to myself and adjusted my emotions
from fright to wonder.
Simon had stopped and was pointing.
'Wow, look!' he said.
We all stopped with him for a moment to look at the birds.
Hundreds of them moving together in a flowing sky-dance.
The freedom in their movement was incredible, but at the
same time, they were also completely unified as a team.
Ollie flitted into my mind again; he would have loved to
have seen this.

Max barked and Godfrey waved us forward when they
noticed we had stopped to gawk. They were obviously
pretty used to the birds.
They turned and were about to continue the trek, and we
began to follow, when Max started to growl, ears pricked.

# Chapter 20 - Prey 

Up ahead, I saw what looked like a wild dog dart between two boulders. Godfrey's shoulders tensed and he bent his knees, eyes fixed on the movement. He waved a palm towards us to stop, 'Desert-wolves.'

As he said it, two more large dogs' heads reared up from behind rocky cover. They were as big, if not bigger, than Max. Then, a mouse scuttled into the open away from them.

Was that Mynos? I started to walk towards the scene, concerned, but Godfrey shot me a wide-eyed warning stare and a raised hand to stay still.

Another of the desert-wolves appeared to the left, from the direction the mouse was running. It burst forward, as low to the ground as its big frame would allow and pounced.

I gasped.

The mouse dangled from the wolf's jaws - dead. The other three padded out to the kill, sniffing the ground around it.

Godfrey turned again to me and whispered, 'It's not Mynos, Bill.' He lowered a flat palm towards the ground urging us to stay calm and still.

We watched the desert-wolves pick the dead mouse apart. It only took them a few seconds and then there was nothing left. Max was surprisingly quiet.

They hadn't noticed us, or were ignoring us. Then they trotted off down a dried up creek to the left and out of sight. It was unsettling but I was relieved that it wasn't Mynos, as cruel as that sounds.

We began walking again on command but, after another few metres, I was startled once more and stood still again. This time, by a girl's voice from behind me. I spun around 180 degrees, stumbling a bit, but only Lorraine was there. 'Bill...I'm not feeling well at all.' Her mouth didn't move, but our eyes met as I heard her words and I knew. It *was* Lorraine speaking, but in my thoughts. And she did look exhausted and pale.
'Where are we? I can't go on, Ed, Simon...I'm sorry.'
Her eyes rolled back into her head and her legs crumpled under her.

# Chapter 21 - Push 

Ed reacted first, darting towards her as she was about to hit the ground, and caught her.

'Godfrey, help!' I shouted. We surrounded her in Ed's arms. Godfrey and Max rushed back to our huddle.

'Move,' Godfrey said calmly, to Simon and I, pushing between us. 'It looks like heat stroke. Does she have any water left?'

'No,' I replied. 'She'd been drinking mine.'

'Give her the end of it so, Bill.'

I handed Ed my water bottle and he poured a dribble into the small opening between Lorraine's lips. She was unconscious. It was serious.

I could feel myself starting to panic, thinking she was dying – we were still miles from anywhere. I tried to control the panic but that almost made it worse.

'Lorraine!' Ed said to her firmly. 'Can you hear me?'

She was still unresponsive.

I started pacing outside of the huddle.

Ed put his trembling hand on her brow to check how hot she felt, not knowing what else to do.

A moment after he did, Lorraine stirred.

'Ed?' she spoke again, fraily, without opening her mouth, and her eyes still closed. 'Your hand's...cold...'

Her eyes opened. I stopped pacing.

'She talked!?' Simon exclaimed, looking around at us as we stooped closer in towards her again.

Ed kept his hand on her brow; whatever was happening, it

was working.

'Thank you,' she said, again without moving her mouth – in our heads. 'That's helping…'

Ed looked up at us, like Simon, for more confirmation - that we had heard her too. We had.

*This* was Lorraine's ability. She *could* talk, but with her mind. All of those times I thought I imagined her saying something back in Pleasant Pines, she actually really was, underneath the medication.

As I knelt next to them, I felt the coldness coming from Ed. It was like an aura, mainly coming from his hands. Things started to replay and click in my head then. I remembered when he brought me the cold coffee a few weeks back in the mess hall. This cold force-field must be something to do with his ability too. As well as the turning invisible? A multi-ability?

'Ed, I can feel cold air from you,' I said.

'Yeah, I've been noticing different things for the last while in Pleasant Pines, but didn't want to make a big deal out of it at all.' His voice trailed off insecurely.

'I think I can...stand up…' Lorraine uttered internally.

'Let her up, gently now,' Godfrey instructed.

Ed gingerly stood up from his knees, while still holding Lorraine, and gravity returned to her feet.

'Stay next to her, Edgar, but let her find her strength,' Godfrey added, watching her closely as she stood and balanced. 'Well done,' he said, slightly quieter to Ed. And then louder, 'You're learning about your hyper-ability and using it. We all are.'

He didn't seem as surprised as the rest of us by these 'abilities',
like he expected them.
We were relieved that Lorraine seemed to be ok again.
'I think the coldness is going a bit, though,' Ed replied, keeping
one hand on Lorraine's shoulder but rubbing his palm with his
fingers on the other hand. Godfrey responded, 'Ok, but stay
with her, and drink the rest of the water, Lorraine. We don't
have much further to go now.'

With that, Godfrey turned and started walking purposefully
again in the lead, but slower now than before.
Max had been keeping watch in a circle around us and joined
the rhythm of the group again as we moved off.

Up ahead, towards the horizon, I noticed the ground become
more rocky and jagged.
Ed and Lorraine walked in tandem just in front of me,
Ed's arm around Lorraine, trying to hold his cool. She
gave him a kiss on the cheek.
It was nice to see after all the panic, and Simon even refrained
from making a joke out of it.
My anxiety was still concerning me, in the background, but at
least I didn't have a full blown panic attack. I was managing
it, just; focusing on the dusty ground beneath my shoes and
each step.

After another short stretch, Godfrey turned to us while
walking backwards, 'Up ahead, we must pass through fire-
beetle territory. Beyond that is where The Haven is,' he said,

pointing behind him with his thumb, towards two large, uneven rocky columns shimmering with the heat near our horizon. 'Through and beyond those rock formations. Just one last push.'

# Chapter 22 - Fire-beetles

After a slight dip in the terrain, the ground looked sandier than before in front of us. A strong wind blew through our group all of a sudden. My focus jumped a bit further ahead to where the ground was covered in big patches of black.

In between the black parts were sandy mounds with tufts of brownish green grass.

'Is this where the "fire-beetles" are?'

Just as Simon asked Godfrey we heard a small bang and a spark flashed from one of the tufts to our right.

'They are a relatively new species,' he responded, still walking, while we had stopped, looking in the direction of the bang.

'Their larvae get nutrients from the soot and ash.' He pointed at a patch of black on the ground. 'They have special exoskeletons that, when they click their legs together, create sparks. And, of course, they're fire-resistant.'

We kept going. My eyes followed a line of the brownish grass off to the left, and ahead of it, there was a burnt building with no roof, half-hidden by rocks.

Another small bang came from behind us to the left.

Then the wind picked up even more. It made me have to shift my balance against it. Very different compared to the dead air from before here on our journey. It was probably the strongest wind I'd ever felt.

'We'll have to move a bit faster now, I'm afraid,' Godfrey advised.

'Don't want to get caught in a fire.'

We picked up the pace. My concern for Lorraine grew again.

Ed was still helping her to walk.

As the wind swirled around us and the sand was thrown up to mix with it, another crack came from behind us.

I turned to check it, out of fright more than curiosity this time. A small flame flickered amongst the desert grass. A spark had caught.

'Si, look, they started one,' I said, still looking at the small fire.

'Whoa,' he replied, turning around with me.

The wind kicked up again. With it, the fire grew, latching onto more tufts.

'Bill, Simon! Come on!' Godfrey shouted.

Another gust. But this time it didn't die off. More sand was sucked upwards. Then the fire was whipped upwards with it into a cyclone. I stumbled sideways with the wind.

'Run!' Godfrey yelled.

The wind-storm had created a small tornado of fire. I didn't have time to be amazed or worried by it. We sprinted away from it after the others. The wind blasted in my ears as we ran through the patches of scorched soil. I had to squint to keep the sand out of my eyes. Ed had lifted Lorraine off the ground as they ran just ahead of us.

We kept going, heads down, until the ground became rockier and plain again. I looked over my shoulder.

The fire tornado had become thinner again but was still swaying from side to side about 100 metres back. Some more patches of grass had caught fire around it.

'Okay, we're safe here,' Godfrey reassured. 'But let's keep moving. Lorraine, you can rest up ahead. Ed, try to keep her cool.'

I walked half-backwards for a minute, watching the fire and wind die down behind us again to a few smokey flickers. I imagined the beetles jumping in the embers.
This place sure was different.

# Chapter 23 - The Valley 

The wind died off completely again after ten minutes of walking away from the fire-beetles. But then the Sun came back to the fore in our minds and bodies.
It was still uncomfortably strong and high in the sky and made my scalp itch. We marched towards the now close and big rocky outcrops and another ridge behind them. I clung to the fact that Godfrey had said we were nearly there, because the heat felt relentless again, and things could get very messy if we had to go much further. The stone ahead was sandy yellow coloured; boulders of various sizes scattered in front of us.
Godfrey told us to rest and we gratefully sat on the rocks.

Ed let go of Lorraine's shoulder and gave her some space. Despite the close-call with the fire and Lorraine, he had an unusual slight smile on his face and kept glancing back over at Lorraine. They actually seemed good together. She was still very weak but seemed to be managing a bit better.
Simon had a dribble of water left and he gave it to her before we moved on again. Ed linked back up with her as we restarted the march.

I looked behind us again for a moment, at the land we had traversed. We had actually been going slightly uphill. When I turned back towards the yellow boulders, I realised that Ed was powering ahead, with Lorraine's shoes barely touching the ground and his arm tight around her. He accelerated right past Max and Godfrey.

'Ed, slow down, man,' Simon shouted after him. 'Is he on some kind of energy-high after the heroics, or what?'

'Yeah, I think she'd prefer to walk at her own pace,' I added.

In agreement with us, Godfrey boomed, 'Edgar, STOP!'

Ed stopped abruptly and looked at Lorraine, squeezed next to him, as if he had just snapped out of a trance. He let go of her and looked back at us following, and then at the ground.

'Oh...sorry, I didn't realise,' he said, sounding confused. They both looked at each other awkwardly before walking back to rejoin us.

Another few minutes' walk and the two columns of rock on either side were now behind us. Ahead, it looked like there was another valley beyond the ridge.

We followed Godfrey through a narrow path then between mounds of boulders that had been hidden from further back. Simon asked me to help him navigate it. We were all glad that the rocks around us were providing some shade now. And with that gladness, we found ourselves noticeably curious again about the terrain as we moved through the rock-walled passage.

'Imagine if there are, like, ancient stone carvings around here somewhere?' I said to Simon, wiping sweat from my face with a forearm.

We stepped carefully through the tight, snaking path for

several minutes before reaching an opening. What was in front of us was both incredibly daunting and confusing, *and* sort of amazing, at the same time.

Godfrey was standing there with Max panting next to him. We were, indeed, on the verge of another valley; but this one was ten times as vast as the last. The opening in the rocky passage, on the down-slope of the ridge, created a natural viewing perch here.
The first thing that caught my eye in the view before us, was a thin river in the middle of the valley, at the end of which was a distant mass of glinting grey; a giant circular city.
At the centre of that distant city were several skyscrapers. The buildings in it generally seemed to get smaller as they radiated out to the edge. It was like a silver mountain.
I saw green too. I could just make it out, in patches around the city's buildings. Movement caught my eye in the valley then; a couple of silvery dots, reflecting the sun, flying slowly through the valley off to the east of the city; drones.

'That's Ferfa,' Godfrey said, as we surveyed the biggest expanse we had ever seen.
'Also known as "The Last City".'
'Wow…'bit dramatic,' Simon chirped.
'We can't stay here for long, come on, we're exposed,' Godfrey warned while pointing at the silver dots. 'And there are more of them around…I will tell you about everything, soon…keep moving.'
He started off again, continuing through the narrowing rocky

path downhill amongst more boulders. Max followed behind him obediently.

I could only see glimpses of Godfrey's head and the tops of his shoulders then between the boulder-walls. As they walked – us following once more – I noticed, down at the base of the slope ahead of them, our 10 o' clock, a huge crevice.

It was about fifty metres wide and maybe half a kilometre long; a few miles from the city.

I was just about to point it out to Simon, when Godfrey shouted back and pointed right towards it before me,

'That's where we call "home".'

# Chapter 24 - The Haven

We shuffled quickly down-slope through the passage to catch up with Godfrey and Max. We had to lean backwards slightly on our calves against the incline. The valley floor sprawled off to our right at the end of the slope.

Godfrey and Max were waiting for us when we reached the flat ground, at the edge of the big crevice. I realised that we had another bit of steep walking to do as we stood briefly at the top, looking down into it. There was a narrow path that hugged the wall of one side and looked like it led to the bottom.

The drop was at least as high as Pleasant Pines was tall and I discovered that I was scared of heights as well (added to the list!).

Godfrey waved a hand gesture towards it, behind him,

'This thin canyon was formed nearly twenty years ago after an earthquake.

Fortunately, I was able to make it my home soon after.'

He pointed at the sky. 'They don't fly in. They find it hard to map.'

He walked forward a bit, before crouching and touching a crooked thin piece of metal sticking out of the sandy ground.

'These help to scramble their sensors too; house-keeping, if you will.'

Max' tail began to wag as we eased onto the downward path behind Godfrey and into the canyon. I decided to strike up a conversation with the huge dog again while concentrating on my steps, ''You excited to be home, Max?'

''Sure am,' he replied. The little surge of excitement from being able to talk to a dog returned to me and the others looked up from the path, for a second, at our chat.

'I was on that last patrol since dawn.'

'We've been going since then too,' I added.

The anxiety had eased a little since I started helping Simon, I noticed, but the exhaustion hadn't.

'You'll like The Haven.' Max continued. 'It's our own little paradise. And you can rest.'

His tail kept wagging as he then moved up along our single file on the narrow path to Godfrey's side again.

I peeked tentatively over the edge at the ground below; stupidly, actually - my heart rate felt like it doubled when I saw the drop.

The Sun was hitting most of the canyon and it was high in the sky now. I reminded myself that the shade would grow in a few hours.

The rock wall next to us jutted inward to the right about halfway down. The path, Godfrey and Max, disappeared around it.

Then, I heard a faint gushing sound. As we turned that corner, we saw what they called 'The Haven'.

The cliff-path widened at the bottom where it met the canyon floor and ahead of that we faced a big wood-cabin, built right into a hollow at the base of the rock face. It had a shaded step-up deck area in front of it. There were green plants popping out between rocks and in pots all around it, and away from the cabin to the left in another recess in the cliff was a small waterfall that came from a crack in the rock above.

At the base of the waterfall in partial shade, was a rockpool. Between that and the cabin were two deck chairs and a fire pit. To the left of the fire pit and us was one big tree. Its upper branches splayed up and outwards like a fountain. Boulders and wiry bushes littered the canyon floor around us.

On second glance, I saw that the cabin was decorated with small, mutli-coloured ribbons fluttering gently in different spots on its wooden frame, and I noticed two antennas sticking out of the bit of roof that was exposed from the rock wall. A thick wire snaked from the cabin roof up to the top of the canyon wall, on one of two cliffs on either side of us. It was amazing. We all wheeled slowly around, taking in the space. It just felt totally new and free, but hidden and safe too. And it wasn't completely dead. I had never really seen natural, flowing water like the waterfall up close in real life before. The gushing echoed slightly around the canyon. And it was cooler and more shaded down here, even with the high Sun.

The four of us just stared at things for a while and caught our breath. I noticed what looked like paintings of animals on parts of the rock-wall opposite to the wooden cabin. Godfrey must have done them. There was a snake, one of the desert-wolves and birds among others.

We had made it.

'Lorraine, take a seat,' Godfrey said, while walking over to one of the deck chairs and moving it under the tree's shade. 'Max, fetch some water, please.'

'No problem,' he barked back. He padded up onto the cabin deck and picked up a wooden bucket with his mouth by its handle.

It sploshed about as he carried it back to us.

We joined Lorraine under the tree and drank ladles of water in turns after her. She seemed okay now.

After rummaging on the deck, Godfrey came back with a small solar powered fan and set it up in front of Lorraine.

'That was *arduous*,' Simon said after a few sips, his energy for commentary returning. 'Drones and fake news, exactly as suspected, really.

The pawns have left the table though, baby!' He lifted the ladle above his head to toast, water spilling out of it, and hung his other hand in front of me in a fist as I sat. Not one to leave him hanging, I bumped it with mine but rolled my eyes.

Then, the door of the cabin opened and my eyes moved from our fist bump to it. A girl backed out from inside holding what looked like an open laptop computer.

She pulled the door shut with her leg and swiveled to face us from the deck. Her shiny black hair flicked around and back over her shoulder to reveal her face and she said, 'Hey.'

A strange feeling came over me when I saw her. It was a bit

like anxiety but more enjoyable. And I kind of felt a bit sick like when I looked down into the canyon from the top but also amazed like when I saw the Sun-rise this morning. It was a lot to process.

But already, I thought she was the new, most beautiful thing I had ever seen, and that was saying something after today. It was almost too much to experience in one day. I took a deep breath.

'Seersha,' Godfrey addressed her while he walked towards the cabin. 'You've decided to join us? Everyone, meet Seersha; she's lived here with me for the last five or so years.'

She flipped the laptop closed, tucked it under one arm, waved at us, without making eye contact and then joined the circle. 'So, the new recruits...welcome to the weird family, I suppose,' she said. Her eyes were accentuated with black eyeliner and I couldn't take mine off them. 'Is she ok?' she added, nodding at Lorraine. Lorraine smiled in response to indicate that she was, and we all introduced ourselves.

She told us that Godfrey had helped her escape from a Wellness Centre like us. At the edge of my fascination with her, I noticed a scuttling movement from the cabin-deck and then I remembered - Mynos! It was him, my old buddy.

He hopped down the wooden steps and scurried across the sandy ground towards us.

'Well, Bill,' he said, standing up on his hind legs as he reached my foot, a little out of breath. 'You made it. We both did. Congratulations on your new freedom from them.'

'Thanks, Mynos,' I replied, smiling and crouching. 'We wouldn't be here without you, so I've heard. It's good to see you again. Are you ok? I thought a wolf had got you on our way here.'

'No, Bill. You helped me first. Your kindness shone out from the start. I wanted to help you in return. And we had a connection through your gift.'

My smile stuck as he continued.

'I'm fine, now. Don't worry, I'm too smart for those wolves. I had heard about The Haven through a swallow who nested near your facility. He had met Max further out in recent years. I decided to leave and search for him and this place. I had nearly given up when we found each other. It was lucky because I was too weak and had gone too far to make a return anytime soon.'

The others stared a bit at me exercising my ability again with Mynos. Everything was new. I couldn't help glancing at Seersha again too. Our eyes met, I darted mine off to the side and then quickly back to the mouse as if nothing had happened.

'I told Godfrey and Max about you and your friends. Then Godfrey ventured to the city in disguise and from there he went to the Pleasant Pines Centre.'

Godfrey pottered around the cabin deck and disappeared inside for a while as we rested and spoke. The shade slowly grew, which we were all thankful for. Simon began experimenting and managed to make a rock levitate for a few seconds to our delight, but in general, we all agreed that we weren't really feeling well, despite the rest.

Seersha spoke again at this and I gladly took the opportunity to gaze at her again.

'That's the withdrawals. From the meds. It will be a rough few days. Just focus on your breathing and drink water.'

She was a little shy and unassumingly beautiful.

In a weird coincidence, my already raised heartbeat suddenly started to turn rapid, uncomfortably so. I felt a rush of panic; tightness in my chest, and began looking around the canyon uneasily, without focusing on any one thing. My hand was trembling. Was I having a heart-attack?

'It's ok,' Seersha said to me, noticing my quiet distress. The others were focused on Simon who was talking loudly now about what possible technique he would use to levitate a huge boulder near the waterfall.

I looked up at her from my shaking hand.

'Just breath, like I said.' She smiled cutely at me with one side of her mouth and I fell instantly calm again.

Then she spoke out loud to the group.

'I better get back to it,' she said, holding the laptop up off her knees. 'See you in a bit for food.'

My eyes followed her as she went back inside the cabin. I couldn't wait for food, and not just because I was starving.

Godfrey emerged a few moments later and walked towards us at the tree. An exotic smell wafted from the cabin behind him.

'You like her, Bill,' Lorraine's voice popped suddenly into my head and I jumped a bit. I swung around to look at her.
'Whoa, what? Eh...hi, Lorraine,' I blurted, but not too loudly.
'Yeah, she seems nice, I suppose.'
'No, you "like" like her.'
'What? No, we've only just met.'
Lorraine smirked at my reply. Before she could probe further and start me panicking again, I countered with a question.
'Did you hear her just now?'
This was all surreal and awkwardly new.
'No, I didn't,' she replied. 'But you've been *thinking* loudly about her.'
She winked at me.
I grinned awkwardly and glanced at the ground. So, Lorraine could hear thoughts too?
Also, it was curious how Seersha seemed to have noticed me panicking but no one else had.
There was going to be a lot to get used to with these 'hyper-abilities'.

Godfrey stood in front of our tree-gathering and placed his hands on his hips, our attention held,
'Right, everyone; today has been an achievement to say the least, and I commend you on it. This is a lot to take on.' We glanced and smiled at each other, in a back-patting sort of way.

'I trust you all have hydrated well now. Lorraine, you look stronger.' He nodded at her. 'I was preparing the cabin for you. There are two rooms with bunk-beds inside – one for the girls and one for the boys – but we will get to those later. For now, follow me.'

Max bolted down from his perch on the cabin deck and mounted a small boulder in the direction Godfrey was beckoning to, to our left.

I felt really stiff getting back up and moving again. Tomorrow would be painful. The shadows had grown so that one side of the canyon was now in the shade of the cliff behind the cabin. There also seemed to be a slight breeze passing through which was nice.

We followed Godfrey again, obediently and humbly; he had freed us, and got us here safely without knowing much about us at all. My respect and gratitude was big and still growing for him.

He led us over to the rock pool beneath the waterfall. As we reached it, a stream that came from it and followed a gentle slope further away from the cabin into the canyon, came into view. It trickled between a mound of boulders on its way, at which Godfrey pointed,

'Behind those, we have our little garden.'

It was all almost overwhelming to take in, like Godfrey had said, 'a lot', like we had just been born, but it was exciting. We rounded the rocks eagerly. A dusty dirt-bike was leaning against them next to the garden.

Then, the colours of the plants, the pop of contrasts against the surrounding backdrop of yellowish brown rock, took me by surprise – especially given the outside landscape we had walked on to get here.

Vibrant green pea plants. Kind of…lettuce. The tops of carrots. Rich red tomatoes, strawberries, an orange bush, all bursting from well moistened dark brown soil.

Behind those, were a group of very striking tall plants that I couldn't name. The leafy flowers on them were like big stars coloured with zebra patterns of dark green and bright yellow. They kind of glistened.

'This is how we eat, of course,' Godfrey gestured at the plants like they were a prize exhibit of his. 'I presume you all like vegetables? Max and I collect spices too from around the valley, ones we don't grow ourselves, so the flavours are quite nice really, you'll enjoy; but I'm sure you'd eat anything now, after our efforts.

We also have some grain growing a little further down there.'

He pointed beyond the rock walled garden. 'What's for dinner tonight?' Simon asked.

'My speciality curry.'

I made the connection with the smell. I had never tried curry before, don't think the others had either, so another first.

'I will show ye how to tend the garden if you're interested. Good to get stuck in. It can be nice to just sit with the plants too, of course. I talk to them. They don't speak back though, in case you're wondering, Bill.'

After Godfrey named a few of the plants, which I ticked off with my own earlier guesses, and got us to pick a few tomatoes and strawberries, we returned to the fire pit in front of the cabin steps.

He popped inside to check the food. I noticed he hadn't

named the glistening 'zebra' plants. A moment later, he poked his head out of the cabin door to confirm the food was ready. We went inside, for the first time, to eat.

The cabin was fantastic. It felt like a mix between a mad scientist's lab and a very homely, quirky wooden cave. There were all sorts of different pots and cups on shelves, and little carved wooden animal figures. There was a wooden clock that looked like a house on the wall. The cabin was big too, bigger than it looked from outside.

We could all stand apart and spread our arms in the main room with the kitchen and table. On either side, were two sets of doors. I guessed they were the bedrooms. The air was comfortably cool with the soft whir of fans.

On the long wooden table – one end of which was up against the back wall – the food was plated and steaming. It smelled interesting and delicious.

Everything was so different to Pleasant Pines already; warmer, or something

Seersha appeared again from one of the side rooms and joined us, to my delight, although she did make it a little harder for me to focus on the nice food.

Still, I ate ravenously. The curry wasn't too spicy or anything. Afterwards, we laughed a bit about the close calls we had on our trek here. Max and Mynos ate from suitably sized containers on the floor. Mynos could easily have used Max' bowl as a swimming pool.

Everything was better on a full belly.

'Rest now for the evening. Tomorrow, I will tell you about the City you saw to the north,' Godfrey instructed, while gathering the plates. 'Your rooms are in there, Seersha will show you.'

He beckoned to the two doors on the left side behind us.
'Oh, and my room is off limits, please stay out of it, I would appreciate the privacy.' He left to wash the plates outside.

Simon pulled me aside as the others followed Seersha to the rooms.
'Did you see those plants outside?' he asked stealthily.
'Yeah, they were crazy looking,' I said. 'And he never mentioned the-'
'That's because they're Xantho-leaf, Bill.'
It took me aback. Simon stared at me sternly.
'What?' I rasped. 'Why is he growing that? He really doesn't seem like someone who-'
'It's not a great sign. We still have to be weary of him. We barely know him.
Who knows what secrets he might have.'
'I hope he's not dealing with gangs or something. Maybe we should just ask him? He *has* helped us get here.'
'Look, let's get some rest tonight. Tomorrow's another day. Just keep your guard up; that stuff is bad news.'
Ed had gone into the room on the right after Seersha showed him and we followed. He was already settled, on the top bunk, with his headphones on again, when we got into the room. It was small but there was enough space for the two

bunk-beds on either side and a few feet of space between them. Simon took the bed underneath Ed. I threw my bag down at the end of mine.

I passed out as soon as my head sunk into the pillow.

# Chapter 25 - Night-sweats

I woke, soaked in sweat and hyperventilating. Still dark. I sat up, trying to remember where I was. My hands were trembling badly. The bedroom door burst open. Max bounded into the middle of the room, also dripping wet. Then, a stampede of scuttling on wood.

The bedroom floor was swarmed by hundreds of rats. I heard Mynos screaming from somewhere within the writhing swarm. I tried to get up – out.

I couldn't; my feet were bound to the bed. I ripped the sheets off me. My feet were wrapped up in thick vines with bright yellow and black leaves.

And then, with a huge gasp of air, I woke up. Again. I had been dreaming of a dream.

I sat trembling and heavily breathing in the bed. It was getting bright outside. I felt scared, confused; on the verge of a panic attack. I dove onto the unfamiliar wooden floor – confirming that I wasn't in Pleasant Pines anymore – and splashed cold water on my face from a bucket. What if I was *still* dreaming? What if I was stuck in a nightmare?

I anxiously scanned the dim room and then heard the breathing of Ed and Simon. Simon was snoring. I flicked and slapped the side of my face, and, with the sting, felt more certain that I *was* really awake now. My hands were still trembling though.

I took in some big deep breaths, focused on the sensation of the wood underneath me, grounded myself and listed out each person that was staying here with me in the cabin. It worked, thankfully; I felt calmer.

I hoped these withdrawals wouldn't get much worse, got back into bed and closed my eyes again.

I managed to get back to sleep but woke again after a while with a jolt and in a fever.

This time Ed and Simon were standing over me, which didn't help.

'Do you feel weird, Bill?' Simon asked, his mouth sideways from my bleary point of view. 'Like, really weird, not just normal weird?' They both looked shaken too. 'We can't stop shivering.'

'And, just generally freaking out,' Ed added, glancing around the room behind him.

I blinked a few times.

'Yeah...I do,' I croaked, starting to feel cold. 'I think it's the withdrawals. Splash some water on your face.'

The door burst open and we all jumped violently as Max bounded in.

'Morning, Bill!' he said, ignoring my look of terror. 'Breakfast time. Tell your friends.'

He ran back out towards the clinking cutlery and a waft of baking.

'He said "it's time for breakfast."'

My eyes were still fixed on the door and I gulped the residual anxiety down, trying to make room for food.

My muscles ached all over as expected. I really had to pull myself up out of bed; like some of those vines from my dream were still attached.

We shuffled stiffly from the bedroom to the kitchen table. The girls were already there. Seersha being there made me feel worse and better at the same time. Godfrey was cooking at the stove, his back facing us. He turned and noticed our paleness and shakes as we sat.

'Orange juice,' he said in an 'a-ha' kind of way. 'Drink, it will help. Vitamin C. Fresh from the garden.'

I followed his advice and poured myself a glass while fighting the tremors and spillage. I cupped the glass with both hands and drank deeply, savouring the tanginess. Simon sniffed his before drinking.

'Morning, Bill,' Lorraine said to me, as I put the glass back down, with her blossoming ability. 'I feel horrific too. Godfrey said it will get easier with time.' I forced a smile to agree.

'Yeah, it's no wonder we thought the meds helped,' I replied.

But I replied in my head, without opening my mouth.

When I realised, my smile grew and my eyes widened at Lorraine.

Her ability seemed to allow whoever she spoke too to reply just by thinking it. I think it was private too, or, she had control over that.

It was cool.


Breakfast was nice: fresh fruit and freshly baked bread from Godfrey's stove oven. It would have been even better if we didn't feel so nauseous. It had been over 3 days since we last took our medication but it felt longer.

I changed my attention from thinking about withdrawals and Pleasant Pines to Mynos. He had climbed onto the table and sat next to my hand. I gave him a strawberry which he began nibbling straight away.

Godfrey spoke to us as we sat trembling, quiet and trying to keep the food down.

'The third day is the most difficult. You will all feel quite unwell today; full of worry and doubt; you might even miss the safety blanket of your old routine and medicines. But keep believing in yourselves, and with time, it will pass and become easier.'

His words didn't help much.

'They still have the vines of control around you, and the mental ones will last the longest.'

A rush of paranoia came over me at his last sentence. How did he know about the vines in my dream? Could he listen in to my dreams? Or was he mocking us with the fact that he was growing Xantho-leaf right in front of us, without us knowing what to say or do about it?

The room started spinning. I suddenly felt as if I was losing touch with what was real – my sanity. Maybe we shouldn't have done this at all: left.

With a stranger.

I'm not able to cope with the pressure of surviving in a wasteland with people chasing us and others wanting to rob us or worse...

'You *are* able to cope, Bill,' Seersha's gentle voice interrupted my racing thoughts; amazingly, like Lorraine, inside my head.

'You're a kind, talented person. I can tell.'
With her words in my mind, I instantly felt calm again; it was like she just turned off the anxiety with a switch. None of the doctors were able to do that for me before.
I glanced at her graciously, and then at the others, grounding myself in the setting again. It seemed that they hadn't heard her either; like with Lorraine, she seemed to be able to keep our words private, but there was something *different* about Seersha's ability too.

Godfrey spoke again as we shakily sipped orange juice. Surprisingly, he addressed the issue of the deadly plants outside.
'You may have seen the yellow, striped variety of plants in the garden yesterday…'
Simon's eyes widened slightly and flicked up to mine across the table. He nearly spat out his juice. We shuffled nervously in our seats in anticipation. How was this going to be explained away?
'Those are what you know as "Xantho-leaf" plants.'

Lorraine gasped a little and straightened up. Seersha looked at me again. The four of us grew even paler. That stuff took my parents away.
'Everything you know about that plant is a lie; another lie. You will have the choice to take some tonight.

# Chapter 26 - Truth 

Simon couldn't stop himself from reacting,
'Hang on there, Godfrey, what? You never mentioned this before, and you ignored it yesterday in the garden. We don't want anything to do with that stuff, it's trouble, it kills people. Bill can tell you about it.'
Ed told him to calm down and let Godfrey speak, but it was nice that Si spoke up for me.
'And that is one of many lies they have been telling you throughout the entirety of your lives,' Godfrey responded calmly. 'As you know, there are a lot of changes to your reality that you now have to adapt to, and yesterday, after everything, I didn't want to overwhelm you with information.'
Simon sat back a little with Godfrey's explanation, more intrigued, calmer – we all were.
'You will, of course, have to trust us again; have an open mind and remember, we are together in this. But this *is* the truth: "Xantho-leaf" does not kill people. It can actually help people.'
I resisted a surge of denial.
'It will help relieve the withdrawal symptoms you are experiencing, if you decide to try it, of course. And it actually amplifies and encourages the emergence of hyper-abilities in people; that is why they want us to think it is poison.'
Simon looked stunned. I mustn't have been too different.
I thought about my parents – how they died and treated me – that it had to do with a Xantho-leaf addiction. I *had* to

challenge this.

'What about my parents, that drug killed them, or led them to one that did?

They weren't able to look after me properly because of it.'

Godfrey looked intensely at me, thinking. The other's eyes trained on me too and I felt the anxiety rising quickly again as my past and I became the focus of attention.

'Bill, I know this will be difficult for you to accept, and I'm sorry. I don't know the full history of your parents by any means, but they almost certainly didn't die from taking "Xantho-leaf". Sure, it can be over used, and, like anything – alcohol, coffee even,' he raised his cup. 'Too much of it can be bad for you, but certainly not life threatening. In moderation, it can help people, and it isn't addictive.'

The sky isn't grey anymore, is, basically, what he was telling us.

'They want you to be afraid of it, like, their version of, the world outside of Pleasant Pines. They want to dampen your hyper-abilities until you lose them. They don't want you to know how to consume it safely – the full truth.'

I thought deeply about it for a few seconds, my eyes shifting from side to side. I believed him. The picture was consistent. We would just have to be ready to question everything and reconstruct reality as we went forward. I still felt angry and confused, now, having my past and my parent's story thrown up in the air but also, a new desire to find out what *really* happened.

'We call it the Blá...spelt with an "A-fada"' Godfrey smiled slightly, recognising acceptance in our eyes and body language. 'Finish your orange juice now. We will meet under

the Spirit Tree at noon.'
He rose from his chair and gathered the plates and cutlery.

I remembered that he asked for our trust; and after everything he had done for us in this small stretch of time, why *shouldn't* we trust him. I guess he thought he had *something* to gain from helping us? And Mynos trusted him. And I trust Mynos.
It wouldn't be easy letting everything we thought we knew go, but you have to believe in something, and the real truth and being free was what mattered.
I looked at Simon. He was frowning slightly and watched Godfrey as he went outside with the ware. His eyes met mine and he just shook his head. He still didn't look convinced.
'Hey, so, ahem, everyone, follow me,' Seersha blurted loudly while standing up, to snap us out of zoning into the grain of the table at the revelations and withdrawals.
As we stood up to follow, I glimpsed Ed and Lorraine letting go of each other's hand from under the table. They smiled at each other. I grinned to myself too. It was cute and a nice, positive distraction.
Also, Seersha was a nice distraction. I felt kind of tingly at the sound of her voice, like with the rain. I had to stop myself from glancing at her too much, so that it wouldn't be weird or something.
She led us to the door next to Godfrey's room, on the opposite side to our bedrooms.
'This is where the magic happens,' she said, with a slightly

awkward smirk, looking towards the floor. She opened the door for us.

It was a small room but filled with cool stuff.

The walls were plastered with old band posters and I felt more tingly feelings for her. Some of the bands I knew – Grín Day were there – but others I didn't. In the middle of the room, in front of us, was a cluttered table with a big electrical console, a microphone, the laptop and wires snaking in between them. There were two shelves on the left filled with books and CDs, and on the floor next to them in the corner, a wooden box filled with what looked like vinyl records. LPs I think they were called as well.

'This is the Receiver Room, like Godfrey mentioned. We have a radio receiver and we also pick up what they call "internet" in Ferfa...basically, it's the "spy room"' She made the inverted commas gesture with two fingers on each hand raised.

We giggled.

Seersha showed us the gear in detail for a bit but it was really hard to focus and stay standing with the weakness, nausea, trembling and general anxiety swirling inside us. I made the effort to ask her who her favourite band were.

'Hmm...probably either Disintegrating Darkness or The Beetles.'

I had no clue who Disintegrating Darkness were - although Ed seemed to - but was delighted to hear The Beetles.

'Whoa! The Beetles are one of my favourites too. Do you have

a record player?'
I pointed at the box of records.
'Oh, it's in Godfrey's room, but he takes it out sometimes.'
'Cool,' I replied but then felt suddenly very faint, after the exertion of talking and lifting my hand. The room got darker and started to go wavey.
'I think I have to lie down again.'

Ed and Simon followed me into our room while Lorraine stayed with Seersha. My head felt like I was having to balance one of the boulders outside on top of it.
I lay flat on my back, eyes fixed on the underside of the top bunk. Then Mynos popped up onto the bed beside my arm.
'Just rest, Bill, there's no rush with this.'
With his words, I closed my eyes again.

I woke to Simon poking my arm.
'Bill, it's nearly twelve. Godfrey's going to explain everything, remember?'
'How are you feeling now?' Ed asked me from the top of their bunk.
I had to think for a second. My legs and arms felt heavy, but other than that...
'A bit better...I think. Still, 'hope it doesn't last much longer. How about ye?' 'Rough. Very rough. But at least we know it will pass,' Ed replied.
I forced myself upright. After I splashed water on my face again, Mynos hopped down off the end of my bed and followed us outside.

The Sun's light was dazzling and stabbed at my eyes, but that eased a bit under the Spirit Tree's shade - where we sat.

Seersha and Lorraine came out of the cabin after us and then Godfrey. I shuffled a bit and tried to prepare myself for the next mind-upheaval as he stepped off the deck towards us. He was carrying a wooden footstool from the kitchen and plonked it down behind him before facing us and standing up straight. He cleared his throat.

'We call this the Spirit Tree because it stands for the Spirit of Nature. What they call 'supernatural', is really just 'natural' but not yet understood.'

It seemed Godfrey had prepared a speech.

'And also, the spirit in us to be free and express ourselves...'

'Godfrey,' Seersha cut in.

'Get on with it, they've waited long enough.'

'Right, ok,' he continued, toning it down. 'The city you all saw yesterday from the ridge, it is the *only* city left in Aunn Tír...spelt with an "I-fada"'

I mouthed 'what?' to myself and pictured it. Simon had joked about it when Godfrey had mentioned it on the ridge, but I didn't think the name was that literal.

'Every city you heard about on the news over the years, and everything you were told about diseases, gangs, murders every day, child kidnappings, was also false, like Xantho-leaf; or, vastly exaggerated from a rare event in the past.

For example, there *is* a gang, of sorts, an alternative settlement, really, operating in the remote East, but there hasn't been an actual murder in Ferfa for many years.'

I looked to my left and right at the others, almost for emotional support through their reactions. They all had slightly raised, frowny eyebrows. Simon was shaking his head slowly again. But we were starting to see the elaborate pattern. 'Ferfa is, as you will remember from yesterday, the Last City. It has a strict population of 100, 000 people.'
It made complete sense now, that Godfrey hadn't told us everything at once. This was insane.
All those years thinking we were too unwell, for a totally fake world we thought was out there.

'The question is, why?' he continued. We silently focused on his every word, fighting through the still-strong trembling, chills and tension. He sat on the footstool.
'I will start at the beginning. About fifty years ago, the world was on the verge of disaster; a permanent one. Due to the booming population and overreliance on chemical fuels, the planet was overheating at an exponential rate. The climate mutated completely, but lots of people resisted the austerity needed to reverse it. There were protests. People didn't want to lose their freedoms.
Initially, there were many bad hurricanes, for several years, that left millions homeless or dead, until the dual seasons settled. And even though governments made token efforts to reverse it using solar and wind power generation, it was too late. There was mass migration due to flooding and then, long periods of drought, as you know; after that came the global food and water crisis.'
I remembered the stalled wind-turbines we saw.

A faint patter of paws came from beyond the garden; Max appeared and loped over towards our gathering before slowing, and sitting beside Godfrey, as always.

'Parts of Aunn Tír, at first, generally accepted and accommodated all migrants and their abilities in the chaos, but over time, as more people died and economies faltered, there was a rise in conservative politics, and here enters Elron Hawking Goode – The Hawk. He is the man you heard speaking from the drone yesterday.'

I remembered the bluish hologram I had seen above the drone from behind that car.

A gentle breeze blew past us through the canyon and Godfrey paused. It was a welcome break, for a few seconds, from the heavy history lesson. He patted the top of Max' big head and continued, 'He had a small following for several years initially, based on his involvement with an organisation that uncovered classified government information and championed alternative facts, but that following grew quickly after he went into politics at the start of the climate crisis.

He claimed to have discovered an ancient digital text transmitted by an advanced alien race that had evolved soon after the Big Bang. He presented the discovery on television with his team.'

This was going to get worse before it got better.

'This text exalted the human race. It foretold that through commitment to classical science, humanity could evolve to become Gods. But, the most important thing, it said, was to survive global catastrophes, until that evolution point had been reached. Some of course thought it was madness. But more and more people grasped onto it. The media coverage certainly made it plausible.'

I realised my mouth was paper-dry because it was hanging open. This was not the ideal thing to be hearing with the medication withdrawals gnawing at us, but at the same time, we all wanted and needed to hear it now, not later.

'Another important aspect of The Hawk's text was its advice to utilise science and genetic analysis to further humanity; and that's where people like us come in. Hyper-abilities do not show up in the genetic code, they are blank spots, anomalies, and so, they were deemed unnatural, unscientific. His politics emphasised strict population control and consolidation to the cities, but more comfort for the few. And, despite thirty to fifty percent of the population, at one point, exhibiting hyper-abilities, especially in younger years, they were ostracized; seen as a threat to genetically "natural" humans and part of the problem for the prophecy, like the migrants and the burgeoning population.

Hyper-abilities were painted in a way to appear like disabilities, burdensome, and after birth-rate restrictions and genetic selection therapies were employed, anyone born with these abilities were deemed "unwell" and so, were placed in what became Wellness Centres. There, as you know, individuals were either made to feel sick or had existing conditions emphasised and exaggerated.

It was rumoured that The Hawk's own brother was in fact, hyper-able, and that there was emotional abuse and favouritism from the parents, which fueled his ideas.

As support for The Hawk's existential, new age religious politics grew, his control over society did too, of course. Hundreds of millions of people had died at this point due to food and water scarcity and extreme weather events.

Concern for survival was paramount, of course, even more so in light of this sacred text.

He must have felt his control wasn't acute enough however, and so, set about covertly spraying the remaining farm's crops with poisons from the skies and heavily taxing water supplies outside of Ferfa; crop toxicology reports from other regions surfaced briefly, before being censored. The irony was monstrous given his own anti-mainstream past.

He also withdrew funding and personnel from other cities and restricted exports from the Ferfa farms. In other words, the refugees and other cities were left to die, but the weather did most of the work.

Ferfa became a utopia for those that lived and worked there, at the expense of the rest, but the carrot was always dangled that people would be accommodated, and "it was for the greater good.'"

I looked down for a second to digest it all and noticed Mynos was sitting on my lap, my body had gone a bit numb as my brain reorganised itself.

'Everyone in the city began to wear black clothes to represent the full absorption of colour in the visible spectrum, but also, of course, as a kind of uniform for those committed to the Last City's cause.

Only 100 babies are born there every year; parents are carefully selected. I.V. fertilisation is utilised because it is deemed more clinically accurate.

Hyper-abilities are getting rarer, but those that are born with them, are placed into institutions, like you were in Pleasant Pines.

I was about your age when these Wellness Centres started to gain favour and become more established. My parents worked in healthcare. We lived in a city in the west called Írrhur. They helped me escape, after it became known that I had an ability and was put on trial-medication, and after we found out that I might be considered for segregation.'

He paused in thought.

Lorraine said 'oh my God' telepathically.

Two questions jumped from my mouth, 'How many Wellness Centres are there?

Are there many people out there like us now?'

'There are at least two hundred in various remote parts of the continent.'

Then Simon jumped in with his own question, sounding restless again, 'Can you tell us more about the hyper-abilities?'

'You have heard enough for now. Let us eat lunch and we can talk more about it later.

Keep drinking fluids. You are all in delicate states at the moment so rest is as important as information.'

I was glad for the break, my head felt like it might explode.

# Chapter 27 - Sick-art and tunes 

There was a lot more silent staring at the table and slow chewing during lunch, even though we were having soup. The reality of everything that we had just learned about was jarring; in some ways, it felt slightly better, and in other ways, worse. Us, and others like us, were being controlled without even knowing it, being kept sick - stuck.

'I don't trust him,' Simon whispered to me amongst the slurping.

I looked up at him from my bowl for a second but didn't respond. I checked the door. Godfrey was still outside.

'He keeps avoiding questions…'

I shook my head and spooned another mouthful. A bit of doubt crept into my head but I ignored it. Godfrey had helped us, was my mantra.

We had been puppets, or pawns, like Simon would theorise in Pleasant Pines with his tongue in cheek. But at least we were out of there now. I tried to remember that that was all that really mattered now. No point in looking back – ironically, like the Nurses used to say – or being paranoid. The whole thing was diabolical though.

I couldn't stop clenching my jaw in between reluctant mouthfuls of the tomato soup. I felt freezing one moment and roasting the next.

I wondered whether Ed could somehow regulate his own temperature flushes with his hyper-ability, or abilities, but as interesting as that should have been, it was hard to think about for long because the withdrawals were coming on in excruciating waves again.

I kept hearing negative voices in my head too, more than ever, despite trying to ignore them, telling me that I deserved to be back in Pleasant Pines; that I was a freak; that I was an arrogant, bad person; that my friends didn't really like me, and that Dr. Akbar would find us with a team of Nurses any minute. The thoughts became incessant, playing on a loop as I sat fluctuating at the hard table.

I winced down another spoonful of now-tepid tomato soup but as soon as it hit my stomach this time, I knew I had to escape.

I toppled out the door into the white glare and puked in the dust. My eyes were tightly closed and I could see stars.

Then, a splash of ice cold water slapped my neck and the back of my head. I opened my eyes at the jolt. The water mixed with the red soup between my planted arms on the ground.

'Bill, go to the water-fall and put your head under it.' It was Godfrey. He was standing behind me on the decking with the empty upside down water bucket. I heaved myself up from all fours. Just as I began to stagger towards the waterfall, the cabin door burst open again. Max bolted outside with Mynos on his back. He was whimpering.

'Godfrey, we have another one,' he barked, bounding off the deck and circling back around quickly to face the cabin, ears pointed.

Ed came stumbling through the swinging door and fell to his knees at the edge of the deck. More fountains of tomato soup.

I continued towards the waterfall in a daze and submerged my head. It was glorious.

When I pulled it away from the gush and turned, I saw that the others had joined Ed under the Spirit Tree, he was gulping water from a bucket and his hair was wet like mine. Lorraine and Simon looked drawn and sweaty too but so far, there were only two pieces of instant red sick-art on the ground in front of the cabin.

Godfrey returned from the cabin with a tray of orange juice in cups.

'Drink. It does help,' he said, as I joined the others again. 'But the Blá is better. Go back to your rooms now, use the fans if need be. Rest as much as possible until dinner, and after, we will sit down out here again with a fire and the stars.'

We rested in our rooms again for a few hours as instructed. I couldn't sleep with the worry but lying down at least helped the nausea. I could really see now how the pills could *keep* people feeling unwell. It was a terrifying experience trying to come off them. Doubt was still creeping too; I wondered would it really pass, or was I genuinely unwell and unable to function normally in everyday life, like they told us?

Just as my thoughts started to spiral darker, Mynos appeared again at the edge of my bed next to my arm.

'Have you got any biscuits, by any chance?' he said with a smile.

'Don't make me laugh please, Mynos,' I replied, forcing a slight smile back.

'Go to the table yourself.'

'How do you find talking to non-humans?' It was nice that he was trying to distract me.

'I see what you're doing...well, right now, I almost wish I didn't know anything about it, like two weeks ago. But you're *alright*, I suppose.'

'Look, Bill, Max said that with Seersha, it passed after three or four days, so you're nearly there.'

'Mmm,' I had closed my eyes again as I felt another wave of yuck.

'Try some of the plant later.' I opened my eyes again. 'It's natural. Not like the pills. Oh, and when you feel better,' he leaned into my arm with an extended tiny elbow and winked, 'good luck with Seersha.' He scuttled back to the kitchen before I could respond. *That* distracted me.

How did he know? Wait, I don't even know. Well, ok, maybe I do, but I'm not used to this. Is it that obvious? Could Seersha tell? Or had Lorraine somehow told him? It would be nice though. She's nice.

Mynos' probing kept my mind occupied and somewhat positive until dinner when Godfrey shouted for us.

Thankfully, it was a light meal of boiled potato and veg with a honey dressing. Godfrey told us about the beehive down at the end of the canyon, as we ate, not very enthusiastically. I tried a piece of pickled gherkin which I never had before. It was nice, I think; sort of tangy.

We all managed to keep the food down this time but my anxiety and sweats were still bad.

Godfrey then went to his room and brought out the vinyl record player. He kept making jokes to Seersha, as he was setting it up, about how The Rolling Stones were better than The Beetles. I was worrying that they were actually mocking me; that Seersha must have told him about my comment to her earlier, or was it yesterday?

'There's only one way to settle this,' she said to Godfrey. 'Not play *either* of those bands.' She ran into the Receiver Room and returned a few minutes later with a handful of vinyl.

I had never heard a vinyl record before but I knew of them from books and magazines I read in Pleasant Pines. They seemed a bit old fashioned and all the people who played them seemed to have beards.

Godfrey had set up the record player on the wooden floor and Seersha connected two small speakers on either side of it.

I noticed that she had lovely hands too, as she delicately lifted the needle arm onto a spinning black record.

There was this cool crackly sound before the music, and then a weird but funky humming and a disco beat.

It was a cool song called, 'I Heard It Through the Grapevine' by a band called The Slits, according to Seersha. I had never heard it before but we were all bopping our heads despite the sweating and chills, and it sounded very original. Even Ed had abandoned his headphones for a listen.

After another few tracks, Godfrey lifted the needle again, and picked up the record player after the record stopped spinning; we all followed him outside. It was nearly dark.

'Seersha, you might grab some wood, please,' he said while stooping to set the record player down on the deck. 'Could someone get the speakers too?' Lorraine turned back inside to get them.

As Seersha jogged to grab the firewood from a pile beside the cabin, we sat down on the deck chairs in front of it. Lorraine returned and Godfrey set the needle down on another record. Crackle. Then, a punchy rhythmic group of what sounded like saxophones, a piano and light drums in a kind of voodoo waltz. I looked up at the sky; the stars were starting to pop out. Godfrey was fixing the fire. We arranged the chairs around it.

The vocals kicked in, 'I put a spell on you, 'cos your miiiine…' He sounded a bit menacing. I started to feel paranoid again. Was Godfrey trying to intimidate me with the song? I had heard it before sometime, but I think this was a cover version. Seersha told us it was a guy called Screamin' Jay Hawkins. What if Godfrey was using the song to imply that he had a secret plan to hurt us? Simon was right before.

Seersha looked at me and that sort of broke the negative thought pattern. 'Bill, don't worry like that,' Lorraine cut in with her power from the other direction. She must have heard my thoughts. 'Sorry for kind of eavesdropping, but you're reading into things, it's the withdrawals, Godfrey is good people.' That helped.

'Ok, Lorraine, thanks,' I thought back while nodding at her, and took a deep breath. It *was* a good song. Maybe it could be about The Hawk actually. Our team song.

I lay back in the deck chair and looked at the stars, focusing on my breath going in and out, as the fire and vinyl crackled along.

# Chapter 28 - The Antidote 

'So, how are you all feeling?' Godfrey asked, finally settling after all of the arranging. He sat down on the pile of remaining fire-wood Seersha had gathered. Simon answered, 'It feels a bit like we've eaten a load of gone-off fish and are also hanging from the edge, at the top of one of those really tall buildings in the Last City.'

That was fairly accurate, I imagined; a mix of food poisoning and impending doom. Godfrey took a few seconds to respond,

'Can you see how this would feed into a belief of being too sick to cope?' Lorraine and Ed nodded. 'Two days without medication and you feel worse than ever.'

His words resonated strongly. My brain kept urging my head to turn and look up at the path that bent around from the cliff-top into The Haven; that a drone or a Pleasant Pines staff member would appear or a whole team of them.

In general, I felt slightly better now, than earlier today, but still very unwell.

'Compassion, openness, loyalty and friendship can be just as potent as medication in helping us get through life,' Godfrey added. I glanced at Simon, his eyebrow was slightly raised.

As the fire grew stronger and embers floated up to mingle with the stars above the canyon, Max padded his way down from the deck and lay down flat in front of it, resting his head on his paws. Mynos followed too, from the shadows.

A sense of togetherness and freedom welled in me between the discomfort, for a moment.

'You asked earlier about your hyper-abilities, Simon,' Godfrey offered, prodding the fire with a stick. Simon's gaze shot across to Godfrey and he nodded. I could tell he was a bit surprised that Godfrey was now answering his question from earlier. It went against his suspicion a bit.

'I want you all to know that they're wonderful gifts, and you should cherish them, now that you can.'

I glanced up from the fire's glow at Seersha when it looked like she wouldn't see me and felt that tingle again. I wondered what exactly *her* hyper-ability was other than causing me to feel tingly.

'As I told you, somewhere between 30 and 50 per cent of the population pre-The Hawk's governance had a hyper-ability, but it wasn't talked about widely. Some didn't even realise they had one. Then, for a few years, it became more accepted in society; globalisation, a culture of equality developed, but the coincidence of a worsening climate, famines and migration surges allowed his new religion and opposing conservative politics to grow and take hold instead.'

'You mentioned that people can lose their abilities?' Simon asked, he and the others still looked pale even in the shifting orange light, and no doubt, I did too.

'Children usually start to display abilities as early as two. Various mandatory tests began to be carried out by the public healthcare system. If left to develop naturally, a person's hyper-ability becomes strongest around the age of 18, which, of course, you are all around now. It's why you started to notice them more in recent years.

But it is crucial then for a person to use his or her ability during these and the following years, to allow it to establish in the body and remain. Like a language. If the ability is not reinforced during those peak years, it will fade and often disappear by the mid to late 20's'

Another baffling part of what Godfrey told us earlier popped into my head.

'Godfrey,' I asked. 'What the hell is the story about this religion of The Hawk's? An alien race?'

'I know, it sounds hard to believe, but he had funded a team of official astronomers and researchers that intercepted the transmission and recorded it. The message led them to a dig site where they uncovered a capsule that was independently dated millions of years old. As I said, he unveiled the discovery to the media and television and his following exploded.

This alien civilisation was apparently very similar in genetic make-up to humans, and may even have seeded life here, they said.'

Simon interrupted. 'But, how do you know all this?'

'It was all over the news when I was young, as his influence grew all over Aunn Tír; there were multiple news outlets before, until they took control of the media.

From the start, I've had the radio receiver, and have listened into the City's radio broadcasts. Seersha uses the laptop to connect to their "internet" signal. But enough discussion for

now. Seersha will show you their internet websites and the files that we have compiled over the years that document it all.
The key point is your hyper-abilities; you have the chance now to explore and use them, when, for so long, they were hidden from you; and from so many, they have been taken permanently.
And by the looks of it, you are all still suffering with the awful effects of their drugs'

Godfrey reached into his jacket's breast pocket and withdrew a leather pouch. He squeezed the middle of it and spread the top open with his thumb and index finger.
'You have the chance now to fight back against their lies and against their attempts to steal yours and others' innate abilities, with this…' He held the opened pouch out towards the fire and then in front of Simon's nose. Without hesitating, Simon sniffed it.
'Whoa, that smells weird,' he commented, his head snapping back in response.
'I can't tell if it's good or bad…' He looked up at me, unsure.
'Remember, this will ease your discomfort *and* increase the prevalence of your hyper-abilities,' Godfrey added.
Suddenly Simon looked convinced and eager. We all took a smell; it *was* hard to explain.

I felt another wave of sickness starting.
Mentally, I started dwelling on my parents, and before Pleasant Pines. Even though I couldn't remember anything,

the beliefs I had about them and that time were still lingering. I suppose anything could be the truth now, but all I knew, before a few days ago, about them, was that drugs took them from me, and this stuff played a part.

And prescription drugs were fed to us for most of our lives. What if this was really just another poison? Who could we trust anymore? Should we trust Godfrey so easily?

My breathing became shallow because my diaphragm felt stuck, and my heart started to race again. What if I just ran to the top of the canyon and ended it all now?

'Bill, snap out of it!' My eyes refocused, as if I had pulled my head out of a deep pool of water. It was Seersha this time, crouching next to me. She was staring at me with a serious but sympathetic look. 'Don't let these withdrawals take control. You really *can* trust us. I've taken this before, it will help you, if you use it properly, carefully, it's good for you, and different. Don't believe the lies from the Doctors and the news.' She smiled a little, very cutely, and I felt a little lighter again.

'It's totally your choice now, but this is like…an antidote.'

I was grateful for Seersha's distraction again. She had noticed me freaking out, I guess through her hyper-ability somehow, or maybe my blank stare at the ground made it obvious.

These withdrawal effects were dangerous. Another two days of this would be unthinkable.

I suddenly decided.

'Ok, I'm ready,' I said out loud and straightened my back.

'Me too,' Simon insisted before I had finished the words.

He now looked more eager than all of us, even Godfrey.

And then Lorraine's voice popped into my head again.

'Bill, I don't know about this…' None of the others noticed her words, so she must have been isolating her ability to only address me. I thought my response like before.

'I know, Lorraine. I'm not totally sure either, but I think we *can* trust this. If it helps with the sickness and goes against everything from before, then maybe we should. I think it will be ok.' Lorraine thought about it for a second, eyes on the ground, and then we smiled slightly at each other and nodded. 'I'm just going to try a little bit. But you know it's completely ok if you don't want to.'

Godfrey rummaged in another pocket and pulled out a small wooden pipe. He then pinched a little of the dried 'blá' from his pouch and packed it into the pipe's bowl.

'Now, the essence of this,' he said, while raising the pipe to the dark sky in the firelight. 'Is that you all have complete and utter choice. Whether or not you decide to try some is entirely up to you; it's perfect either way, because, if you decide not, philosophically, it will still be a display of antagonism to what The Hawk and your old way of living did to you. You have *choice* now, whereas before, you did not.'

Then he smiled slightly.

'But I do recommend trying some because those withdrawals are nightmarish, and it's a bit of fun'

With that, Godfrey rose from his cobbled seat and crouched down at the fire's edge. He plucked a half-burning, small stick from the edge of it and angled it into the bowl of the pipe now in his mouth.

His cheeks puffed in and out a few times and the end of his nose lit up a bit with the pipe-glow before he breathed in the smoke.

A couple seconds after blowing it out again, he held the pipe towards Seersha,

'Fine maiden, show them how it's done.'

We giggled. Myself and Lorraine probably nervously.

Seersha drew on the pipe, a little less assuredly than Godfrey. The bowl glowed orange again and she breathed in deeply, paused a second, and then exhaled. Before the complete cloud of smoke had left her lips, Simon had maneuvered himself between her and Ed out of blatant eagerness.

'Don't be so shy, Simon,' Ed jibed lowly, which was funny in itself coming from him.

'Crikey, you're a changed man!' I said to Si with a wink.

We were all reacting to this in our own way, I suppose; the realisation of new freedom filled me again. This was a bit of a party, really. My shoulders dropped an inch.

Godfrey put another record on as Simon had some of the blá. He coughed a bit as he exhaled.

It was the album 'Dark Side of the Moon' by the band Pink Floyd, from way back in the 1970s. I knew it from Pleasant Pines.

The start of it, a building crescendo of weird noises and screams, always freaked me out a bit, so after the pipe was passed to me, I waited a few seconds for the music to kick in. The stars were covering the sky now and at full brightness.

I looked down my nose as I put the pipe in my mouth and sucked. The bowl's glow illuminated my nose like with the others and I breathed in, closed my eyes, and breathed out again.

My eyes opened again slowly with the exhale and the music enveloped me as I sat there; the fire's warmth too and I zoomed into the song's lyrics:

> 'Breathe,  breathe
> in the air/
> Don't be afraid to
> care/
> Leave,  but  don't
> leave me/
> Look  around,  choose  your
> own ground.'

I felt the anxiety, nausea and muscle tension melt away.
This was...nice.

I smiled. We were all smiling, slightly goofily.
'Ah, that's class,' Simon said with a chuckle.

Ed finally passed the pipe to Lorraine after his turn. He smacked his lips.
'It *is* nice, Lorraine. I think it's ok,' he said, noticing her uncertainty. She looked at him trustingly before trying some.

'Well done, guys,' Godfrey said.
We all laid back and looked up at the thousands of stars

between the canyon walls. They kind of had trails of light to them as you moved your head. So many possibilities out there. I looked at the glow of the fire dancing on the different rock faces and boulders surrounding us. Those and Godfrey's animal paintings were much more vibrant than before, beautiful.

I could hear someone humming along to the music, but not from beside me, from the fire.

It was Mynos, sitting in half-shadow next to it.

'Ha ha, nice humming, Mynos!' I said to him.

He quickly turned to me, 'You could hear that, Bill?'

I nodded.

'Great, good ears, see? I told you it would help. I nibble on it sometimes myself.

My singing might get annoying after a while, though…'

We chuckled.

Then, Simon started floating in his chair. He was looking around him, about two feet off the ground, slightly out of control, amazed and startled. We all laughed heartily.

'Hey guys!' It was Lorraine, louder than ever, to us all. 'This *is* cool. Thanks for reassuring me. It feels nice to be able to talk, and I don't feel like I'm being constantly stabbed in the stomach today anymore.'

We all laughed together again.

Seersha looked amazing; Simon was floating, and rotating; and then, Lorraine gave Ed a kiss. It was the happiest face I had ever seen on him.

# Chapter 29 - Joyride to the Purple Moon

'The lunatic
is on the grass…'

The last two songs of the album played, the needle getting close to the middle of the record. Seersha got up from her seat again and flicked through the box of records by Godfrey's feet, looking for something new.

Simon had stopped levitating uncontrollably but instead was making pieces of burning wood float and dance above the fire; it was cool, and slightly dangerous. Godfrey was particularly delighted with him.

'Excellent, Simon,' he exclaimed over the end of the song 'Eclipse'. 'That's what I like to see.'

Max shouted, 'very impressive', which, of course, sounded like barks to the others.

Seersha placed the needle back down on another record she had chosen. After the crackle, an acoustic guitar played from the speakers. Our eyes met as she stood up to go back to her seat; I glanced away nervously. But what was the point in that?

I defied the self-doubt, looked back and asked her about the song that I didn't recognise.

'Who's this?'

'It's called 'I'm fine' by bÚkl, it's spelt weird. It came out around the time The Hawk got into government. I found it scavenging an empty town with Max.'

'So, it's more recent?'

'Yup,' she leaned closer to me with a mischievous glint in her pretty eyes.

'Wanna go for a spin on the dirt bike?'

I felt a burst of excitement at her invitation. We didn't have to be in bed any time soon like back in Pleasant Pines.

I controlled my eyebrows.

'Yeah, sounds like fun,' I replied, trying to be cool. We stood up together. Coincidentally, the song started to get livelier, and Seersha told Godfrey we were going for a 'walk' further down the canyon. Simon let the bits of wood he was levitating drop back onto the fire. Nothing gets past him.

'Swit swoo!' he said, grinning and flexing his eyebrows at us.

'Shut up, Si,' I said, the fire's glow camouflaging the new redness in my cheeks. We walked over to the garden with the music fading behind us and the orange light touching less of the dark ahead. The shadows still danced a little around us as we passed the cabin and made it to the boulders in front of the garden.

'The stars are cool,' I said, nervously wanting to fill the silence between us, even though the waterfall was fairly loud. She lifted the dirt bike away from its leaning spot. I continued, 'I've never seen so many.'

'Yeah, I love them here. My favourite constellation is The Tiger. See it there,' she pointed up past my right shoulder at the sky. 'The three bright ones there make up part of its head, and then, see the stripes?'

I did…I think. The Tiger's body was a bit vague, but the

lines of lots of small stars made the stripes clear.

'Cool. That's unreal!' I said. The blá's effects were still there but even so, it *was* cool. I've been saying 'cool' a lot.

She swung her leg over the bike and kicked it into ignition.
'Hop on!' she shouted over the engine.

I hoped Godfrey wouldn't be annoyed.
'No doubts,' I said to myself and climbed on.
I wrapped my arms around her waist – for safety purposes – and felt all tingly again.
'So, Seersha,' I said, thinking of a question. 'What's your hyper-abilityyyy…' The bike shot off into the dark of the gorge beyond the garden, before I could finish asking. My eyes adjusted.
The dark canyon walls, and rocks, scattered on the ground, zoomed past us as Seersha zigzagged between them.
'Woohoo!' she cheered, and I echoed it. I felt like Luke Starwalker from that old movie Star Trek.
I looked up while holding on to her tight. The stars all had luminous trails again as we sped along. I really liked her and hoped she liked me.
The canyon narrowed. It looked like we were reaching a dead end but Seersha sped up.
Slightly concerned, I switched my view to up ahead, over her shoulder. There was a narrow path that ramped up out of the canyon. She took it at high speed. We zoomed upwards.
The bike left the ground as we shot out to the top. I closed my eyes for a second. The bike landed.

We were out on the open valley plain above. It felt almost like flying.
Then I saw the Moon near the horizon, purple in colour, like the Sun had been.

The usual anxious side of my brain started nudging me towards thinking about the drones, but instead, I squeezed Seersha a little tighter and focused on the ground flying past us and the wind on my face.
I think the blá was helping with that too.
Then, a voice shouted from right behind me,
'Hey, slow coaches!' and I felt a tap on my left shoulder. I looked around, confused; nobody.
I turned to the other side, and there was Ed. He was running alongside the bike.
'What the?! Ed, how??' I shouted.
'I can do this now!' he laughed and then sprinted ahead of us. We must have been going at least 40 mph.
All I could do was laugh. How many abilities does he have?
'That's crazy,' I shouted to Seersha as we continued the spin.
'Yeah,' she laughed back, turning her head slightly to me. 'I think it has something to do with his emotions. He's really happy at the moment.'
She abruptly hit the breaks and skidded the bike sideways on the dusty ground until we came to a stop.
We hopped off. I looked around, slightly disoriented; the Last City's lights were in the distance.
Then she grabbed me and kissed me.

Her lips felt amazing. My eyes closed after the initial surprise.
I didn't really know what to do with my lips but just went

with it. This was like some brilliant dream that I flowered up with creative writing times ten. I didn't want it to end, but when it did, I felt even more disoriented.

My eyes took a few seconds to adjust and fully open; wow.

'I can sense strong emotions in people, Bill, to answer your question.'
'Oh…' I replied, still dazed.
'And I can change them.'
'Cool…' I said. 'Did you sense when I was freaking out at the fire earlier?'
'We should get back,' she continued and then pointed ahead of where we were, where Ed had shot off too. 'About a mile that way is the empty town I mentioned, we could go there someday.'
It almost felt like she was changing the subject.

A flurry of rapid steps rushed towards us from the dark path ahead and back past us within a second.
'Last one back is a rotten eeegg!' It was Ed, returning to the canyon at hyper-speed, his voice trailing away after him.
It was really unlike him, but I understood his happiness. This was the best night of my life. A month ago I could never even have imagined a night like this.
Seersha didn't shirk the challenge. We zoomed back through the valley, weaving between rocks and back down into the canyon again to the fire in the nearing distance.
I hugged Seersha from behind and thought about the kiss

again, as if I knew the fun might be coming to an end. Fancying someone is another thing that never occurred to me in Pleasant Pines.

So, if Ed's ability is linked to his own strong emotions, then maybe he turns invisible when he's scared, like he did on the back wall, the night we escaped? And he's super fast when happy...

There were so many thoughts going through my head as we arrived back at the garden, but for a change, they were all good and exciting. So different to before. Seersha propped the bike back against the boulder.

'Ah, the joy-riding lover birds are back,' Simon commented as we reached the now dying fire.

I smiled again but this time a little bit more confidently. One of Godfrey's eyebrows was slightly raised at us. Ed was already back sitting with Lorraine, their arms around each other.

'Good of you to tell us exactly where you were going,' Godfrey put to us sarcastically. 'Right, the fire is going down. Can I take it, you're all feeling *somewhat* better now?'

We all laughed again together and affirmed 'yes,' before helping to tidy up.

It took me ages to get to sleep, between the occasional fountain of colours behind my closed eyes and the fresh exciting memories replaying. But eventually, I did, and it was a lovely sleep.

# Chapter 30 - Time to Die...

I dreamt of birds; that I was a bird, part of a flock, and we were flying in formation above all the different cities they would mention in the news before – how I imagined them at least. We were so high up; the cars and buildings looked like little toys, and you couldn't see any trouble at all. I was just flying in our formation saying 'hi' to as many fellow airborne birds around me as I could.

Morning came. The withdrawal symptoms were almost completely gone now. It was such a relief. The blá - it would take a while getting used to these new names - really did help, and I didn't have a hangover or anything.

I looked across at the lads' bunk. Ed had his headphones in, of course, and was writing too.

Simon stirred and looked over at me after a few blinks.

'Last night was class,' he yawned.

'It really was.' I replied. 'You can basically fly, Si.'

'Yeah, well, I wouldn't go that far, but maybe with practice. I can definitely move stuff on command now, I think.'

He faced the palm of his hand down at one of his shoes on the floor. It started floating upwards.

'Un-limited power!' he announced theatrically but also with a slight morning-croak in his voice.

Max bounced in through the door with Mynos on his back. I jumped a bit in the bed. Mynos made a tiny trumpet fanfare sound.

'Good morning fellow Haven dwellers, hope the heads aren't too sore!' he announced, followed by Max adding,

'Breakfast is ready soon, and then, you will die…' they turned and left.

'Did he say "we will die"?' I murmured to myself. That was a bit ominous.

Simon's shoe was on the floor again.

'They said breakfast was ready, but also something about… dying, I think?' I translated to him.

I felt the familiar twinge of anxiety return. Still there. The blá hadn't cured that.

'Yeah?' Simon asked and then shrugged. 'That's a bit…weird.'

'Morning,' Ed said while lifting his headphones. I was glad he interrupted my train of thought.

'Breakfast, Ed,' I replied. 'What 'you listening to?'

'Eh…'Shiny Happy People' by R.E.M.,' he murmured. Simon and I burst out laughing.

'What? Lorraine likes them,' he retorted, trying to reestablish his more natural grumpiness.

'You really have been changed by love!' Simon added, looking across at me and popping his tongue out a little.

'Whatever, Simon. It's a pretty good song, actually. I'm surprised you know it.'

We got up and put on our clothes to go to breakfast. Ed was ready and in the kitchen before I had even put on one shoe. He was definitely still hyper-speed-happy from last night. It was interesting but also slightly annoying that he seemed to have loads of abilities now depending on his mood.

Simon used his telekinesis to lift himself up and into his chair. There was a nice smell of baking coming from the kitchen, and coffee. I rushed my other shoe on and followed the scents.

'Ooh, coffee!' I exclaimed, as I sat down with Ed and the girls. 'How come we didn't have this yesterday?'

Seersha and I smiled at each other.

'It's not good for the withdrawal symptoms. Makes them worse,' Godfrey replied while carrying a baking tray to the table.

'Date and orange cake,' he clarified. 'They used the coffee to manipulate you in the institution too, you should know.'

'What? Really?' I questioned, my eyes darting up at Godfrey 'It's just coffee.'

'Coffee is a mild stimulant. They gave you enough to have a craving, a routine, and be satisfied by it. It would have played into your consumption of news there. When your brain is stimulated, you have more energy to absorb information. And the reward centres in your brain would then make associations. Everything in these Centres, you see, is designed to brainwash and manipulate. You had to *believe* that it was "home", that you had freedom, choice and quality of life; feel satisfied enough not to want to leave.'

Seersha chimed in while cutting the warm cake.

'It's like a soft drug. But, the main thing is learning that, and at least then, you can step outside of it with awareness.'

'"Keep awareness in mind and the mind will be aware", so goes the Aunn Tírian proverb. My father taught me that,' Godfrey added.

Simon arrived at the table after me and went straight to the question without hesitation or caring about the light mood, 'What were Mynos and Max on about "dying"? Bill said they mentioned something?'
Godfrey blinked at Simon, then turned to Max, who was now lying on the floor next to the table. I refocused on my coffee cup nervously at the sudden awkward seriousness.
'Ah, Max,' he rolled his eyes to the sky. 'Don't be messing with them, they've been through a lot.'
'It was Mynos' idea,' Max mumbled. I saw Mynos' tail go behind the stove. Godfrey turned back and addressed us at the table.
'My apologies for those two's mischief. You're going to be "dyeing", spelt with "y,e", your *clothes* after breakfast today.'
Simon and I let out an extended, 'oh', in relieved realisation, and then I felt the urge to find Mynos and string him up by the tail, but he had fully gone into hiding. I took a breath instead.
'Choose your colour,' Godfrey continued. 'Ye can't be stuck wearing that white from before. It's Haven policy.' He winked. That was that explained.

Breakfast was nice again, but I did find myself examining my coffee cup with new suspicion now. It was my first in ages but I think, from now on, one in the morning would be enough.

We followed Godfrey outside when everything was cleared.

It was such a relief to not have the feeling of the Sun's rays stabbing into my eyes anymore now that the withdrawals were almost gone.

We walked to the waterfall; the gushy sound grew, like turning the sound up on an out of tune TV. In front of the rock pool, there was a row of about ten cups, full of different coloured powders and a stack of buckets.

'Godfrey, when will we be trying some of the blá again?' Simon asked, glancing over at the garden as we stood in front of the cup and bucket display.

'Not for at least a month, Simon,' Godfrey replied matter-of-factly. He sat down facing us on a raised rock next to the water.

'It's not particularly addictive at all like the media told you, but, like coffee, it can become habitual and rewarding, so I always practice balance.

Mindful awareness of what we consume is my recommendation. That, and moderation is the safest way to consume the blá.' He nodded at Seersha. 'Seersha and I have some about once a month on a weekend. Discipline and not over indulgence, in anything, is important in life, so, even though you enjoyed it, Simon, I would ask that you be aware of your thoughts, and have patience; you will have a chance to partake again.

Better to have had a taste than to have had too much.

Until then, practice your hyper ability within your own natural consciousness.'

'That's fair, I suppose,' Simon agreed with a thumbs up.

'Now, pick your colours,' Godfrey changed the subject by directing.

I picked green; Simon, red; Ed, dark blue, and Lorraine picked a dark purple. We filled our buckets with water and then Godfrey told us to strip. Ed and I glared, horrified, at him and I could feel my face reddening while Ed went pale. 'You can leave your underwear on,' he confirmed with a chuckle, but it wasn't much consolation with the girls there. Seersha giggled a little.

Down to our underwear, we mixed our chosen coloured powder into the water with sticks and then submerged our white garments.

I noticed Seersha glancing at my body. I didn't know where to look or what to do with my hands.

Godfrey must have been happy that I had suffered enough, 'Seersha, while they do this, I want yourself and Max to go for a scout patrol. Collect the usual.'

She nodded at his instruction and her eyes flicked back to me for a second before she waved jerkily and turned to leave. Max lifted himself up from the deck and joined her. At least I could relax a bit more now. Ed remained paler than usual.

The Sun was nice on my back and shoulders as we waited for the dye to stain in. After about an hour we pulled them out. They looked very cool. The colour wasn't fully solid but wavey.

We laid them out on boulders to dry, went and got the other change of clothes we brought in our bags, and dyed those too. I went for yellow the second time.

The Sun got hotter so we waited under the Spirit Tree's shade and practiced our hyper-abilities. Godfrey encouraged us as we did.

Lorraine started chatting to us all about anything that popped into her head, by popping into ours; questions about the City, the people there, the Religion, she asked me what happened between Seersha and I on the dirt bike - as if she didn't already know - why our abilities don't show up in the DNA tests, whether they were searching for us.

After answering some of her questions, Godfrey went to the garden then and left us chatting, so we just guessed at things. I noticed Simon's gaze following Godfrey as he walked off. Before he got to the garden, he glanced back at us before pulling something out from inside his canvas jacket. Then he disappeared into the garden. I thought nothing much of it but Simon stayed squinting at the garden boulders. He shrugged. We refocused on Lorraine's telepathic chat.

She asked Ed about his ability. He echoed what Seersha had thought and recalled how he was really angry when he crushed the controller in Pleasant Pines.

We all concluded that he must become stronger when angry, can turn invisible when scared, is fast when he's happy and that he could create an icy cold aura when he is sad. He agreed that 'sad' was his default mood most of the time and that it may have something to do with the music he likes normally.

'You think?!' Simon taunted. 'So, instead of The Smiths or

Nick Cave, what if you listened to angry music? Will that make you strong at the push of a button?'

'I don't know,' Ed replied. 'I'll try it later on.'

We laughed. The Haven was starting to feel like 'home' already.

I remembered some of our daily routines from Pleasant Pines; where we were being held captive without even really knowing it.

'Si,' I said, thinking. 'I suppose, us dyeing our clothes means we're really not those pawns anymore...'

'Exactly!' he said, clicking his fingers and pointing at me with a smirk. 'When have you ever seen multi coloured pawns? My theory becomes Law by the day. Although, I could get used to this naked thing. Maybe we could turn The Haven into a nudist colony...Godfrey?!' he shouted.

'Alright, Simon, relax!' I stopped him, tapping his arm while we giggled. Simon then turned his attention to moving himself forward in his chair without using his hands. He managed it.

We were cheering ourselves when Godfrey returned from the garden.

Then we removed our freshly dyed clothes from the water. It was crazy how we took for granted so little colour before.

Thankfully, I was dressed again when Seersha and Max got back; although, part of me now *wanted* her to see my body.

She had collected wood and Max was carrying a bag filled with, I guessed, other supplies in his mouth.

'You weren't seen?' Godfrey asked Max, who barked they

weren't. 'Good. Let's have lunch. Seersha, you can show them the radio properly and "the internet" afterwards.'

# Chapter 31 - The Internet 

The small radio speakers fizzed and buzzed with static and interference; dodgy signals bouncing around out there over our heads. Seersha twisted the tuning dials on the receiver, with us gathered on either side of her at the small table.

'It should be around here…' she mumbled, inching her face closer to the frequency display in concentration, looking for the exact spot.

The Aware FM music ambushed us from the speakers. Our heads jolted backwards. Seersha quickly moved her hand to turn the volume down.

'…I'm Thomas Dentridge…' I felt sick when I heard it. She was picking up our propaganda news.

'Another 806 people have died this week due to the effects of Sun induced ultra-melanoma. Scientists are suggesting that Solar radiation is still intensifying across the spectrum, and that, coupled with atmospheric lensing, any prolonged period in direct Sun-light is deadly. Meanwhile, sales of bone-marrow harvested antheochrome have exploded on the black market, with…'

'Still at it…' Simon quipped.

'So, ye know this well,' Seersha said, settling back into her chair, satisfied with the signal. 'As Godfrey explained, there are over two hundred Wellness Centres out there and this gets pumped into every one.'

We listened to the 'news' with that new perspective for a

minute. It was disgusting, really; as much as I still felt the pull of slight anxiety and self-doubt that they had cultivated in me, us, over the years, I also started to feel anger, at what they had done and were still doing.

'It's so wrong…,' Lorraine said, in our heads. 'How does everyone in that City just let this happen?'

'They think they're helping people, doing the right thing,' Seersha replied out loud. 'They believe in The Hawk's policies, and that the Wellness Centres really are humane, rehabilitative places; in some ways, they are, I suppose, but not really.'

We listened to the twisted news without talking for another minute before Seersha interrupted, 'Heard enough?'

She reached for the tuning dial again. We nodded.

Ed's face was red. He looked more upset by hearing the news again than the rest of us.

Seersha turned the dial slowly again and the flickers of static and faint, nondescript signals popped in and out of the speakers as it moved.

'Wait 'til you hear this…' She had stopped twisting the dial. A faint unintelligible chatter was just audible.

'What next?' I thought. She flicked a switch on the receiver and the signal became much louder and crystal clear.

'…and basically, the world really opens up to you when you achieve ISC3. My life changed completely. AF was laid right out in front of me, it was amazing, and I really felt like I was making a difference to the world at that point.'

'What's this, Seersha?' I whispered to her, confused, impatient. 'Just listen for a bit.' Her answer didn't help the tension but I did as I was told.

'That's a really prudent insight for the listeners of Ferfa. Certainly something to aim for, for us all,' the radio presenter commented.

'Anyone can get there, if they put the work in,' the first speaker chimed back. The presenter continued, 'Just to change the subject a little, a question from one of our listeners: "As an approximation, what kind of timeline, from today, do you think we have ahead for fruition of the Navsplauk Forecast"?'

At that point, I zoned out from listening, trying to make sense of what I had heard. The jargon-filled radio conversation continued. Seersha sat back again and turned to us.

'That's the short-wave radio signal that is broadcast throughout the City,' she pointed through the wall in the direction of Ferfa. 'We're just in range of it here. They have regular talk shows with guests from different faculties. This guy is a well known Level 3.'

'A what?' Simon blurted. Seersha raised her index finger to her nice lips to get us to listen again.

'...certainly within the next millennium, *Life Extension* will be vital, but I must speak highly also of the infrastructure and staff of our Wellness Centres, without which the vulnerable of our society wouldn't be looked after, and allowing those living and working in the City to work towards AF, which, as we know, our future holds.'

Seersha could probably feel our confused looks zeroing in on the side of her head so she tried to explain again, 'The Navsplauk are the aliens.

In the City, Level 3 is one of the 5 levels of society...Look, I'll show you.' She turned the volume on the radio off and reached under the table for her laptop.

She was just about to open it when, instead, she spun around towards Ed, who hadn't said a word.

'Ed, calm down, are you ok?'

We all looked at him then.

The frown above his eyes was rigid, and his face was glaring and even redder than before. He unclenched his jaw to growl, 'That.Is.Sick. They can't *do* that.' I edited his words a bit to be less colourful.

His fists were clenched and trembling slightly on his knees. We silently scanned him for a moment, slightly concerned.

'Oh, wait, Ed,' Simon again blurted. 'You're raging. Pick me up or something.'  Ed's angry-strength! It was a good call, he looked like he might break something otherwise.

He glanced at each of us, as if snapping out of a trance.

'I am sensing you,' Seersha confirmed. 'You *should* be able.'

Ed stood up and grabbed Simon's wheelchair by the wheels, a hand on either side. Simon watched him open-mouthed in delighted curiosity. Lorraine and I were still a bit nervous.

And, like it was one of the dye buckets from earlier, he picked Simon up in his chair and lifted him up above his shoulders.

A 'whoa' escaped from my lips.

'Cool!' Simon said, ducking a bit as the ceiling came closer to his head. 'Down with the City!'

'You're getting heavy again though,' Ed replied.

'Yeah, you're less angry now, you should probably put him back down' Seersha explained, using her own emotion-sensing ability. Lorraine and I began to smile as Ed lowered Simon down again. Seersha told him to take a few breaths. He sat down again.

'Will we get back to it?' she said. We agreed and re-focused.

'Ed, I have to play you some Rage Against the Machine later, alright?' Simon laughed, still excited. 'You'll be able to lift the cabin!'

Ed smirked, slightly embarrassed, without reply. But he was a bit more composed again in himself.

Seersha opened the laptop and tapped a few keys on it when the screen loaded.

'So, the laptop will connect to a signal from that box in a minute.'

She pointed to a small black box on a shelf in the corner. It was a few inches wide with pulsing lights on it. There was a wire coming out of it that went up the wall and out to the roof.

After a few seconds, a small icon appeared on the screen that said, 'searching for network', then it changed to, 'connected'.

'Through that box, we're now connected to what they call 'the internet' in the City. Godfrey says it used to be available in every city, but that was like, at least, twenty years ago.

I leaned in closer with interest.

'It's basically a city-wide network of information exchange. The information is coded, and then read by a computer and displayed as a "web-site".'

Another type of media, I thought.

Lorraine must have heard my thought and echoed it, as a question, to Seersha. Seersha clicked and typed as she responded, 'This is different from the normal media you know because people can interact with the information, and form communities online. There's a website that everyone from the City interacts on, it's called *Saylella*.

There's a tier system, like I said, and it carries weight on this too.'

She typed again.

'This is the government's website, people can search for all other websites from it, but it also has all their policy and history information on the home page.' She clicked the mouse cursor on the laptop and a big black emblem with gold wings popped onto the screen. It was almost like a football team's badge. I recognised it from the glimpse I got of the drone a few days ago.

I squinted to see the title of the page at the top of the screen: *atw.advancedfurtherment.org*

Seersha then clicked onto another page of the website with lots of writing and some small pictures of people in suits shaking hands and different official-looking, fancy buildings.

At the top of the page was a title with big bold letters:

'Advanced Furtherment:

Nurturing Citizens to Build a Better World.'

It was nuts.

And *we're* the ones who are supposed to be unwell?

'Do people actually believe this stuff?' Simon blurted once more.

Lorraine followed with, 'How did he get so much support from the start?' her telepathic voice sounding exasperated.

'Godfrey says after he rode the initial wave of "opposition to mainstream politics", he used people's fear to brainwash them, but it's hard to explain fully,' Seersha replied while scrolling the web page upwards.

'It plays on people's egos too, I suppose,' Ed said, now fully calmed. 'Self-importance, self-preservation, status; this, "path to becoming a God" thing.' He made the inverted commas gesture with his hands.

'Yeah, definitely,' Seersha continued. 'And on *Saylella* people love getting "likes" from others who agree with them. Look, here's the tier system.' Another heading appeared, after a click, with a small picture next to it of The Hawk talking at a lectern to an audience.

The heading said:

'T5LEE: The 5 Levels of Enhanced Enlightenment'

Below it were the five levels – each with a small distinct emblem, again like weird soccer team badges.

# Chapter 32 - T5LEE 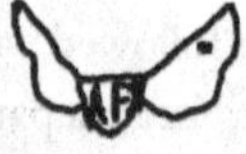

'Level 1: Citizen of Ferfa.'

It seemed like you could click on each Level's title, like a button. Seersha did that and a paragraph of information appeared beneath. I didn't have time to read it as she moved the mouse-cursor quickly onto the next level.
'Level 2: Qualified Science Operative'
'Level 3: Influencer Science Chief'
'Level 4: Master of Enhanced Survival'
And Level 5 just said 'Classified'

'That's crazy…' I said, shaking my head – Simon was finally blurt-less. 'Does that make us "Level 1's" so, or?'
'Yep. Anyone born in the City, even the "unnatural invalids" are. I suppose it helps keep the other levels feeling good about the morality of it. Everyone's included, like.
They have a University and Laboratories then, for the Science-education paths. Remember I said there were online communities?'
She clicked down to the bottom of the page where there were buttons for other pages.
'These are links to other websites that are closely linked to the government; that they "like", basically.'
She pointed the cursor at one titled, 'AISC3: The Association of Influencer Science Chief 3's'
'Remember what the radio-guy was talking about? Everyone who achieves Level 3 has built up a huge online following on

*Saylella* and presence on their Internet in general, together with a high level of Science knowledge. People from lower levels can interact with them online. They're pretty much propaganda masters. It's kind of a machine designed to make everyone feel good about themselves. Where people with status promote each other and stuff.'

'This is heavy, Doc,' Simon remarked, puffing his cheeks, he had regained his quipping composure; I think he was quoting some movie but I couldn't remember which one.

After clicking through another few pages of Internet, Seersha was about to close the laptop again when I noticed another one of those 'links': *Citizen's Archive*

'Wait, Seersha, can you go into that?' I smudged the screen a little with my index finger.

'Oh, yeah, they probably do have you listed, but we don't know your second name, and you can't access much information without being logged in directly from a computer in the City.'

'Can you search for me anyway, please?' I was intrigued by the possibility of reading the details of my family history, from their end. It was worth a try.

'Oh,' her head jerked away from the screen a bit. 'You *can* search by first name...'

She typed quickly and a page with an incredibly long list of names came up. She started to scan through it with me.

'You wouldn't be under "William" would you?'

'Em, I dunno. I don't think so...'

She scrolled the list upwards and after a few moments, she came to a group of 'Bill's. There were only seven! It mustn't have been a very popular name. There were loads of 'Blake' and 'Byron'. She jumped in and out of each name file with the mouse cursor, scanning for clues – my birth year, physical features.

'That must be you…,' she said on the fourth name down. I jumped forward slightly to check the information.

'Blythe! My second name is Blythe? Wow,' I said, scanning frantically for more details but there was only my date of birth, eye colour and my parent's names, Annabelle and Marcus.'

A surprising sadness welled in me, along with the familiar insecurity. I had never known their names, or my second name.

Seersha looked at the side of my head as I remained looking at the screen, my eyes out of focus in thought. She put her hand on my back and rubbed it.

It helped.

There was one other information label under my name – *Citizen code* – but it was blanked out.

'What's that, Seersha?'

She turned to check the screen again.

'Everyone has a Citizen code. It's kind of for weird security and data purposes, but we can't access it unless we're in the City.'

There was a knock on the door; Godfrey opened it. Max bounced in ahead of him with Mynos on his back, his big paws thudding and clicking on the wooden floor.

'Seersha, I think they've seen enough for now. Too much of that stuff can fry the brain cells of even veterans like me.'

A part of me did want to keep searching and studying the City's Internet, especially now that I had seen my record and my curiosity had gotten a boost, but maybe a break would be good too.
Simon was annoyed that he didn't get to see his file but we agreed that we would look again tomorrow.

As everyone got up to go back out to the kitchen, I heard the laptop snap closed and Seersha grabbed my arm and spun me around to face her.
'Whoa, whats-' I started but she shut me up by pushing me against the wall next to the door and kissing me. I obliged. It was more intense than our last kiss; in a good way; there were tongues and all; last time was the polite trial run. Then I felt a new sensation in my pants, stronger than a tingle, but it went away again after we stopped.
We held hands for a bit afterwards in the kitchen. I felt good-tingly and instead of thinking about my record from the City's website, I thought about how the meds in the last place probably numbed us towards the opposite sex too. I certainly never really thought or felt much about it before I met Seersha. It was nice.

We rested for the rest of the day into the evening and it was then that I thought about the new bits of information I had learned about my past. New questions stirred in me. I wondered what else they have locked away in their 'archives'.

# Chapter 33 - Surveillance 

A few days later, we had a visit from a drone, or, at least, one flew over the canyon a few times.

Lorraine and I were practicing some newly learned gardening skills before dinner, when the Sun had calmed a bit. Max had been on a patrol and we heard him shouting to Godfrey, faintly at first, from the top of the canyon wall.
Lorraine just heard him barking, of course. His calls got louder quickly as he bounded down the path towards us and the cabin. Godfrey burst outside and immediately hissed for us to get inside. We dropped our trowels and hurried to the cabin – confused, obeying – but then we heard the faint buzzing coming from the cliff-top facing the cabin and realised what we were running from. That's when the fear kicked in.
Just as we stepped onto the deck, Godfrey pulled a cord that was hidden above the cabin's door. A spring-loaded sheath ejected from the roof and covered the entire front of the cabin, that was protruding from the hollow in the cliff-face behind, in about a second.
Lorraine and I stood, ducking slightly and facing outwards, in the doorway. The others scrambled to meet us from inside to investigate the commotion.
Godfrey then hurried to fully secure the camouflage from underneath at the edge of the deck.
It was speckled from what I could see through it and I guessed there was some type of heat deflection built in, like

Godfrey's portable insta-tent.

The buzzing drone got nearer. We made way for Godfrey who backed in through the door gingerly, He pulled out a device with a small screen and showed it to us.

It was connected to a surveillance camera that looked like it was positioned at the cliff's edge looking into the canyon. And there was the drone, almost level with the camera, hovering and moving slowly above the rocky chasm below. It twitched from side to side as it searched beneath it but wouldn't descend any lower; like Godfrey had said - they didn't like it.

I looked up from the small display to listen to the bad buzz overhead, like a giant wasp. My anxiety swelled with the noise's volume. It was almost right above the cabin deck.

But it didn't see us or make any alarming signals. It stayed at pretty much the same height, thankfully, before passing over another few times and disappearing again.

We all exhaled as the buzzing faded back to silence.

Godfrey pressed a button on his device. The clifftop camera rotated slowly, scanning the horizon.

He clicked the screen off after it made its full rotation and walked back out to the deck to flick some tags at the bottom of the camouflage sheath. It sprung back up into the roof slot again.

'Did the job,' he said, turning back to come inside again, the evening Sun's grey brightness back in full behind him. 'That happens from time to time. Not often, but good to keep eyes and ears peeled. Good boy, Max.'

'Just doing my duty,' Max barked and growled a bit.

We all went and sat down at the table, unsettled by the encounter. Ed had his head in his hands for a moment. I couldn't help but start worrying in general again about people, either from Pleasant Pines or the City, finding us. I tried to reason that it was unlikely, according to Godfrey, but that didn't really help the thoughts from coming.

I decided to ask, 'Godfrey, will they, will Pleasant Pines be searching for us?'

'From what we have gathered,' he responded without hesitation, as he was good at, while pouring us orange juice. 'The security staff will have sent a team to survey a few miles radius around the Centre, for a few days. After that, they will likely have reduced efforts. Your identification details and clinical histories will be relayed to the City and then onto the drones' memory bank programming for them to take over the search. But they won't put huge resources into finding you again and will likely presume you dead. They have no reason to suspect much from you, they aren't fully aware of the recent emergences of your hyper-abilities, and I believe I covered my own tracks diligently.'

I felt the tension ease a bit from my chest and shoulders.

'So don't worry. Once we keep our low profile and remain vigilant like today, we will go unnoticed.'

We talked it out for another while at the table to fully calm down and the conversation got more casual as we did. Then we agreed to go back to what we were at before the intrusion for the remaining day's light.

Lorraine and I planted carrots and beetroot as the sky got purplish in the direction of the Sunset.
The thought of having to stay on alert lingered in my head though for a while.
The Haven's homeliness had been diluted a bit for me.

Before going inside to bed, I sat on the cabin deck at dusk - when some stars were starting to peek out - for a few minutes and closed my eyes. I took in three deep breaths and concentrated on my lungs and belly moving in and out. The feel of the air coming in through my nose. It helped ease the tension. I just focused on the present moment; the sound and sensation of the soft breeze, my breath, murmurs from the others chatting inside the cabin. Even though my brain started thinking again about worrying things, I just noticed it, and then brought my attention back to my breath and the cabin deck beneath me.

In bed, I reminded myself of Godfrey's assuredness and knowledge, and how well The Haven was hidden too to help me get to sleep.

# Chapter 34 - Unfamiliar Skies 

A month passed uneventfully but in a good way. I made a routine of doing that little breathing meditation before bed and Godfrey has been encouraging me. He says that it's good to simply live in the moment instead of documenting or analysing the whole time. 'Anti-me-media' he calls it. We've talked about meditation too in that sense, and I've been practicing that most days; I like it. The funny thing is, Dr. Akbar and the nurses would say similar things for treatment before, that's where I first learned mindfulness from, but it's different now, because it's not in the context of their manufactured mental illness; we know this is real now and that we have real choices and challenges for ourselves.
Godfrey's been encouraging us to practice our hyper-abilities every day too. Simon still doesn't fully trust him though and he's trying to influence Ed that way.

Last week, I went to the beehive at the far end of the canyon to see if I could speak to them. I had noticed them going to and fro between the garden and other weedy flowers in different parts of the canyon.
It was amazing. Their way of speaking is a bit different. I couldn't really talk to them, like with Max or Mynos – maybe they were too busy – but I heard them communicating with each other. It was hard to make out exactly everything that they were saying amongst the crowd, but things like, 'Bring more food to the young', 'Hive is clear. Safe at honey

chambers.', 'Attention workers; make way for the Nectar-bringers!', 'Human near!', 'The Queen needs clean!'.

It was interesting; we're all living and surviving in communities in similar ways, no matter how different our languages or bodies are, big or small. We're probably more connected than we know.

Sleep has been good. I've been dreaming a lot about being non-human animals; seeing, smelling, hearing the world through their senses. The two that stood out were; one, where I was a hedgehog travelling slowly through an old, green countryside, and then curling into a ball to protect myself from being stamped on by all the stampeding people when I reached the city, and another, where I was with Mynos, as a mouse myself, and we were running from an eagle. We couldn't get away from it, but just as we thought it was about to catch us in its talons, it actually said, 'Hi', instead and carried us over the city.

I told Godfrey about them and he said there was this guy called Signul Fried, or something like that, who would interpret dreams, and he would probably have told me that I wished my Mum was a hedgehog deep within my subconscious. Which sounds a bit mad, but apparently he was one of the founders of human psychology.

I suppose these dreams are part of my ability now, in some way, and also because of being medication-free, maybe they're clearer. I've become really sensitive to animals in general.

There's a flock of birds that pass over The Haven who – maybe with my eagle dream in mind – I shout, 'Hello' to.

I've just been feeling way more connected; *part* of this new world.

It's nice. And I've been attempting poetry writing, and drawing a lot, so, more creative as well. Devendra would be delighted with me!

> *Buzz of new community rings*
> *true*
> *In the green-purple desert*
> *Sound waves sea above us*
> *And crash in*
> *static*
> *Now is the time*
> *to be alive*
> *And wise and able*

The others' hyper-abilities have gotten stronger and more consistent also. Simon is probably the most fluent of us. He did actually play Rage Against the Machine to Ed one day, and it worked! It was the song 'Killing in the Name Of'. A couple minutes into listening to it in his headphones, Ed started frowning and bopping his head, then he picked up a boulder by the Spirit Tree that was about three feet wide and threw it over and beyond the garden. After that, he put on Nine Inch Nails and Geoff Buckley and froze a bucket of water.

Simon is pretty jealous of Ed's multi-abilities at the same time, even though he won't admit it. He just keeps calling Ed 'privileged'.

Ed hasn't been able to turn himself invisible with music though, or anything really, which in another way is good, because it means he hasn't really been scared of things.

Lorraine has been able to communicate with us in our heads from other rooms in the cabin and even from one end of the canyon to the other.

Simon has been able to make his chair levitate and move around with him in it at will for over ten minutes without stopping. He, Ed and Lorraine go on servicing patrols up top once a week now to change memory cards in the camera, move antennas, check the solar panels or collect some supplies that we don't have in the canyon.

Seersha and I have been going on scout patrols sometimes on the bike, along with Max. We have to be careful though, of course, because it's loud.

One day, we went to that abandoned town she had mentioned before. There were so many old, dusty buildings there. It was eerie being so empty but kind of fun too, and different seeing somewhere built-up instead of just desert. We practiced kissing there for a bit which was nice.

Then, we picked up some old canned food from, what she called, a 'Supermarket' and then she brought me to an old record shop called 'Ray'z Recordz'. It was cool to be able to pick anything we wanted from the shelves; proper looters we were.

She picked an album by a girl called Feebee Bridgerz –

apparently she released it right before things got really crazy and the arts got censored – and I chose Nirvana. An album I hadn't heard before called In Utero. It was fun playing them on the turntable later that night.

Between those things, we've been gardening, cooking, surfing the web – as Seersha calls it – and listening to music. It's been good.

Godfrey has been great to us, despite what Si, and now Ed, sort of, think; almost like a Father. My anxiety is still there a bit but he has helped me talk it out and has suggested things; exercise is good; I jog a few laps of The Haven every day and slap each of the rock-painted animals as I go.

He's also gotten us to help Seersha keep note of the City's radio broadcasts, stay ahead of them. And he's talked more to us about Ferfa, The Hawk and mostly everything we want to know, really.

But there are *some* things that have been bothering me, and Godfrey has kind of dodged some of my questions, which Si keeps reminding me of:

The Citizen's Archive from the Ferfa website. We've gone back to it a few times and the others have seen their files; Simon's second name is Oeshay, Lorraine's is Bradbree and Ed's is Russleworth; Seersha told us hers is MacAdam. And they seem happy with that but I can't stop thinking about my parents now that I know our names, and what other information they have about my past, for better or worse. What other truth was there to uncover. I have the taste for it now and I just want the full picture but Godfrey doesn't seem to want to talk about it.

He disappears into his room too for ages sometimes.

Documenting the news broadcasts most days, knowing that The Hawk and the AFs are brainwashing thousands of people above our heads every hour is upsetting and frustrating. It's hard to just stay neutral about it. Godfrey told us that Aunn Tír is actually a continent on a round globe, not flat with an edge which is mental to think, but it kind of makes sense. He explained it well.
And the other day, I found out that the Citizens are encouraged to get themselves sterilised, 'for the good of the population'.
I asked Seersha if we could broadcast something ourselves from here, even just some music, to be another source, but Godfrey says they've scrambled any external signals. And it would alert them too much.

We were off on a patrol after dinner – drone spotting with Max. Godfrey likes us to keep track of how many they have in the sky above the valley, without being seen ourselves, of course.
'Don't go ramping up rocks again, ok, Seersh?' I said, with a smile and a small kiss on her cheek as she pushed the dirtbike over to me from its usual spot at the garden.
'You're some wimp, you know that?' she wry-smiled back. 'Here, put these in and shut up.' She handed me a set of earbuds. They were connected to her MP3 player in her pocket. She popped in her own pair too. I hopped onto the

bike behind her and just as she kicked the engine into ignition, the start of 'Welcome to Paradise' by Grín Day came on.

'Niiice!' I shouted over the music and the revving. 'Good choice.' And we shot off past the garden.

Max didn't need to be told, he bounded up onto the boulders and leapt into a sprint after us.

I loved going on patrols at this time, when the Sun was on its way down and was all purple and greenish, like the day we first got here. The City even looked pretty, glinting in the dimming light, if you just forgot about everything else about it.

The sky was so different, especially down at the horizon, compared to the greyness of it during the day, and again, I felt grateful that I was able to see it nowadays.

As we sped along through the rocks and small scrub-hills of our side of the valley, with the City in the distance like a model, a flock of birds scattered into the air. They swooped together like smoke, then wheeled around towards us and back over our heads.

I thought about Ollie again. One of the people that didn't make it. A friend. But what about all the ones out there across Aunn Tír that we don't know, that go unheard of; the ones who die quietly without adventure, imprisoned like we were, without hope or even knowing about it?

I kissed Seersha's neck through the head-wind to remind myself of how far we had come and shake off the sadness.

I checked the sky and where the City was oriented before realising that we had passed the turn off to the abandoned town.

We were now further away from The Haven on the bike than I had ever been before.

'Seersha!' I shouted. 'I think we should turn back now.' She didn't respond. I was about to call her again, moving my mouth closer to her ear when she slowed the bike.

Max appeared up ahead of us, barking back. We both pulled our earbuds out. He bolted towards us and barked, 'Hide! Drone…'. Just as he said it, the whirring metal shape appeared from a dip in the cracked road behind him. We couldn't outrun it now without making more noise and drawing attention to The Haven. Seersha skidded the bike abruptly towards a mound of rocks on our left next to a fallen dead tree.

We dove off it and got as low as possible behind the cover with Max.

The drones buzzing blades zoomed loudly towards us. My head was bowed below the brow of rock, facing the ground, hoping against the likelihood that we had been seen.

The buzzing got closer still, like that giant wasp again, within a few feet of our hiding spot. There was nowhere for us to run to. The hiding wasn't working this time.

And then, a short blast of a siren. My heart jumped with shock. We were caught. We covered our ears at the blare. A robotic voice boomed from it – not The Hawk's, like before, 'Show yourselves. This is an "Official Government of Ferfa Autonomous Security Unit".' It moved even closer. I could feel the vibration and gust of its rotors on my back and shoulders.

I moved to stand and face it but Seersha pushed my head back down to the ground. It was hovering right above us.

'Please present your Identification and Citizen Code for verification immediately.'

Max launched himself at the drone, like he had done the time by the car at that factory, but it saw him coming and darted backwards and up higher, away from his snap. It repeated its command, again starting with the insincere, 'please'.

I was now hyperventilating, the dusty soil on my lips and in my nose close to the ground, my eyes darting around. What were we going to do?

Its siren erupted again, above mechanical gears moving into place. Should we try to run?

Then, from nowhere, two heavy slapping clunks. a flurry of wing flaps overhead and a bang. Seersha and I scrambled backwards on our hands in surprise and looked up.

The drone had been blown forward and smashed into the boulders right in front of us. The siren was suddenly dulled and distorted and out of tune, the hologram of The Hawk on it flickering. The buzz of the rotary blades stuttered.

It was damaged, not destroyed, and was clearly recalibrating, yo-yoing in the air close to the ground. A voice came from the sky. It was one of the birds, 'On the ground, next to you!'

My eyes darted across the ground, zeroing on a hefty rock. Without hesitating, I jumped to my feet, grabbed the rock and swung it hard at the wavering machine.

The light metal of the drone's shell crumpled upon impact. It flew backwards through the air in a haywire loop before smashing into the ground. This time it went fully quiet and motionless after a few sparks.

I looked up to the sky. There were the flock of birds again, shifting off into another direction away from the incident. They had saved us. Some of them had dive-bombed into the drone from above and knocked it out of control.

We didn't say anything to each other, just picked the bike up, together with ourselves, to go back, and watched the birds drift further away above the valley.

# Chapter 35 - Secret

'Don't tell Godfrey, ok?' Seersha said to me sternly, finally speaking as we got off the bike near the garden. It was what I was thinking. 'Can you warn Max too?'

'Eh...ok,' I said uncertainly, still shook. Max padded along behind us, whining slightly and sniffing the air . I turned towards him.

'Max, we were...hoping you wouldn't tell Godfrey about this?'

'Why?' he replied, still sniffing. 'This is important to know for our records.'

'He will worry, and he won't let us go out again.'

'Please, Max?' Seersha added, following my responses and hoping Max would understand her.

'So, this is for selfish reasons?'

'Well...we don't want anyone else to worry either.'

He lifted his head to look me in the eyes, concerned.

We pleaded for another few minutes while Max sat switching his eyes back and forth between us and sniffing.

He eventually agreed.

Mynos hopped towards us from the cabin as the discussion ended and we continued walking.

'Well, how did that go guys?' he asked, his usual inquiry after a patrol.

'Oh, fine, *fine,*' I quickly replied, as casually as possible. "Kind of tired now though. Think I might hit the hay...'

'Ah, you can't go to bed now, Bill,' he replied cheerily, up on his little hind legs.

'Godfrey wants us to have a bit of a party again, with a fire and music and the blá!'

Seersha and I looked at each other with concern at the announcement; the worry from what happened was still in our heads and a party was the last thing we had in mind.

Max grumbled and trotted up onto the cabin deck.

The worry started to grow in me, about the fire and the possibility of another drone spotting it, but I talked myself back; Godfrey has said that there is 'rarely ever' more than one in the same area within the space of a few hours of each other.

Maybe the blá was just what we needed now.

The cabin door swung open. Simon wheeled out, hands-free, holding the speakers, ahead of Godfrey.

Max lifted his head from his paws and his ears twitched backwards but he said nothing, thankfully.

'So, what's the report guys?' Godfrey asked as soon as he saw we were back.

'Oh, normal,' Seersha responded instantly.

I jumped in, 'There were six in the valley from our count.'

He blinked at us for a second from the deck before moving again to pick up a bunch of firewood.

'Great, good job. Well, get comfortable, we're having a fire.'

I let go of my held breath a bit.

# Chapter 36 - Get up, stand up 

The fire and the music got going and we tried to relax and forget about the patrol incident but Lorraine, Simon and Ed could definitely tell something was up.

Godfrey was busy filling his pipe with the blá. We each had some, like before. The happy, relaxed wave washed over me again. I started to enjoy the distraction.

The fire danced in almost slow-motion with a tinge of purple in it like the setting Sun. Simon went floating again, this time above the fire, where he stated it was, 'toasty warm!'. I just stared into it for a while as the others chuckled and chatted but then realised that I could hear something to my right. It was Max, grumbling to himself on the deck. My hyper-ability was heightened like last time, so I could just hear him.

'...That was dangerous...too close...I've never had to do this before...keep quiet...a dog shouldn't have to do this…' Those were the bits I picked up.

I stopped tuning into his angry murmurs and thought to myself again about what happened with the drone, pushing back against the relaxing buzz of the blá.

Were we dealing with this properly? Was it dishonest? It was clearly having an effect on us.

Then, I felt a pang of shame and frustration and defiance all at once. We couldn't just ignore it and keep quiet. This was wrong. We were still living in fear. They still had control over us. We weren't really free. We *should* be fighting back instead of hiding and running.

Seersha and Lorraine shot looks at me just before I opened my mouth.

'Godfrey,' I called over everyone, he was humming loudly to Bob Dillon. 'I want to fight back.'

He stopped swaying in his seat.

'Hmn? Sorry, Bill, what?'

I stood and walked to the record player by the fire in front of Godfrey's feet and roughly lifted the needle; there was an abrupt scraping sound as the music cut out.

Everyone looked at me, silent, apart from the crackle of the fire, above which Simon was still hovering, now seriously and awkwardly.

'I want us to fight back, Godfrey, we should *go* to the City and confront The Hawk. Do something. I don't want to keep hiding and worrying and letting this happen.'

Godfrey put the pipe down by his side and thought for a moment about his response. Simon floated back to the ground.

'Bill, it's impossible, I'm afraid.' he calmly responded. 'Security around the City is too tight, ten times that of the valley. And a Citizen Code is required to enter a gate, even if you managed to avoid detection up to that point. To have a meeting with The Hawk is impossible. Even high ranking City officials have never spoken with him.'

'But-'

'Your spirit is admirable, but I'm sorry, it can't be done, and it's not safe for any of us.'

Anger welled in me. I knew for a fact that *he* had gone into the

City undercover before. What was he hiding from us?

'I've had enough of "safe". We've been locked up in supposed "safety" our whole lives. This is just another version.'

'Bill, calm down,' Lorraine interjected inside our heads, but I kept going.

'We know the truth now, Godfrey. We owe it to ourselves and everyone else locked up out there…to fight.'

He echoed Lorraine's 'calm down' but more composed,

'I have spent a long time building The Haven for us to live in. We're free from their regime here. You're free to practice your abilities here. Perhaps, in a few years, we can attempt to infiltrate another Wellness Centre and bring more here, but for now, we lie low.'

'A few years? No, Godfrey, I can't wait that long. I want us to do something now, or soon.' The adrenaline was simmering in me again and my hands were gesticulating automatically. 'Let's go into the City and send a message out from their radio tower to the world-'

'I SAID NO, BILL!' It was the first time I had seen him angry and heard him raise his voice.

We stared at each other intensely for a few seconds, everyone else staring at us. I could feel my hands shaking a bit, and they were scrunched up in fists.

Simon broke the stare-off by pushing himself away from the fireside, then next to the girls and Ed. I dropped my glare from Godfrey and looked at them before swallowing,

'We were nearly caught by a drone earlier.'

I admitted it.

Godfrey blinked in thought and switched his severe stare to Seersha, and then Max at the cabin. They said nothing, just bowed their heads slightly.

I scrambled an explanation. 'It came right up to us out of nowhere and asked for our Citizen Codes and set off its siren. But a flock of birds helped us; they attacked it.'

'How long did the siren go off for?' Godfrey snapped, if a little calmer again.

'A few seconds, maybe...'

'Right, Ed, put out the fire, please. Everyone, get to bed. This is serious. Were you followed?'

'No,' Seersha replied timidly.

Ed put on his headphones to tune in quickly to something morose, then emitted an icy fog from his palms to fizzle the fire out.

Godfrey slapped Max on the nose and said, 'Disappointing.' He continued ranting to himself as we marched mute into our rooms, his voice trailing into a mutter. 'I don't know why they can't just be grateful for this. He has no idea...'

# PART 3

# Chapter 37 - Night Time Running Out

Simon immediately spun to me once we got into our room after Ed closed the door behind us,

'Jeez, Bill, you kind of lost it a bit there…'

'Yeah…sorry, Si. I just realised that we shouldn't just-'

'No, you don't need to apologise, I kind of agree.'

'You do?'

Ed had quietly hoisted himself onto his top-bunk and moved one headphone off his ear to listen to us.

'I told you there was something not right with him,' Simon continued. 'We *should* think about fighting back. We all have hyper-abilities, so why not use them to make a difference. Instead of just *not* being pawns in their game anymore, let's become, like, knights or bishops.'

'Yeah…exactly,' I said, uncertainly, surprised at the support; I thought the others might have been happy just to be 'safe' here, outside of Pleasant Pines like Godfrey wanted. But Godfrey's reaction had me doubting myself too with a hint of guilt starting in my stomach.

We laid down in our beds silently for a while, listening to Godfrey passive-aggressively put things away in the kitchen.

'Never seen him this annoyed…' I said, softly to the underside of my top-bunk, during a pause in the cupboard banging and forceful plate stacking.

'He's lost it…' Simon added.

It got louder for a moment as the door squeaked open an inch or so and in crept Mynos, checking over his tiny shoulder before heaving the door shut again. He scuttled towards my bed, climbed up the post and sat by my legs.

'He only wants to protect you, Bill,' he said.

'...I know,' I replied, the twinge of guilt finding its way into my low voice.

'It's dangerous to go to the City. Godfrey knows. If they recognise you, they will lock you up in a *real* prison, or wipe your memory and put you back into Pleasant Pines, or another one, on more drugs than ever.'

I stared off into the wall behind him, propped up on my elbows.

'And remember, the drones *will* recognise you now,' he added.

'Mmn,' I responded flatly.

'I like your thinking though. It's your kindness coming through; you want to help others with what you have now.'

I looked up at him, from picking at a fingernail, after that bit of positivity.

'But he won't change his mind, I'm afraid,' he continued. 'It's safe here for all of us.'

I didn't respond and Mynos curled up next to my leg.

Godfrey still wasn't finished venting in the kitchen. We were stuck listening to him for another while; he was giving out to Max now for not telling him what happened on the patrol.

'Guys?' A girl's voice suddenly came from all around the room. I jumped a little in the bed. It was Lorraine. Ed sat up on the top-bunk, pulling off his headphones completely and looking around the room. We looked at the wall between our rooms, even though her voice came from all directions.

'It's me, Lorraine.' She was in all of our heads.

'Me and Seersha have been talking. We think the radio station in Ferfa might be a good idea.' I sat up further, wondering if Godfrey could hear.

'But we can't let Godfrey find out...and we won't be able to get in without one of those Citizen Codes...' I guessed he couldn't, that Lorraine was only including us in her telepathy.

'Oooh, top secret mission-plan,' Simon quipped typically, but that was also his way of showing serious interest.

'Oh, cool...' I added, obviously surprised again by the support. 'You're on my side?'

'Of course,' she replied.

'Tell Seersha I said "sorry" for telling Godfrey, I just got angry and it came out'

There was a pause as Lorraine thought the message to Seersha separately. A bit of nervousness stirred in me ahead of Seersha's reaction. Mynos' ears were pricked but he was licking his hands. I wasn't sure whether he could hear her too; I realised Godfrey definitely couldn't because he was still giving out to the kitchen.

'She said it's fine, but if you seriously want to do this, we'll have to do it ourselves because Godfrey won't let us.'

'How can we get in there, so?' Simon asked eagerly, in Lorraine's thought-channel. It was like she was amplifying the others' thoughts so that we could all hear each other, at least on our side. I remembered we were all probably still under the effect of the blá too; maybe *it* was energising this idea in us?

'We don't know…short of paragliding in.' Lorraine said.

'We shouldn't rush this,' Ed cautioned, more so towards Simon than in general.

'You're awake?' Simon scoffed at the underside of Ed's mattress. 'Could you put on some Abba or something, Ed? There's a draught coming from you.'
Ed rolled his eyes but didn't reply.
'What if you hacked into the AF website, Seersha?' I suggested. Mynos jerked his head up at me, ears pointed. I still wasn't sure if he could hear us. 'You said there's more information stored on there somewhere?'
There was another pause as Lorraine relayed the message to Seersha and we awaited the response.
'She said she tried it before but got nowhere, it's too well secured. We would need back-end access to the database software.'
The idea seemed like a dead-end. How else could we get a code?
'You don't know anyone from the City, do you, Seersh?'
Again, Lorraine relayed my question by tuning back over to Seersha's mind on the other side of the wall. We could *just* hear Seersha's muffled voice replying to her out loud.
Simon chipped in again, 'What about that drone that nearly nabbed you? Could you find anything out from that, if you went back to it?'
'Lorraine?' I followed up, wondering if she had heard Simon.
'Two seconds…' she must have. We waited again for Seersha's response. Then, 'duh duh duh.' It sounded like an, 'oh my God!', from her at the other side of the wall.
Simon turned to look at me from his bunk with a raised

eyebrow at her exclamation. Ed cupped his ear to the wall trying to catch what the following more excited murmuring was.

'Guys, Seersha says that that is definitely worth a shot, she can't believe she didn't think of it before. She might be able to-'

There was a pause and murmuring from Seersha to Lorraine again.

'-to interface the laptop with the drone's...CPU hardware, now that it's down; but they will be sending a human team to recover it soon.'

'So we have to get it back here before they do.' Simon countered, still eager but now fully serious.

'How soon, Lorraine?' I asked.

'She says by tomorrow afternoon, most likely.'

The doubts immediately jumped back into my head, 'Seersh, we can't go, Godfrey will be checking on us, and he'll definitely hear the bike, and it's too far on foot.'

There was another silence. Even Simon was stumped.

Uncertainty and frustration in our silence; this could be our only real chance. Mynos hadn't said anything but his concerned gaze had been switching between Simon, Ed and I. At the very least, I think he had figured out what we were talking about.

I noticed Godfrey had just stopped shouting in the kitchen.

'I'll do it,' Ed said, quietly.

Simon and I looked at each other in surprise. After a few seconds, it dawned on us as to how Ed might be *able* to 'do it'.

'Good man, Ed!' Simon exclaimed without raising his voice,

pointing up at the underside of Ed's bunk.

'Are you sure, Ed?' Lorraine asked gently, still tuned into the conversation from their room; the pair had gotten really close over the last few weeks.

Ed didn't hesitate, like would have been normal for him to do in Pleasant Pines, 'Yes, I'm sure. I've been out that way before with ye, and I can cover distance…fast.'

'Abba!' Simon reminded us, snapping his fingers.

It was decided: Ed would get his hyper-speed going and run to the downed drone location to bring it back before morning, for Seersha to work on.

We outlined the details and precautions with him, Lorraine passing Seersha's notes through to us with her hyper-ability. I drew him a map, as best I could, of how to get to it. It was mainly straight out to the east and he knew the path, but the left turn at the end and the distance there was crucial; he was to look for the mound of boulders and the dead tree before the hill, which would be tricky now in the dark.

'Sounds like a good plan,' Mynos said unexpectedly from my bed behind our huddle on the floor. He definitely knew what was going down now; but I thought he was against it? 'The whole lot is well worked out,' he smiled tinily with a thumbs-up.

'Could you hear all that? Lorraine and everything?' I swiveled around on the wood to face him.

'I told you I have good ears, Bill, certainly better than human ones'

'But Lorraine can't speak to animals like me or Godfrey?'

'I can't talk back, but I can hear her sometimes.'
'What about Godfrey, now?'
'He's asleep. I can hear him snoring,' I couldn't hear that but took his word for it. 'I think she has aimed it exactly into this room anyway,' he continued. 'I can help with letting you know he's not awake, keep an ear out? And don't worry about Max, I'll have a word.'

With that, Mynos hopped down off my bed and scurried to the kitchen.
Simon continued the momentum, 'Seriously though, Ed, what *are* you going to listen to?'
Relishing the chance to put music to work, Ed picked up the two headphone ear-cups from around his neck and stretched them out, a couple inches away from each ear.
'Well, first up is, "Two Princes" by the Spin Doctors, it was the first song I remember loving as a child. And then, maybe I *will* try Abba…"Waterloo"' Simon looked delighted at that.
Ed was just about to let go of the headband to snap his headphones in place when Lorraine's voice filled our heads again. 'Hey, Ed…love you, good luck.'
He went a bit red and quiet.
'What power do you get from mortification?' Simon jested.
'She's only saying that to make you go faster.' We all chuckled, but it was on top of nervousness.

After a few more happy songs of his choosing, Ed said he was 'readyashe'deverbe' and hopped down off his bunk. You could hear the speed in his words even. It reminded me of

Ollie.

Mynos poked his head inside the door while pushing it with both hands I walked over and held it for him.

'Max is fine with pretending to be asleep,' he told me from down by my shoe. I peered through the inch or so gap between door and frame, confirming the kitchen was quiet and empty apart from Max ignoring us under the table.

Mynos scuttled out and across to Godfrey's door where he placed his miniature hands on the wood and leaned his head into it.

I was worrying about Ed now - but this is what our abilities were for, surely. I just hoped he would be back quickly, without trouble.

Ed and Simon got behind me at the gap in the door. Ed's knees were bent a little and he leaned forward, waiting to spring. Mynos turned to me from Godfrey's door and gave the little thumbs-up again.

I turned and put my hand on Ed's shoulder and opened the door fully.

He was gone before I said, 'Go!'.

# Chapter 38 - Every possible way

The wait was tense. Simon hummed a made-up tune and I bit my nails. There wasn't any muffled chatter coming from Seersha to Lorraine on the other side of the wall. Mynos stayed by our ajar door, ears pointed at Godfrey's room, standing upright, hopping slightly from one hind foot to the other. A minute felt like ten.

I tried to just focus on my deep breathing, and it helped a little, but between flicking my eyes to Mynos every 10 seconds for any sign that Godfrey might have woken up, and the thought of Ed tripping and breaking his ankle, only to be picked up by another drone, I had no nails left.

Then, Mynos' ears twitched forward. A rattle and squeak of floorboards came from the main room. My heart rate accelerated by at least 20 beats a second. Godfrey was coming to check on us. How would we explain this away? Mynos backed away from the door and the footsteps behind it. It opened slowly. I gulped.

It was Ed!

He was back already, the damaged drone in his hands.

'How…did you?' Simon blurted, as amazed and surprised as I was. I looked at the clock.

'You were only gone, like, eight minutes?' I added.

Simon's breathing was, unusually for him, shallow and anxious, like mine. We had both been convinced it could only have been Godfrey but we were delighted with the surprise and massively relieved.

I rushed to close the door behind Ed. Mynos scuttled up to the nearest leg of my bed and climbed up.

'It took me and Seersha nearly twenty minutes each way,' I remarked.

'Abba,' was his deadpan response, with a wink to me. Simon burst out laughing. We put our index fingers to our lips at the loudness of him; we still didn't want to draw Godfrey's attention, especially after Ed's feat.

We covered the dented, broken-down drone in a bed sheet, holding together any pieces that were hanging off it and pushed it gently under my bunk.

Lorraine checked in with us to see if the commotion was good news and Ed confirmed he was back by thinking it back.

I felt a little bad that we had to go behind Godfrey's back, but it would feel even more wrong if we just did nothing, kept hiding. I was convinced of that. We had to, now that we had one real opportunity to get into Ferfa.

It took ages to get to sleep. I was thinking about what real steps we would have to take to actually get into the City, and what message we would send out on the radio, and also, about the disagreement with Godfrey, how angry he got, I had never seen him like that before. Simon's distrust of him popped into my head again. What if that was just the start of his angry side?

There were also still little slivers of colour on the dark of my eyelids amongst the thoughts; leftover effects from the blá.

I thought about the people living in Ferfa, the AFs, how they were living in a manufactured reality too. It was similar to those in the Wellness Centres, they were just more conscious of it, wanted it that way, or, at least, thought they had a choice.

I suppose we're always living in some kind of manufactured reality, with the illusion of choice.

I wondered too about finding out more about my parents; how I ended up in Pleasant Pines and exactly what they did. It might be wishful thinking, but maybe it wasn't all true. Xantho-leaf was different, so why couldn't other things be? It was hard to know what to believe anymore. Ironically, like the Nurses used to advise us, the present moment was really all that we could trust, and that's why the breathing focus helps – I crossed my hands over my rising and falling belly – but even then, our senses are manufactured by our brains and electricity in a way too.

When I did slip off to sleep, I had an odd, vivid dream: I was a hedgehog again, but some of my spines were actually sticking into me and I couldn't reach them to pull them out. And I was worrying that I might actually be a porcupine. Ed, Simon, Lorraine and Seersha were dogs. We were running through a green forest. I couldn't keep up with them. A small black dog that I didn't recognise looked at me and ran past me off into a sunny field in another direction at the edge of the trees.

When we got to the end of the trees, I was completely out of breath. There were birds in the sky and Ferfa was in the near distance, towering. It was glowing with a golden light around the edges of the buildings. The sky was deep blue. I tried to get the birds' attention but they couldn't hear me, I was too small. I felt a crunch under my feet.

The ground was covered in insects, mainly bees, they weren't flying for some reason. I felt an urge to stop and eat them, but I didn't.

Then, booming footsteps came from behind me amongst the forest. I turned, frightened, to see a giant human towering over me.

I curled into a ball. Those ingrown spines made me wince. I was lifted up into the sky.

I peeked. It was Godfrey. He smiled at me and carried me forward, and then I woke up.

# Chapter 39 - The New Normal 

I woke to a warm, sloshing sensation on my ear; it was Max licking me. Then, the smell of breakfast from the kitchen wafted in after him and I realised why he was in good form again - food.

I hung my head and shoulders out over the side of my bunk – he turned and padded back out – to look under it at the covered up drone and regather more wakefulness. I recalled all of last night and the plan ahead.

It didn't sound like Godfrey was still annoyed either.

As long as he wasn't on high alert, we were going to start the work on the drone after lunch in the Receiver Room; Mynos would keep his ears pointed at the door and all going well, we would start working out a plan to get into Ferfa too.

With a slight headache – I guessed from the blá – I dressed myself and nodded at Ed and Simon; we went tentatively to the kitchen.

The smell was warmed watery oats and honey (thanks to the bees). Seersha and Lorraine were already at the table eating theirs. Lorraine glanced up at us, then reverted back to her bowl trying to act like everything was normal again since Godfrey's freak out, but Seersha held eye contact with me for a second and then looked to the side towards Godfrey at the hob. The cuckoo clock went off; it was eight.

He turned and smiled slightly at me with the corner of his

mouth and I did the same back, looking away for a second, sort of apologetically.

'Smells good,' I said, breaking the awkward silence.

'Of course it does,' he replied and put another bowl down in my spot.

We tried to forget about the disagreement and enjoyed our breakfast with a few laughs. Subconsciously though, I was probably still a bit unsure as I avoided eye contact with him. Simon was pretty quiet for a while and kept glancing at me.

Lorraine offered to clear the bowls and spoons. We sipped on coffees while she did.

We were almost fully at ease again when Godfrey brought it back up, but calmly.

'So, I just want to have a word about our issue last night at the fire.'

Everyone apart from him shuffled and stiffened a bit again.

Max, on the floor near the table, lifted his head from his paws, and his ears pricked up. I couldn't see Mynos; hiding again, most likely.

'I apologise, if I lost my temper,' he said gently. 'I just don't want you to put yourselves in danger after everything we have done to get you all here. Ferfa, and The Hawk and his followers, particularly those of the higher AF levels, are quite dangerous, and won't be reasoned with.'

He took a sip of his coffee. Max lowered his head again, hearing Godfrey's calm tone.

'The higher they get in the dogma – that hierarchy – the more they learn about and believe the philosophy that was derived from the Navsplauk text. It makes them feel important, rewarded, privileged, they feel it is the right thing for the world but in fact, they become more discriminatory to those outside of it or who don't align with it.

My own parents were harassed into sterilising after it was found that I had a hyper-ability. They helped me to flee, as I told you, because I was going to be sterilised too, and put on medication and segregated. But most people willfully accept the rules, unfortunately.'

He paused for a moment. None of us said anything. His explanation was fair, and it wasn't the right time to get defensive again, even if I did think it was a bit hypocritical of him to complain about people just accepting rules.

'They interpret "science" in a twisted, narrow way, to suit their belief system. They won't be reasoned with,' he continued, still gently. 'Hyper-abilities just *aren't* part of that. The average citizen, below level 3, will generally be under the illusion that those in Wellness Centres *are* being looked after – segregated, but looked after nonetheless – and helped to adapt to Ferfas's vision of normal.' I still thought he was missing the point.

'...if a drone or high level security member was to discover us, we would be classified as disruptors of order, dangers to the prophecy. I was never able to prove it, but from the information I gathered, the few dissenters of the last two decades were supposedly lobotomised. At the very least, you would be sedated to the point of leaking saliva.'

Impulsively, I started, as he paused, 'I know,' The others shot concerned looks at me. 'I just feel we could do more to push back against it all.'
'And that's admirable of you, but think of what we all have here, now, in The Haven, Bill. You would be risking this new life here, and that of your friends.'

I was about to reply again but Godfrey cut me off, still calmly. 'That's all I will say on it for now. Does someone want to begin garden duty, please?'
I suppose it was nice that he had apologised and explained his side of the issue. It was fair, but nothing would shake the new feeling I had that we couldn't let fear and a comfort zone paralyze us again, and I think, deep down, he knew that too.
I apologised for shouting but I still didn't feel satisfied inside. When we came here, Godfrey asked us to trust him, so why couldn't he trust us on this? Simon and Ed volunteered to go to the garden while me and the girls got up to follow them and clean the plates under the waterfall.

It was another roasting day. Even though we had been here a couple months, I don't think we would ever get used to living without proper, government funded air conditioning.
Lorraine popped into our heads as we carried the clanking pots, cutlery, bowls and mugs in the heat.
'That's interesting about the Citizens under Level 3...maybe we could find out online what Level the Gate Security are?'
Seersha replied, thinking back in the bubble, 'Yup, it is. If they were Level 1 or 2, it might be easier, might even be able to negotiate, plead our cause or something.'

After we had finished at the waterfall, Godfrey was waiting at the decking steps and ushered us under the Spirit Tree. He asked each of us how the blá had encouraged our abilities last night in general, and noted his own pleasant experience apart from the disagreement. We discussed supplies, maintenance and general Haven activities too, but all the while, I felt distracted and determined to get into the Receiver Room and unlock that drone.

We had a salad at lunch, then Godfrey said he would head out on a short patrol with Max. This was our first chance to jump on the plan.
We waited on the cabin deck, doing our best, casual 'see ya later' acting, until he had turned the cliff-path corner. We rushed back inside to our room.
Simon levitated the sheet-covered drone out from under my bed. I held the door open for him as he moved it out into the main room like a magician. Mynos scuttled up to my leg and nodded.

Seersha was already setting up things on the laptop in the Receiver Room. She connected different cables into the back and side of it, maneuvering around the table in the process. Lorraine helped clear space on the table for the drone. Ed flicked on a fan.
I pulled the sheet off it as it floated in through the Receiver Room door ahead of Simon and between Ed and Lorraine.
It felt almost like it was a small alien spaceship that we were examining. There was a light, metallic thud when the

crushed aluminium frame landed in the space on the table. Part of it was hanging off the side. Simon wheeled in after it. Mynos held a position outside the door keeping watch. Seersha typed and clicked fluently. You could see how much practice she got living here with Godfrey for years. I felt a belly-flutter at her coolness. Her hair was in plaits and she looked particularly cute too.

On one side of the laptop screen was a black box into which she was typing computer commands, and on the other, the AF website was opened on its database page.

'Ok,' she said, standing up from her chair, eyes still fixed on the screen. 'I'm going to try to hook it up now, but we have to find the right part of it first. Bill, could you get the tools, please?'

Godfrey kept a tool box in the corner of the kitchen; I went and lifted it in.

'Hammer please.'

I handed her one. She used the back of it to wedge a loosened metal plate off the back of the drone. Inside, were dimmed lights, wires and mechanisms. Her eyes darted from one part to another and we watched her work without much of a clue ourselves.

'A-ha!' She spotted the potential connection and leaned in to connect a cable.

Suddenly, the deafening drone siren we had heard yesterday blared again and the dimmed lights flashed brightly. My heart nearly exploded. An electric blue hologram of The Hawk flickered menacingly in front of us above the table and the bent rotary blades began spinning unevenly.

The drone must have been restarted through the cable connection. Ed and Lorraine stepped backwards. I went to pull the cable.

Seersha jumped back in front of the laptop while batting my hand away from the cable. The others ducked and covered their ears.

She quickly stooped, tapped two keys, and it stopped again instantly.

'Whoa!' Ed said, raising his head back up from his hands and opening his eyes in relief.

'Is it safe now?' Simon asked, slightly shouting - he was still covering his ears.

'Yeah, it's fine now. Sorry,' Seersha replied. 'I've disabled its behaviour now...never actually seen one up close like this before, obviously...'

'Lucky Godfrey's not here,' Lorraine said.

'But do you think he heard it?' I added.

'Coast is clear for now,' Mynos shouted to me from the main room which I relayed to the guys.

The panic-rush settled then and we hunkered down next to Seersha again in front of the laptop.

As she worked with the drones innards on the laptop, we tried to follow along with her typed codes and commands. It was impressive to watch her; I was happy that we were kind of boyfriend and girlfriend now, even though we had never really talked about it 'officially'.

She muttered her thoughts out loud, 'Just need to...so, I'm in here, with that...run this, and it should come up...'

'Sounds promising,' Simon commented.

'What?' She snapped out of her focus on the screen. 'Oh...yeah, sorry, I think so. I just have to start this program here, to find the password for its internal memory. The full database should be in there then.'
She tapped the big space button on the keyboard and rows of letters and numbers started scrolling downwards in a new small box on the laptop display. We glanced at eachother, nervous, uncertain, but excited, waiting for Seersha to tell us what was happening.
I worried that the thing might re-awaken again after it realised that we were breaking into it, or that Godfrey might have silently avoided Mynos' ears and would burst in on us.
'It's taking a bit longer than I thought...' she said.
I picked at some dead skin on my thumb. Then, after several silent minutes,
'We're in!' Seersha bolted upright with the words.
The numbers and letters had stopped moving. 'Access Granted' flashed on the screen. It worked.
We *were* in.

# Chapter 40 - Vital Information

My Citizen Code was 73652B.

We had found all of our codes; that was the good news.

The bad news: the only other information stored on the drone about us was that we were considered 'high-risk-to-society-or-selves' SPs. 'Should be arrested on site and brought to the attention of Level 4 Security or Media Personnel immediately.'

There was nothing more detailed about our past, although an alert appeared on the file page of the website saying, 'See City Archive for full background bio'. It was disappointing, but at least there was *something* to follow.

Seersha switched to the AF website, back to that first page. She typed in a search there for the City Archive.

'Oh, this is interesting,' she said, scanning the results with a squint, then jerking her head back. 'One of the "City Archive" locations is in Ferfa Library and Media Centre.'

My eyes moved aimlessly out of focus around the room as I worked out the significance. Ed and Lorraine looked at each other for ideas. 'It's where the Radio and TV are broadcast from…,' she added.

Realisation hit me.

'Where we're going to send the message from!' I replied, energised by the possibilities. I could find out more about my past in the same place where we would execute the plan.

'How do we get there once we get in?' Simon asked. Seersha

searched for a map of Ferfa.

She clicked on the first result. A 3D image of the City appeared on screen. It was daunting and impressive at the same time, to see it in such detail. I couldn't forget the coldness of it too though, because of what it was built on – crazyology.

The tallest buildings were in the centre of it, like we had seen from the ridge above the canyon, and the smallest at its edges, so that it was shaped like a mountain. Everything looked modern with lots of glass and green plants popping out of evenly spaced ledges on the buildings all the way up.

The main skyscraper at the centre had the winged AF emblem on it at the top. Seersha clicked on a two-dimensional, top-down map.

'It's there,' she said, pointing to a part of the circular map near its edge, and then she zoomed in.

'What's the nearest access gate?' Simon was thinking 'tactics' already. He moved his chair a little closer to the screen. 'Can we find out what security staff are on duty?'

Seersha pointed to a gate. He leaned in to trace a route with a finger on the screen but just as he did, Mynos hissed, 'guys!' loudly from outside the door. Godfrey was back.

Ed was nearest to the bits of drone on the table and acted sharply. He jumped up and gathered them together in the sheet and hurried, rattling out across the kitchen with the bundle to our room. He wasn't moving at hyper-speed but quick enough.

I stood in the Receiver Room doorway, heartbeat hastening, waiting for Ed to come back out. My eyes darted from his rattling in our room to the front door. Seersha yanked cables from the laptop and closed the hacking programs.

Ed was just about to come back across the kitchen when the front door opened forcefully and Godfrey strode in, followed closely by a panting Max.

Ed and I dodged backwards into our opposing rooms again, just before Godfrey saw us.

'All clear out there apart from four drones spread out from the central plain to the Western horizon. One was making it this way, which is to be expected, but should be fine,' he announced to the quiet cabin. 'Where are ye?'

'In here, Godfrey,' Seersha replied, a bit too quickly. We exhaled, sitting around the laptop again, pretending to be doing something boring.

He poked his head inside.

'I was just showing them the history of the climate crisis and some of the IVF websites...and also hydroponic farming stuff,' Seersha elaborated.

He blinked at her. 'Right, thanks for the detailed report. Try to get out for some exercise before dinner,' he said, scanning the four of us.

As he was closing the door again, his eyes focused on the table behind us and he stopped.

'My hammer. What were you using that for?'

My heart bounced like a basketball in my chest. Seersha scrambled an answer somehow,

'Oh, the, eh, antenna on the receiver was bent, so we straightened it.'

He looked blankly at her and then the rest of us.

'Right.' This time he left.

We could hear him talking to Ed then in the kitchen. Similar small talk, which was a bit unusual for Ed maybe. Lorraine scrunched her nose as we listened to the awkward conversation.

The door opened again and Ed slid in. We all exhaled for the second time.

Meeting adjourned, but we had some new, vital information.

# Chapter 41 - Momentum 

The next few days flew by in a blur of covert conversations, the evolving plan in our minds. We tried to find privacy to discuss it whenever possible, without being obvious. The garden was a good spot.

Yesterday, at Godfrey's request, we got back into the Receiver Room. Every few days he liked us to document the news broadcasts they were sending out, compare the Ferfa ones with the Wellness Centre ones, and deconstruct whatever the agenda was. The latest big headlines being sent to the Wellness Centres were that the gang terror had escalated into a full blown war. The fighting was all about control of water, food and now the cure for UM cancer, antheochrome. And hundreds of kids were being abducted every day in the middle of it.

Listening to their latest fear updates made me angry and sad, but now, maybe less powerless; our plan would have to work.

In the City's short-wave news, the crime rate was apparently less than 1%, whatever that meant. And the Hawk actually made a public announcement that their genetic research centre was to be expanded and invested further in. He added that they have potentially discovered the gene responsible for aging.

His voice sounded much friendlier compared to the drone holograms, unsurprisingly - even though they were kind of oddly friendly too in a way. He also promoted his *Saylella* page telling everyone to follow his updates on it. The City news was usually followed by ads; recruiting staff in various sectors, the latest home technology products, IVF treatment centres, new books being released by famous high-level people. According to Godfrey, people are more suggestable after hearing the news.

And then there was a talk-show about the continuing development of solar power technology with a leading engineer.

It all sounded great – if you were part of the club.

We tried to get through our usual surveillance research quickly so we could move onto the plan. Mynos, again, kept watch, trying to act casual outside the door as he did. Seersha had almost finished typing the latest report when she sat up with an idea.

'We should record this. Godfrey has a dictaphone, he'd appreciate that. Might help to keep him off our tails too. It's in his room, I think.'

'I'll go,' I offered. I ran out to the kitchen and opened Godfrey's door without thinking.

He was there sitting at his own laptop with his back to me. I froze at the door. He rushed to close the laptop. Just before he did, I glimpsed the AF emblem on the screen.

'BILL!' he screamed, bolting to his feet. I winced. There was that anger again.

I said 'sorry' and looked at the floor. He calmed himself.

'I told you, my room is private.'

'We're just looking for the dictaphone, to record the news headline report with.'

He opened a drawer and handed me the dictaphone.

'Here. Please knock next time.'

I didn't tell the others what I had seen but just that he was annoyed that I had stormed in.

After Seersha quickly recorded herself outlining the main points of what we had found in the radio broadcasts, we tackled finding out what security staff along with what number of drones were posted at each access gate around the edge of the City. Seersha found some information under the 'Citizen Security and Immigration' tab on the AF website.

Lorraine stood over her shoulder taking notes with a pen and pad.

It didn't seem too bad. There were two drones posted outside, and one human

'Security Specialist' inside each of the 20 access gates.

'It doesn't say what Level they are…' I noticed out loud.

'At least there's only one…Godfrey said there were millions!' Simon joked,

'They obviously really trust their drone tech…and the propaganda.'

Ed exhaled sharply through his nose in a slight, nervous laugh.

Seersha quickly typed in a search:

'Security Specialist Qualification.'

We waited for the screen to load.

Lorraine read aloud what popped up for us in her thought-channel,

'A "Security Specialist" is an extremely important member of

society,'
Simon chuckled at that.
'Together with teams of our impressive OGOFAS unit technology…'
'See! They love those drones,' Simon then pointed at the screen while looking at the sides of our faces.
She continued, '…they provide continued safety and equilibrium to our delicate and precious population model.

Every day completed by a Ferfa Security Specialist is one closer to our City achieving the ultimate outcome of the Navsplauk Forecast.'
'Here's the important bit,' Seersha pointed at the next part of text on the screen as Lorraine read.
'Most of these members will have a respectable Level 2 achievement in Basic Science, but can be higher, and will also, of course, have had extensive training in successfully dealing with all members of the public and the security challenges they may sometimes face in this chosen vocation.'
'Most members are level 2…' Simon repeated.
'That's good right?' I asked the others.
'Most members…' Seersha underlined.
After uncertain silence, I said, 'Well, look, we'll just have to go on that probability.'
'Let's try not to be seen first before going to the negotiation tactic,' Seersha replied.
We agreed.

On my knees at the table, I drew a rough map on Lorraine's notepad of the part of the city we would be getting into, going off the website. Simon outlined the best route to take on it, which we then all agreed upon too.

We were going for the G13 gate.

Seersha closed things down again after that. We didn't want to push our luck and have Godfrey come checking, even if Mynos was always pretty good at keeping watch.

But a worrying thought popped back into my mind: What *was* he doing on his laptop?

I started working on the script for what our radio message would be in the bedroom. It had to cut right to the point and convince as many patients as possible.

It felt empowering to be able to do it. A feeling I wasn't used to. I was able to vent a bit of my anger with it.

Simon and Ed went collecting supplies before dinner.

While they were leaving, they also bagged some charcoal from the fire pit. We were going to use it to dye our second change of clothes to help us blend in once we got into Ferfa.

Outside the top of the canyon, they scoped out the path through the valley that led roughly to our access gate with binoculars. They noted the boulders, stumps, outcroppings and few abandoned buildings along it, for cover.

I noticed my anxiety rising in my chest whenever there was a break in the planning process, when there was time to think, lose momentum.

We were going out to face the bully, but it wasn't going to be easy, they weren't going to back down without a fight; and what if we lose? They could easily outsmart us if they get a chance. The key was momentum. We had to keep pushing forward, against the

self-doubt as much as the bully; we could be our own bullies too; and against the comfort zone that they would be comfortable with us being in, the comfort zone that they helped create.

Even if they knew the truth, some of the residents in Pleasant Pines and other Wellness Centres would prefer the comfort zone.

Anxiety would perhaps be something that I would always have, but it didn't mean that I wouldn't be able to adapt to it, push through it, accept it and still create a momentum.

We waited until Godfrey went to bed to go outside that night and dye the clothes.

Max grumbled and shook his jowls as we passed through the kitchen but ignored us.

We broke up the charcoal into a powder that matched the dark around us and mixed it into buckets of water.

Again, Mynos kept watch on the cabin deck, near the door, but he assured us that Godfrey was much calmer now compared to the other night, and it was unlikely he would be up.

We went back to bed and left the clothes to soak overnight in the buckets, hiding them underneath the deck.

The following morning, as per the plan, Ed and Lorraine offered to wash up after breakfast. They put the freshly dyed clothes out to dry in the garden on their way to the waterfall, knowing that Simon and I would be going there before lunch.

Seersha snagged some of the heat cloaking tarpaulin from Godfrey's tool box before going to the top of the canyon to check for any drone patrols.

Simon and I collected our, now black, Pleasant Pines garments and snuck them into our room. Things were really gaining that momentum now. It started to feel like it was time to go for it. The anxiety was still there but it had a positive edge to it. I didn't want to wait for it to turn negative.

That evening, as we sat under the Spirit Tree, Seersha's head resting on my shoulder, I decided to speak my thoughts, 'Seersh, I think we should go tomorrow.'
She lifted her head and turned to look in my eyes.
'Really? Do you think? We still have things to iron out…'
'I know, but I don't want to have to keep hiding this from Godfrey, it doesn't feel right. He hasn't suspected anything yet but the longer we wait…'
She scanned my face and both of my eyes for confirmation.
'We can talk a bit more tonight in the bedrooms,' I continued.
'But let's just do it tomorrow, for better or worse. If we wait too long, it might be worse anyway.' She thought about it for

a moment, looking away at the embers of the fire and then up at the stars as if savouring them before a life change.

'Ok, but let's put it to a vote with the others.'

'Fair enough,' I agreed. 'I know Simon will be game. We just have to believe in ourselves, I think.' As I spoke those last words, I looked around the shadowy Haven and savoured the tranquility for a moment like Seersha had. This place was her home a lot longer than mine. But there was also that pull of the comfort zone, the temptation to sit still, not face things.

An hour later, we put it to the vote in the bedrooms. Lorraine passed on her vote telepathically to us, through the wall. Both her and Ed wanted to wait another few days but Simon and I voted to go. Seersha hadn't decided yet.

We waited in silence for her to decide. I tapped my pen against my diary waiting nervously for Lorraine to relay the vote.

She voted to go.

We were going to leave in the hour after breakfast when Godfrey thought we would be in the garden. He usually left us to our little routines before lunch and stayed inside. Also, travelling in the heat of the Sun would make us harder to spot from distance for the drones; heat camouflage.

Mynos had talked to Max again, who agreed to let us leave unchallenged.

We discussed 'plan A and B': 'A' was creating a distraction outside the gate and sneaking in, but we weren't sure how;

and 'B' was the negotiation tactic with the security guard after we presented a Citizen Code.
Maybe Ed and Lorraine were right in wanting to think longer about it, but I still just wanted to move now. Hesitating wouldn't have got us here in the first place. We would just have to improvise in the moment. I could tell they weren't happy, despite Ed being normally a bit like that anyway.

We agreed to decide exactly which plan option we would go for when we got to the scout position near the gate and saw things from ground level there.
Simon was going to use his telekinesis to swat the drones away if they got on top of us and Ed could freeze the gate to stay open if we needed it. Lorraine would signal and navigate everything in our thoughts so we could work together as a team.
I just hoped everyone could fully use their hyper-abilities under real pressure.

Trying to sleep was an ordeal. My mind was wired to the mission ahead.
It felt like that last night in Pleasant Pines again, but this was so much bigger now, and not just about us.
I flipped bed-positions and fretted about everything that could go right and wrong.
But I reminded myself: We had advantages now with our hyper-abilities. We *were* stronger in ourselves - able.

I wrote a note for Godfrey under the light of my small lamp by the bunk:

*'Godfrey,*
*Thank you for helping us to find our freedom. I'm sorry we went behind*
*your back to do this, but it has to be done.*
*Hopefully we see you again.*
*Listen to the radio.*
   *Bill'*

I was going to leave it at the front of the garden before we left.
He'd find it when we didn't show for lunch.

I flicked the lamp off again and squeezed my eyes shut. I
kept picturing the path from the valley to the city, slightly
obsessively. Then I remembered that I used to check my toes
and my face in the mirror before sleep, and that I stopped.
'Bill,' Simon whispered after a few minutes in the dark. 'Are you
awake? Can you sleep?'
'Not at all,' I whispered back, over the subtle sound of Ed's
headphone music, opening my eyes again.
'I'm feeling weirdly confident about tomorrow.'
'Yeah?'
'Yeah, they won't be expecting us. They're too arrogant. It's not
that heavily guarded.'
'True…,' I hesitantly agreed.
This confidence thing was a new venture for me, I didn't
want to go overboard.
'And with our abilities, we shouldn't worry. The pawns are
storming the castle, buddy…'
Simon's pep talk pushed me to speak louder, 'Well, it is
definitely time to use them for real. Let's just make sure we
get the check-mate and get out again quickly.'

# Chapter 42 - The Last Breakfast 

The few hours of sleep that eventually came were as deep as a puddle. The grey of the morning creeping into our room through the gaps didn't help.

Today was the day.

I took note of my anxiety again: it wasn't like the day we escaped from Pleasant Pines; again, there was a responsibility to this; we owed it to a lot of people; this anxiety could be worth it. I suppose that's the difference between anxiety and adrenaline; there's more of a point to adrenaline. One sort of gets in the way while the other clears a path.

I heard Godfrey pottering in the kitchen and glanced over at the lads. Simon was still asleep but Ed was awake, the faint rustling of music still coming from his headphones, like always. He was staring at the ceiling. Sometimes I wondered if he ever slept and just got all his energy from music.
I kept looking at the side of his face until I caught the edge of his eye.
'Morning. 'You nervous?' I asked quietly.
'Not really. Surprisingly neutral.'
He seemed much more in control of, or at ease with, his emotions in the last few weeks.
'Mmn, I'm a little tense,' I responded. 'Found it tricky to sleep, but not as bad as I thought I'd be.'

Simon stirred with our few early words.

'Hhmn? What time is it?' He clearly had had a way deeper sleep.

'Got to sleep in the end?' I replied rhetorically. 'It's time to get up. Today's the day, Si.' I sat up with a wave of motivation. 'Come on, let's get weaving.'

'Sheesh, you're more eager than usual!' He rubbed his eyes intentionally.

'Are we knitting a jumper or something, Bill?'

I giggled slightly but couldn't come up with a clever comeback.

We slipped our normal clothes on and packed a bag with the black ones and some items from the room that we thought might be useful for the mission: matches, a small mirror, a pocket knife, some twine.

Before I followed the lads out to the kitchen, I paused for a second, looking around our room in thought.

I hoped that we would make it back here again.

It wasn't perfect, but the name, The Haven, did suit it. I felt more comfortable in myself here. I think we all did.

'Ah, there they are! The boys are back in town!' Godfrey announced at our arrival to the table. Seersha and Lorraine were already sitting there, like normal. It almost seemed like any other day until the five of us exchanged knowing looks as we settled together.

A silence grew.

I tried to think of something, anything, banal to say but the plan was still filling my brain.

'You all seem a bit quiet…' Godfrey commented, spreading jam on bread and sitting down with us. 'Ye didn't notice my porridge-people!'

I snapped out of the onsetting internal panic and looked down at the bowl in front of me. He had arranged fruit on top of the porridge to make smiley faces. Half a strawberry for each eye, a slice of orange for the mouth and a blueberry nose.

We all laughed unconvincingly.

I felt guilty again, about going behind his back; he was always looking after us, really.

'I was inspired by some reading I did last night on Ferfa,' he continued, and broke his bread in half. 'Old notes…There's only a very small population of children there, as you know. I had underlined how he doesn't encourage horse play or frivolous creativity at all in the school. From a very young age, the children are pushed into thinking of top scientists, in genetics, or robotics, as the explorers, superheroes or rock stars of old. Heroes, according to Ferfa, are those who succeed in the City's academia. A culture of hard-nosed science and pragmatism. Creativity is a big no; it's reckless, wild, inefficient. And that's from a very young age…It's sad really, but what else do they know.'

I shuffled awkwardly in my chair. Seersha nodded. We stayed silent apart from little 'mmn's in agreement.

It was another well made point and insight from Godfrey. I got the urge to tell him what we were planning.

But I held back. Instead, I thought I'd use it as a pep talk for myself, an unintended one by Godfrey, but I'd use it.

'Hence, the smiley faces,' he added, and bit a chunk of jammy bread.
I unstuck my gaze from him and looked back down at the porridge-person in my bowl. But I remembered too how angry he had gotten about us suggesting we go to Ferfa or when I interrupted him at his laptop the other day. There was still a small percentage of mistrust there.
We had to do this without him.

The building nerves didn't help my appetite but I shoveled down most of the porridge – to avoid suspicion if nothing else. Coffee was more important, I felt. We relaxed a bit and made a little small talk about sleep and lied about the day ahead. As soon as Godfrey mentioned the clean up, we jumped into action.
Just clear this now, I thought, and we would be free to get started on the morning routines, then would be our chance to leave for the city.

Seersha, Ed and Lorraine told Godfrey that they would go on the maintenance run, while Simon and I made it clear that we would be in the garden. We filed outside; onward.

Mynos posted himself at the door, again without being too obvious, to let us know with a tiny thumbs up that Godfrey was occupied inside.
Simon and I made our way to the garden, glancing back every two or three steps for a signal or a warning.

Halfway there, we got the signal. We turned and dashed back past the deck, heads lowered. Mynos waved us clear before ducking back inside the cabin door, and we were off, to join the others up top.

Simon hovered up the inclining cliff-path in front of me. I glanced back down at the Haven as we turned the corner, partially out of stubborn fear of Godfrey popping out to the deck and putting a stop to this before it had started, but also, out of warmth, and again, hope, that we would make it back. I thought: the past few months here had been the best of my life.

# Chapter 43 - The Advance 

My heart was pounding as we reached the top. A drop of sweat slipped off my eyebrow onto the dry ground, evaporating almost instantly. The sun was glaring down now, headache-grey mid morning, and it was hot, but we were somewhat used to it. The girls and Ed were a little further ahead on the valley-ridge. In front of them, a few miles away just below the horizon, the miniature outlines of the highest Ferfa buildings. We marched right for it.

After a few minutes of power-walking, to our left, the cloudless sky suddenly twitched with movement. We slowed. Our heads turned towards it.
A flurry of black wings above us. Not drones thankfully. It looked like the same flock of birds again.
They wheeled around us before whipping off to the east. It was as if they were scoping us out. I ignored a paranoid, negative thought - that they might be spies somehow - and followed their lilting togetherness in the sky. They grew smaller and disappeared again over the hills at the other side of the valley.

Simon and I had closed the gap with the others. Every few minutes, while still moving forward, I checked behind us, but it was clear.

Lorraine talked us through the path ahead telepathically,

acting as our navigator through the valley, as agreed. She seemed to know about most of the geography before we got to it which was reassuring. We were to use any cover we passed on the way, stopping at each spot to keep ourselves difficult to notice and to gather our breath, while scanning the sky for drones before moving again.

About a quarter of the way to the city, one neared us. We used a mound of, what must have been abandoned building materials – cinder blocks, iron girders with hardy weeds growing in between them – to hide, and covered our backs with the cloaking-tarp.

It buzzed about fifty feet over us but continued on its patrol. When it had almost faded away into the distance again, we popped back out. Undetected; the first obstacle navigated smoothly. It was a confidence boost for us.

We moved on again as the sky buzzing became silent. The dry scuff of our steps on the ground took its place.

Every one hundred metres or so, Simon had to drop back down from his levitation and push the old fashioned way for a few minutes. He had never had to sustain it for very long in the Haven over any real distance. As amazing as our hyper-abilities were, we all had our limitations with them too.

I wasn't even going to be using mine. But this wasn't about flexing muscles, I quickly brushed the selfish thought away. We were all going to play our part as a team; positive thinking.

The city loomed bigger ahead of us the further we moved through the rocky desert valley.

About halfway there, we came to a withered forest; mostly stumps, but the odd, leafless skeleton with wiry branches. There were tufts of that desert grass in between them. We rested here, but there was no shade at all.

The sun was nearly right above us and blistering. Seersha used the tarpaulin again, this time to create a little shelter over our huddle and Ed, listening to a particularly mopey Radiohead track, was able to provide an air-conditioning icy fog from his palms. It was a big relief.

After catching my breath, I peered out from under our insta-tent towards the destination. I could see more of one side of it than I had before. There was a formation of working wind turbines on the hills behind it, now in view; another sign of resources being centred on the, so called, Last City.

I gritted my teeth and shook my head a bit.

We didn't rest for long, sipped some water and continued.

When we came to the river bed we realised that it had dried out a lot and was more of a stream, a few feet wide. It wasn't a problem to cross but we didn't drink because the water didn't look clear.

We had about another mile to go. More different little details appeared the nearer we got. There was more green around us. Hardy plants poking out of the dusty ground here and there and even some scrawny budding trees and cacti scattered close to the city's boundary; they would help for camouflage, I thought.

There was a wall surrounding the entirety of it like we had seen on their internet thing, and just above it, I could see the tiny movements of, what must have been, flying vehicles at low altitude amongst the buildings; they looked bigger than drones, but I wasn't certain yet.
The tops of, what looked like, palm-trees jutted above the wall also, and big solar panels glinted on the tops of the buildings above the glass.
'This is getting serious now, guys,' Lorraine said mentally, to prepare us for the advance. 'We should probably start staying as low as possible from here, and let's move from tree to tree.'

We bent our knees more the closer we got. I checked in with Seersha as we advanced, to make sure she was okay. She grinned, 'Don't worry about me, you're the noob.'
Simon had been surprisingly quiet but he seemed fine. It was the most serious I had ever seen/heard him.
We were all very focused, really.
The crouched walking became tiring quickly; with the heat as well, we were panting. We darted from boulder to tree to cactus. When one of us moved, the other checked the sky and further ahead. No drones had spotted us or were approaching so far. They had no reason to expect us.

We started to hear the buzz of the City faintly. And then, we spotted the expected drones patrol-hovering back and forth near the wall-gates.

There was about a kilometre between one gate, its assigned drones, and the next.

'This is the closest I've been…' Seersha said, as we surveyed from behind a gnarled, almost-leafless tree.

'There,' Lorraine said, pointing at a part of the wall a kilometre or so to our right.

Squinting, I saw the marking, 'G13' on the gate in yellow letters. Above it, two drones hovered back and forth over a few hundred metres.

'And there's our last cover spot before it,' She jerked her pointing finger towards a mound of rubble and a bit of old concrete wall nearer to the gate. The last hiding place, I thought.

The adrenaline was really building now, but I was almost enjoying the focus of it.

'Ok. Everyone ready? Let's move, quickly,' Lorraine directed with her thoughts right as the two G13 drones were faced away from our position.

We bolted, stooping as low as possible, for the mound of rocks and wall. My eyes darted from the cover, to the City wall to the left, and up to the sky above it.

The skyscrapers towered massively now above us as we ran. They looked almost like upright syringes with their antennas on top. A dart of panic and insecurity hit me; we would surely be spotted from one of the hundreds of windows.

'Nearly there, heads down,' Lorraine encouraged. We drove on, heads near to our knees. When I looked up again, we had made it.

We were all gasping, apart from Simon who had hovered, with our backs to the rocks and the low wall. I winced for a moment, expecting to hear a siren or a drone buzzing quickly towards us. But nothing.
They haven't seen us? I thought to myself in surprise and relief. My breathing started to slow.
'No, they haven't,' Lorraine replied, she had heard me thinking it. 'But, what now?'
We waited – hands on knees, hidden but close to danger – for our breath to return to normal, and realised the time had come to decide on the crucial part of our plan: to actually get *past* the gate. It was time to improvise.

# Chapter 44 - Wait and Bleed

We took turns to peep out over the yellowish rocky mound and dusty wall, gauging what had to be done and trying to spot something that might trigger the decision. We decided against using the mirror to see around it in case it caught the Sun and gave us away.

'Cameras,' Seersha said, turning back around and staring blankly into the valley with her back on the stone. 'They could be a problem...'

We fell silent again in thought, the background buzz of the City behind the wall and the drones in front, more apparent again. We should have thought of this properly before leaving. I worried that we had made a serious mistake, that Ed and Lorraine were right.

'Wait a second,' Simon said, after a moment. 'Let me try something.'

He moved his chair to the edge of the boulders' cover, where he could just see around it to the gate, and raised his palm.

He was focusing on the cameras, squinting. Surely it was too far away, I thought. It must have been at least thirty or forty metres.

His hand trembled at the effort. We peeked towards the gate over his shoulder and back at him straining.

'Got it,' he uttered with a deep exhale.

We couldn't see what he had done, just his reaction. He moved back behind our cover.

'What did you do?' I asked, guessing what it might be but still disbelieving.

'Duh...moved the camera...just.'

'Nice,' Seersha and I remarked.

'I'll point them all up before we make the move. I think we should just go for it.' he followed confidently. 'Use our hyper abilities. Ed, get strong and throw that rock at the wall.' He pointed at a boulder in the mound about the size of one of his wheels.

Si could get a bit cocky in face-off moments, but this was obviously more than a video game or foosball. He didn't have that cheesy grin either. He was being totally serious and...mature. I agreed with him. This is what we had been waiting for, to stand up for ourselves, use our skills, now.

'Once the drones get distracted, we can run up to the gate and enter one of our codes-'

Lorraine cut across him, 'Simon, calm down, and keep it down,' she warned, pointing towards the gate. 'We don't know if throwing something at the wall will distract one of them, or any of them.'

'And what about the security guard, specialist, on the other side?' Seersha added.

Simon backed down again in thought. No one spoke for a moment. We weighed up the risks and possibilities. I felt that doubt again, trying to grow in my belly. We shouldn't have come all this way without knowing exactly what to do. But I fought it, refocused on momentum and thought of something,

'When we get to the gate, we can use a code, talk to the guard and say we were released from Pleasant Pines, show him our

Citizen Codes, and if he doesn't buy it, Si, you and Ed can overpower him, right?' They glanced at each other.

I added, 'I don't want us to stall here, scared, like we would have done before. We should keep moving.'

'Yeah, I'm with Bill,' Simon agreed, still energised. 'Let's do it. It'll work.' Seersha and Lorraine looked uncertainly at each other. Ed still looked surprisingly unmoved and unpale, even though quiet as usual.

But they all agreed.

Ed played some of the metal band Slipknot in his headphones. After a few minutes, a frown had grown in his forehead and he picked up the small boulder with a wave of strength. The plan was maybe a little crazy but it was all we had. We couldn't just go back.

We braced ourselves in position behind our cover for the launch. Once the drones were distracted, we would have to sprint again.

He heaved the rock over his shoulder and whipped it into the sky from his forearm with incredible strength. His head bopped aggressively to the music in his ears as it flew.

I followed the first half of its arc, the part I could see, and then, 'clang!', 'thud!'.

He shook a clenched fist at his shot, pressed his chest flat against the boulder-mound and, on his tip-toes, peeked over the top of the wall at the drones' reaction. I looked out from the left side of the mound.

One of the drones had stopped close to and above Ed's projectile, scanning it with its cameras. The other remained undistracted from its patrol to the right. And then, the one that had stopped, reversed and rotated towards us in the air. We snapped our heads back behind the rubble, gluing our backs to the rock, desperate not to be seen.

'Did it work?' Lorraine asked after a pause.
Ed peeked, looked across her at me, and then shook his head. I pushed back against the onsetting panic and inched my eyes around the cover again, hoping that he wasn't correct, that both drones *were* taking a closer look at Ed's rock instead of looking this way.

# Chapter 45 - Something in the Sky

Relief and disappointment at the same time: we hadn't been seen.

Both drones were patrolling back and forth again, unconcerned with our attempted distraction, as if nothing had happened. Seersha crouched down and leaned out at the other side scanning desperately.

'What now?' I half-whispered.

Simon tried to rally us again.

'Look, let's just run for it, when they're furthest away. I can knock them out if they get close.'

None of us were certain again about committing to Simon's approach. There was momentum, and there was recklessness.

As much as I tried to defy it, anxiety and doubt started to creep back into my brain, wedging between the indecision. This would end badly if we didn't get it right, and we were no closer to getting in.

But going back was risky too, we'd have nothing to show for it, and who knows what Godfrey would do to punish us. I wondered if he had realised we were gone by now.

Then, from the pale grey East, the black flock of birds appeared again from behind a small mountain.

Their airborne group swelled towards us. Without getting too close to the City, they swooped over our heads before veering back out towards the valley plain from where we had trekked.

As we watched, two of the flock broke away and glided right down to perch on the boulder-mound next to us, just above level with our eyes. We craned our necks and twisted towards them as they flapped to land.

They stared down at us for a second, wings settling, and then examined the surrounding scene with twitchy, swiveling neck movements. The slightly bigger black bird spoke to me.

'Don't you humans have a saying, how does it go... "between a rock and a hard place"?'

I stared back, 'Ehhh…'

'You should ask your friends when you need help,' he stated, in a strangely familiar voice. 'And it's certainly a brilliant day for the birds…'

I looked down, to the side, trying to decipher what the words and *who* the voice reminded me of.

An old face popped into my mind. It couldn't be.

'Ollie?' I uttered, and raised my eyes back up.

The others' instantly perplexed faces shot towards me after I said it.

'Is that…?' I tried to ask the bird, gulping instead of finishing my question.

'Yes…it's me, Bill. Good to see you again.'

# Chapter 46 - Wings

A rush of confusion and...joy came over me.

'Wh-how…?' I stuttered.

'Well, let's just say that reincarnation is real, for me at least. Remember GT?

And I seem to be able to remember my old self.'

'...Whoa…' I crouched down, holding my knees, in disbelief.

I looked at the ground and then back at the bird who was...Ollie.

'Your friend Godfrey and I spoke in Pleasant Pines too.'

My eyes widened as he spoke, as did the others', glued to my reaction. The other bird kept watch.

'I call myself Olwynd now. Because, why not; names are only words, and words are like lifetimes, or raindrops in a storm...each one influenced by the last but yet slightly different…'

He raised a wing and twisted his head slightly.

'This is Leonid. Oh, and of course, Ollie is still fine, if you like.'

'H-h-hello,' the other bird, Leonid, said twitchily.

'We usually stay out of these things, but I've had to keep an eye out for you, Bill. You were always kind to me in my previous life, and, as you can see, we pay it forward!' I heard a smile in his voice.

I opened my mouth before actually thinking of words,

'I...don't know-'

'Know what to say? I know, it's probably a bit of a surprise, but we don't have time to waste not believing. Just accept our help.'

I gulped down my reasoning and smiled. I was speaking to a bird after all.

'Ok, thanks, Ollie...Olwynd.'

He flapped himself backwards, higher up the rock, and glanced back over his wing at the gate. I leaned out and my eyes followed his gaze towards it. I waited for him to respond. The others were still silent and fixed on me as the interpreter, but I was too surprised and focused on Ollie's next words to explain anything yet, but they had an idea.

'Don't be too hasty with your approach,' he said, swiveling his head towards me again. 'Once they lock onto your faces, half the city will be hunting you.'

'Ok'

'Think like in your games of chess; two steps ahead.'

I glanced at Simon and the others looking back and forth at us, desperate for information.

Ollie continued, 'What you need is a substantial decoy, taking the *guard* outside too.'

He flapped again, this time spinning around to face the city. Leonid turned with him.

'Get ready to run for the gate. We will do the rest.'

My mind clicked gratefully into focus on our new task.

Just as he was about to push off, Ollie swiveled his head to me again,

'I told you about the birds, Bill. 'Pity what they did to them though… Never dismiss someone who's different, eh?'

A flurry of dark wings. Ollie and Leonid were airborne again.

They gained altitude and wheeled into the sky away from the City.

I hurried at my chance to fill the others in.

'It's Ollie! He's reincarnated…it must be his hyper-ability I guess.'

The others started questioning but I cut across. 'They're helping us. We don't have time to discuss it. Get ready to run for the gate on my lead. We need to keep thinking ahead. Si, move the cameras, now!'

I positioned myself at the edge of our cover – crouching slightly – and looked to the sky again for my old friend. The others primed themselves too, close behind me. Simon moved next to me and, with his palms raised, squinted at the cameras. The two birds were really high up now. They were almost black dots, but were descending fast, getting bigger. We could see their streamlined bodies and beaks pointed downward in

dive-bomb positions. They were going straight for the two patrol drones like the day they saved Seersha, Max and I with the dirt bike. The drones were now close together and near the access gate.

# Chapter 47 - Diversion

Ollie and Leonid were at top speed, hurtling directly for the hovering City robots from the sky. One of the gang behind me sucked in a bracing breath. I winced before the impact.

'Thwack!' A tinny crack echoed as the two birds crashed violently, talons first into the nearest drone. It bobbed and catapulted into the other's rotary blades. 'Boshhhzzz!'

Both were launched out of control and whacked against the city wall before dropping to the hard ground. The birds flapped hard again, slowing just above the wreckage, and pushed themselves back up into the sky.

A cloud of dust billowed up. Mechanical spluttering and damaged whirring followed by another loud bang.

We ducked behind our cover at the startling and obvious sound.

I checked after a few seconds. A small flame flickered from the pile of drone metal. A slow beeping began, and then the G13 access gate hissed open.

One of the Security Specialists we had read about appeared outside – in black clothes, as expected – and rushed towards the crash site. The gate hissed closed again behind him.

I glanced over my shoulder at the others, raised and held my hand in a gesture to signal that it was nearly time to spring for it.

'Get your codes ready, everyone,' Lorraine noted.

The Ferfa guard stooped over the beeping wreckage, out to the left of our position, in front of the City wall.

We were pretty much in his blind spot. This was it.
I flicked the fingers of my hand gesture forward and we bolted.

The yellowish ground blurred beneath my short strides. I switched my focus between the ground leading up to the gate and the Security Specialist as we ran. He didn't see us and was spraying the electrical fire with a small can of foam that expanded on impact.
Ed made it to the gate first – something happy in his ears. When the rest of us reached him, he was already keying in his Citizen Code. The gate hissed open for him.
It worked.

He flicked a button on the mp3 player in his pocket to change song, and ran through. He was in.
The gate closed again.
I checked the guard once more, so did Simon. Still crouched over the drones, the fire damage alarms still beeping. Seersha keyed her code in next.
This time, when the gate opened, Ed crouched down from the other side and focused on the metal seal-track that the gate moved on. Seersha jumped through, past him.
He placed his hands just above it. A silvery mist billowed from under them forming an icy sheet over the track and on the wall where the gate had disappeared into.
The hissing sound started again, but this time, the gate jammed and stayed open, stuck with Ed's ice. It jerked back and forth from the wall it was coming out of a little but couldn't close.

Lorraine ran through, followed by Simon.

Just as I was about to go next, an alarm rang out from the gate. Louder than the drones'. The guard jumped to his feet and spun around, catching a wide-eyed look at me as I leapt forward through the gate into the City.

Lorraine quickly stamped on Ed's ice, cracking and kicking it out of the gate's way.

We didn't wait to see if it closed but I heard the hiss again as we legged it.

'Follow Seersha!' Lorraine exclaimed, coming up behind.

The City streets were a blur, but it wasn't packed with people, just a few onlookers in black clothes wondering what the commotion was. They clearly weren't used to commotion. An electrified train zoomed against the direction of our getaway route. We ducked into an alleyway after Seersha.

The alarm in the distance stopped and I felt a little relief. We stayed there for a moment, two silvery buildings on either side of us providing cover.

I took in several recovery breaths with the others – hands on my knees – and looked out into the bigger street from where we had come. A very clean-looking, glassy building stood across the street from us. Green plants hung down from spaces between its windows.

The electric cabling and track for the train ran down the centre of the paved street. No cars, but bigger, longer versions of the drones, with people in them. They were what we had seen from outside just above the wall. They buzzed by not far above head height. But again, not many of them.

It was hard not to get mesmerized by the place.

'Come on, let's keep moving. They'll be looking for us now,' Lorraine said. Seersha agreed, and the girls strode off further into the unfamiliar alleyway. We followed.

It was, again, very new and clean-looking. Everything was, even the back-alleys. I checked over my shoulder at the alley-entrance from the main street: no one was following, yet.

We turned a corner and jogged down another empty alley before coming out onto a busier open space. Seersha slowed her stride and said, 'We can blend in here a bit, hopefully,' to Lorraine.

Lorraine nodded and said, 'act casual' to us all. We fixed our pace to a brisk walk. I lifted my view from the spotless street paving for a second to take in the skyscrapers. I had to, they were the biggest things I had ever seen. I felt dizzy looking up at them. Towers of shiny grey and glass, with gold details here and there, and plumes of greenery in pods at each level up. There were visual advertising boards like giant TV screens at different positions outside the lower floors. I stopped myself from looking for too long in case I started to look out of place. Maybe that's what being a tourist was like?

More citizens on the streets here than before, everyone again in black. Some looked at our clothes and us suspiciously, especially at Simon in his chair, but most didn't take much notice. It seemed our disguises were kind of working. In the middle of the space in front of the surrounding buildings was a square area marked with a thin gold border in the paving. Inside that, a small statue. It looked like The Hawk.

Seersha pulled out the City map we had made and looked back and forth from it and each building in sight. Ed and I stood in front of her as camouflage.

'There,' she said, nodding to the right of the space and pushing between us, straight for it.

We all moved quickly after her again, keeping our heads down. She knew the City best from all the years she had spent studying their internet stuff.

The recurring thought of looking behind every few steps and worrying about a group of security staff arriving happened again for me - but no one so far.

Sure enough, as we followed Seersha, I saw that we were approaching a medium height building with two big, shiny metal antennas sticking out of its roof. Craning my head again, I saw that they reached nearly the height of the skyscrapers. They had red pulsing lights at their tips.

On the front of the building, above two glass doors, a gold sign that read:

*Ferfa Library and Media Centre*

Simon grabbed my arm, and not too loudly said, 'That's it, Bill! The radio station's in there. Let's get them in check.'

# Chapter 48 - The Celebrity

The big glass doors swung closed behind us. Thinking ahead, Ed changed his music selection again with a couple of quick button presses. A head popped up from behind the reception counter that we were now standing a few feet away from.

'Can I help you?' The receptionist asked. Another staff member stood up next to her looking at us uncertainly.

Simon pushed himself suddenly forward and raised a palm at them. They both flew backwards off their feet and to the floor.

Ed followed up by running behind the counter and grabbing the dazed staff by their collars. He lifted them roughly off the ground, up into the air, above his shoulders. Something angry was in his ears again.

They struggled, legs flailing, but couldn't shake his hyper-powered grip. Seersha stepped forward.

'Show us to the broadcasting studio *now* and you won't be hurt,' she said aggressively, more than I had ever heard her before.

They, of course, weren't prepared for such an attack at all as they agreed immediately, stuttering an 'ok, yes.'

Ed lowered them back to their feet slowly while still keeping grip of their collars.

'It's on the second floor, that way,' one of the reception staff gestured to our left.

I could see a flight of stairs through a glass panel in a door where he had pointed. No lift.

Again, automatically, I checked over my shoulder for company at the entrance. Still clear.

Ed walked the two staff members out from behind the counter. Even though he had an angry scowl on his face, he was surprisingly emotionally steady in that state. He kept his hands on their shoulders and we followed them up the stairs. So far, the plan was going well.

When we got to the second floor, I opened the door for Ed to drag them through. We came to an open area with a couch and some computers along a wall in front of some windows. Two more staff members were there; one was typing, the other drinking a cup of something.

With an obvious wave of his hand, Simon made a vase with flowers in it fly across the room and shatter against the wall. The staff sprung upright and backed away from us while glaring in confusion and disbelief at the shattered vase.

'Get down on the floor *now*, or he will break your legs next,' Seersha again threatened. The others and I glanced at her, again a bit surprised at her aggression. This was dead serious. They raised their hands at us, urging restraint, and did as directed. Lorraine hurried towards them and pulled out rope from her bag.

The receptionist that had been directing us pointed shakily at a door in the corner.

'That's it, in there…'

A small sign read, 'Studio 1' above it.

Ed pushed the receptionists towards Lorraine, who had finished tying the other two up.

'You won't get away with this, you know?' one of them said brazenly, sitting on the floor.

'We'll see,' Simon replied nonchalantly, hovering his chair closer to them.

'Once we get our message out, it's "job done", really.'

'Seersha,' I said, looking into her eyes 'let's do it.'

Seersha opened the door to the studio, Simon and I followed her through while Lorraine and Ed kept watch on the staff outside. Inside it was a tiny corridor with another door at the end; this one had a red light above it and a neon sign that said, 'On Air'.

I checked through the thin window in the door and saw a thickly built, short, bald man in black clothes speaking into a big microphone. He was sitting in front of a desk covered in lights and controls and a computer screen.

It was the sound desk and he was the radio presenter. Our eyes met as he was mid-sentence. I opened the door.

Simon rushed forward between Seersha and I. He picked the presenter up into the air with his telekinesis.

'What in Navsplauk is going on?' he exclaimed, his voice worryingly familiar. He writhed and looked, wide-eyed, to the floor on either side of him and back at us, as if he should have been able to escape with sheer eye-brow power.

I noticed the gold name tag on his black shirt as he levitated and flailed;

T.D….it was Thomas Dentridge.


'Do you realise you're interrupting essential news broadcasting? Official business of Ferfa?'

'You mean essential lying and brainwashing?' Simon snapped back, his arm outstretched to guide his hyper-ability. He moved the floating, furiously struggling Dentridge out from the desk and up against the wall.

I followed Simon's snap-back, 'You've imprisoned thousands like us over the years, made invalids of us,' I said with anger, to the voice I had known too well. I moved into the centre of the studio after Seersha – in front of the sound desk – my stare fixed on Dentridge. 'It's going to stop. And we're here to broadcast the truth now.'

Still writhing against Simon's telekinesis, Dentridge kept talking. It obviously came naturally to him.

'You don't know a molecule of it. You wouldn't even be here if it wasn't for Ferfa and EHG's progressive policies. We tell the *necessary* truth here–'

'Si, can you do anything?' I asked, interrupting. 'We need quiet, and he won't shut up.'

Simon nodded and twisted his palm around towards himself. Dangling above the carpeted floor, Dentridge continued to rant at us until Simon clasped his thumb and index finger together at him. Dentridge's mouth snapped shut.

'Perfect,' I said, with a thumbs up to Simon. I took out my notes.

Seersha – now behind the sound desk facing me – clicked and typed at the computer before looking up at me,

'We're ready, Bill,' she said, pushing the microphone on its mechanical arm out in front of the desk towards my mouth. She pushed a red button and said, 'Go for it.', and – with momentum – I didn't hesitate.

# Chapter 49 - Side-mission 

It was done.

Seersha tapped the red 'record' button once more to end the broadcast. She tapped and clicked furiously to complete the technical side.

It had gone into the system.

'There. I've programmed it to go out an hour from now, every hour, until they locate the file, which will be difficult.' She winked. 'It's going out on LongWave and VHF. Well done, Bill.'

'Good. I'll get Lorraine to tie *him* up,' I added. I stuffed the notes back into my bag. 'Oh, and don't forget the playlist…'

Lorraine tied Dentridge up, as Simon held him levitating, before leaving him flat on the floor – still jerking, like a just-caught, bald fish – and we left the studio.

'Where's the library?' I asked the less brazen receptionist. Seersha then exited the studio after us – the broadcast fully in place.

'It-it's down that way…' he replied shakily and motioned with his forehead to the opposite end of the corridor from the stairs.

'We'll be two minutes…' I said to Ed. I nodded at Seersha. One last task before we got out.

Seersha and I ran down the corridor. Sure enough, we passed

a sign pointing to the library down further. It was exciting, we were making a difference, we were in control, and my first thought wasn't fear.

We reached the door to the library. I looked out a window next to it before we went in, at the muted city; more busy and alien than anything I had seen before in my life, but with the familiar hot grey sky above it.

A beeping keypad. Seersha typed in her Citizen Code. The door clicked open. I followed her through.

We walked as casually as possible past another receptionist. She was clearly unaware of what was happening outside of the library and didn't look up at us.

'Excuse me, where are the computers?' I asked mischievously.

She looked up over her glasses, barely moving her head at my inconvenient question and nodded towards the long line of computers about ten yards in front of us before refocusing on her screen.

We went quickly to a computer. Cautious excitement and adrenaline whirled in my chest. I imagined it was what a rollercoaster in one of those theme parks that used to be around years ago might feel like. I was about to see the hidden parts of my life in their archive.

I pulled a chair over next to Seersha and sat on the edge of it. She had instantly got to opening the right software. I scanned the screen eagerly with her. The loading pages seemed to take forever. We had to hurry; word had no doubt been circulated, about our incident at the access gate, to all City security staff by now. She skated the mouse cursor over the various folders inside the database.

'Oh, there's one for the Wellness Centres...I could probably find you that way...'

She clicked on it.

A list of all the centres in Aunn Teer popped up, in alphabetical order. She scrolled down the page. Over half way down.

And there it was: *Pleasant Pines*

A voice from behind us, 'Guys...'. We looked around, startled. No one there.

'It's me...' It was Lorraine. 'Hurry!'

She was talking to us from the corridor outside the library. 'We have company. They're looking for us, we can see them from the window.'

Seersha clicked hastily on the folder. Inside it, there was another one titled *Patients*

There we were, amongst the other names from Floor 1 in Pleasant Pines:

Ed, Simon, Lorraine, Dawhee, Nadine, Gregory, Andrew, Kweeveen, Eugene, me...

Seersha rummaged in her bag and took out a memory stick.

'Can I?' I leaned over to put my hand on the mouse.

'Sure. Just be quick,' she replied while plugging the stick into the computer. I clicked on my name and chewed my lip.

A recent picture of me popped up above a column of information. It didn't really surprise me that they had it but I couldn't work out *how* they had it.

Bill Blythe. My date of birth. Born in Fortuna Hospital, Ferfa. Hair colour. Eye colour. Height.

The date I was evaluated.

Hyper-ability: Zoological linguistics. Vulnerability: Anxiety; Self-esteem.

Parents: Annabelle and Marcus Blythe. My heartbeat sped up as I read their names.

Seersha reached over my arm controlling the mouse and typed a command.

I clicked on my mother's name. *Disappeared.* In bold letters above her physical attributes. Nothing else. Strange.

I went back and clicked on my father's name.

His date of birth. Qualification. Where he worked...Where he *worked?*

Fortuna Hospital. Eye colour. Hair colour. My eyes raced down the paragraph to find the part about his death...

There was nothing about his death. He was alive!

He was *in* the city. Currently working in the hospital. I clicked on a link to the hospital, eyeballs scanning manically for information. It was nearby...

I swallowed the realisation. Another huge part of me had just been flipped upside down again in an instant.

Seersha looked at the side of my face as I stared at the computer screen, sensing my emotion exactly, of course.

'It's ok, Bill. This must feel crazy. But, it was part of their sick plan, to isolate you and-'

'I have to find him,' I cut across.

She looked at me lovingly but seriously in the eye and grabbed my arm,

'Bill, we don't have time.'

'You go ahead with the others,' I persisted. 'I won't be far behind.'

'Bill, we can't…'

'I'm going to find him.'

She knew I wouldn't be swayed.

'Well…I'm going with you so.'

'No, Seersh, it's not safe.'

'One rule for you is it?'

'But-'

'No. I'm going with you. This is a team plan.'

'Alright,' I accepted. I was about to zone off into worried thoughts but she interrupted,

'Come on, don't dwell. I have everything.'

She hit a large button on the keyboard while standing up, pulling the memory stick back out and tugging my arm.

We were off again.


'Thanks,' she said to the receptionist as we left, to keep up the cover. I was still a bit dazed by the news.

We ran back down the corridor to the office lounge area outside the radio studio and rejoined the others.

They started moving towards the stairs exit, eager to go. Seersha looked at me, concerned, waiting for me to tell them about the developments.

'Eh, guys, before we go,' I started. They stopped and half-turned impatiently. 'My Dad's alive. He's here. In the hospital. It's near the route to the gate, I saw it in my file.'

They turned fully towards me.

'Seersha and I are going to go find him. You go ahead and we'll catch up.'

After a short pause, Simon moved towards me with his pokerface.

'Sorry, dude,' he said. 'You're not getting rid of me that easily, even if you're practically married these days.'

Ed and Lorraine stepped forward too, next to Simon.

'Yeah, Bill, we're in this together,' Lorraine said, gently, but convincingly. Ed nodded.

'Eh, guys?' Seersha interjected. 'We don't really have time to get all epic and emotional about this.'

'You're right,' I said. There wasn't time for arguing either. I snapped into movement, and with it, conceded that my friends were coming with me on the side mission.

We rushed down the stairs and scrambled across the empty reception area at the bottom, to the glass entrance doors. Seersha and I checked that the way out on either side of the doors was clear. The search patrol that Lorraine had warned us about had moved on, for now, luckily.

We bundled through the Media Centre doors, back onto the City's weirdly, almost empty streets. Even the buzz of those flying car things seemed to have quietened.

We stayed close to the building walls, moving fast and with a purpose. Nearly back at the alley off the thoroughfare, I pointed to the right, 'It's over there.'

I moved to the front of the group with determination. Anxiety had weeded its way back into my head again - that I was putting the others at risk - but the only option was to recognise it, carry it and keep pushing forward.

I glanced warily behind us once more, into the open space with the statue in the middle, expecting to see a group of

Ferfa security or drones zooming towards us.

Still clear.

We reached the hospital doors undetected. I rushed through, leading.

Being inside calmed me a bit again; it felt less exposed and concerned with us. Without much of a plan or direction, I continued forward, still with that momentum into the white foyer. I looked around. The staff were dressed in black here too and stood out against the white.

'Bill!' Lorraine called with her mind. 'Over here. What department is he in?'

She was standing at a glossy board that mapped out the hospital.

'I don't know,' I replied by thought and shrugged my shoulders. I decided to go to the reception desk, trying to act cool and deliberate.

'Excuse me,' I said to the top of a light haired lady's head. She looked up from her screen. 'I'm looking for Dr. Blythe?'

She blinked at me.   I hoped this would work. 'He's in obstetrics. Do you have an appointment?' Her tone trailed into a suspicious one.

I didn't answer and turned towards the map by the stairs. Third Floor.

'Excuse me?!' she exclaimed, as we all bundled into the stairwell.

The steps flew by in three's beneath my feet as we leapt up them. At the third floor I was out of breath but wouldn't stop. The others were struggling to keep up, even Ed and Simon.

I didn't hold the door for them and powered on into the ward.

'Dr. Blythe?' I asked between breaths at the reception there.

I didn't even know what obstetrics was but I could hear babies crying.

The man behind the counter gestured over my shoulder. They really weren't used to trouble. I guess the 1% crime-rate meant something. He went back to typing and I spun and drove in the direction he had gestured as the others arrived.

'He's down here,' I told them on my way.

'Hey! Do you have an appointment?' he called after me, remembering suspicion.

I hurried down a long corridor with doors on the left and windows on the right. I checked the name-plates on each one. At the fifth door, I stopped. This was the one.

I looked back along the corridor. The others were following but slowed as they saw me standing still, facing the door. I pointed at it and they understood, and I went in.

# Chapter 50 - Only Way Out

He was reading at his desk, down through a pair of silver-rimmed, round glasses. He didn't look up as I stepped inside, easing the door closed behind me. His hair was the same colour as mine with a few flecks of grey. I could see the resemblance. Was this really happening? It felt like a dream, totally surreal.

I tentatively stepped closer – transfixed – towards my father, who had been dead only twenty minutes earlier. He was a doctor, not a drug addict.

'Have you an appointment?' he asked, still reading; his voice was kind of husky.

'Hi...my name's Bill...Blythe. I think I'm your son.'

His eyes instantly widened and his head lifted from the book, turning slowly towards me.

He took his glasses off and stood up. We just stared at each other for a moment.

'Bill?' he said, realisation setting into his face. 'Bill!'

He quickly walked out around his desk towards me and we hugged without hesitation.

I squeezed him back. I didn't know what else to do, but it felt natural somehow, despite all the years and the false-grief and mire of questions in my head.

'You shouldn't be here. It's dangerous for you,' He said, pulling away to look into my eyes, his hands on my shoulders.

'I know. I won't stay long, but can we talk?'

'Yes. Of course.'

He went back to his desk and pulled his chair out around it to face the one in front. 'Don't worry, we should have some time, it's not busy here.'

'My friends are outside. We came to do something. I just had to...see you before we left. They told me you abused me. Why didn't you come find me?'

His facial expression changed from a surprised, bright one to a solemn, regretful one.

'Sit,' he said, locking the door and returning to sit in his chair facing mine. 'Did anyone see you?'

I shook my head, deciding not to worry him.

'Bill, I don't know how much you know about...all this, but I presume, since you're here, you know some.'

Sitting at the edge of the chair, I nodded without blinking. Almost every emotion possible churned around in my chest and stomach. I had a Dad.

'We should be quick, but everything they told you about your Mother and I is a lie, ok?'

Again, with a gulp, I nodded.

'You were two when things started happening. Lots of people had died, people were scared. More and more started latching on to a radical way of thinking. They started to do tests on children. That went on for years. After you were tested, we started having visits from government staff. You were evaluated as having unnatural traits and being a threat to yourself and their version of society.

Your mother stood up to them. Soon after that, she disappeared. No trace. From then, I lived in fear with you, just the two of us. They threatened to take you away. There were rumours about what was happening to other children. And they watched our house and my workplace in Tymblia. In the end, I agreed to work in the hospital here in Ferfa, while you would be placed in a safe, secure facility that they called a Wellness Centre. I agreed because at least I thought you would be looked after. They said you would. It was the only choice I had'

My eyes drifted down to the ground for a second as I processed the truth.

'I was promised they would send me yearly reports about your health and education, which they did, but I was forbidden from contacting you. I was never told where in Aunn Teer the facility was anyway, and there are hundreds.

The AF movement is in total control now. Anyone who defied it was ruined or imprisoned at best. And sadly, most here even support it.'

There was another silent moment between us. I pursed my lips and looked at him. Anger welled in me, but then, also, sadness and a vague nostalgia. At that moment, everything happening outside the room didn't matter.

'When we were together...was it...happy?'

He heard my question intently and then kneeled down in front of me. He put his hand on my shoulder and we smiled a little. A tear formed at the corner of my eye.

'Yes, Bill. It was. Your mother and I loved you, and still love you, very much. You used to love drawing with crayons, and we would play you vinyl records on our stereo at weekends.

You loved to dance. The three of us did, together.'
We both giggled at the memory, the tear dropped down my face as we did. 'The first song you really loved was 'Live and Let Die' by Wings. You used to jump up and down in excitement like a madman when it got to the lively part.' I laughed again. A second-hand first memory.

'Cool,' I said happily, wiping my cheek. 'I always thought the first song I knew was by Boyzone, and I couldn't really remember you or Mum.'
The anger rose in me again, thinking about how my memories had been twisted.
'I hate them,' I said.
He stooped his head to draw my angry stare up from the ground and touched my hand.
'Well, son, it's a gift that you're here. Focus on that.'

Just as he said it, the air trilled suddenly with a piercing alarm. I jumped to my feet and spun to face the door. Instantly, the City came flooding back in.
A commanding voice came from the intercom system,
'This is Ferfa security personnel Captain Bryant. We know your party has illegally entered the City and that you are on the third floor of the hospital. Present yourselves in the foyer now, or you will be taken by force!'
'Bill! Get out here. They're coming up the stairs,' It was Lorraine in my head, through the wall.
I stood and stumbled backwards away from the desk and looked at my father; a twinge of paranoid doubt about him

being in on it entered my thoughts along with panic, but he read my face and moved to quell it, placing a hand on my shoulder.

'You could stay here with me, Bill. They respect me here now. We could apply for your asylum in the court.'

A new life with my Dad flashed through my mind. A chance for normality. And then I remembered my friends outside.

'What about my friends?' I pointed to the door.

He looked behind me and back into my eyes, less confident.

'I'm afraid that wouldn't be possible, I'm sorry. It would just have to be me and you...'

A sadness etched the wrinkles at the corners of his eyes. A weight pulled downwards on my stomach as I thought about the possible futures.

I couldn't abandon them.

'I can't. They're my friends. *They're* my family now.'

He didn't hesitate and stooped in closer, our eyes locked. We didn't have much time now.

'You're sure, son? This might be the last time we see each other.'

I looked into his eyes – they were blue like mine – and nodded. Lorraine popped back into my head, 'Bill! Come on, they're coming.'

My eyes started to dart from the ground to the door behind me and back at my Dad. My breathing got quicker. The panic began to take hold. All at once I felt stuck with indecision and fear about how we would get out of here now and generally overwhelmed by everything that was happening.

My Dad noticed again. He squeezed my arms.

'Don't worry son, follow my instructions. There's a small ladder from the roof. I'll show you the way to the back stairs.'

I snapped back out of it and refocused. He burst past me to the door and unlocked it. The alarm swelled even louder as he opened it and beckoned me out in front of him.

The guys were waiting just outside, anxiously checking back down the corridor for the security staff's arrival. Guilt flashed in my mind again. What had I gotten them into?

'We have to get to the roof,' I told them. They looked warily at my Dad. He brushed past me again and forced his voice above the blaring alarm,

'I'm Bill's Dad. Sorry we can't chat, you'll have to use the roof ladder, now. They'll be swarming this floor and down below soon.'

As he finished the sentence, he began striding towards the end of the corridor to our left and we followed. We *had* to trust him.

He opened a metal door at the end of the corridor and used his planted foot to hold it for us.

'Through here,' he shouted. 'Go!' The guys didn't hesitate.

'Another two floors up. When you get out onto the roof, turn to your right. About 100 yards, at the edge, there will be a ladder. They won't expect you to use it.'

The others rushed up the concrete stairs ahead of me. I stopped and turned to him one more time.

'Thanks, Dad,' I said and hugged him again.

We looked directly into each others' eyes once more and he squeezed my arm again for a moment, and then I ran. That was it.

The sprint up the stairs was a flurry of movement, breath and noise. I caught up with the others after one flight. Seersha stopped for a second to grab my hand. Above the slapping of our shoes on the steps, the alarm kept screeching. Again, it was interrupted by the security Captain's warnings,

'Present yourselves now for immediate processing! You are surrounded and deemed a high level threat to the safety of our City and its people until we verify your identities.'

'Cool, we're "high level threats", ha!' Simon panted. Only Simon could see the light side of a situation like this. We ignored him and kept pushing up the stairs. Then, from the flight below us, there was a bang and a surge of footfall.

'We know where you are! Stop evading arrest, now!' a voice yelled up at us, echoing off the concrete and metal.

It was the security team Lorraine had flagged.

They were worryingly close. I started to consider that we wouldn't make an escape this time. Seersha squeezed my hand, sensing my emotions. We moved as fast as possible.

We turned into the last flight of stairs and the black door for the roof came into view at the top.

Simon waved it open while still hovering forward. The heavy footsteps from below gained on us.

The grey glare from the Sun dazzled us as the exit-door swung open. But it was also a slight relief in my mind - we still had a chance.

Simon, followed by Lorraine, Ed, Seersha and I bundled out onto the open roof. We spun around to find our bearings and look for the escape route. The door swung shut. I spotted the top of the ladder, to the right, as my Dad had directed.

But then, my heart dropped like a stone in the well of my chest when I heard the buzzing. Two drones hovered upwards into sight just above the ladder at the roof's edge, the City skyline behind.
They ascended and twitched to face us, jittering up and down in the air, scanning us for confirmation.
The lights on the front of them glowed red like eyes. They began moving towards us.
We backed away into the centre of the roof. The ladder was our only way out.
I caught Si's eye, urging him to swat them back, but they stayed at a distance to contain us, out of reach.
The exit-door burst open again and the gang of security men filed out. They wore the City's black, helmets and red-lensed, advanced-looking monocles. They raised weapons at us that looked like guns, but with fizzing blue electricity between forks at the end of the barrels.
We were completely trapped.

One of the drones above the ladder swooped over towards the squad and hovered in the air above them. Just above its centre on top of it, a blue light flickered and an image formed.

It was The Hawk.
We backed further away.
He folded his hands and addressed us,
'Ah, the Pleasant Pines escape artists. Good to finally meet you.'

It was a live feed, not a recording. We glanced at each other, hoping desperately that one of us would come up with something.

'What if...we ran at them?' Lorraine stuttered a desperate idea. 'Simon, could you knock them back? Ed, could you help?'

I checked Ed and Simon's reaction. Ed was pale, paler than I had seen him in months, his eyes flicking unconfidently from us to the advancing security unit. He didn't reply.

'There's too many of the-,' Simon conceded.

The Hawk's hologram cut across him, 'Don't try to resist. Our Security Specialists' weapons are well within range and I can immediately set them from stun to kill.

Get down on the floor now and cooperate.'

This was the end of our road.

Everything we had gained in these last few months, after so many years locked away, was about to be torn away from us again. They would probably erase our memories. We wouldn't remember any of this, and that's if they let us live. I had been reckless coming to the hospital.

I felt the panic pulsing upwards in my chest with each breath again, and with every one my chest got tighter. Seersha squeezed my hand harder but everything was going numb and out of control.

I started to feel dizzy, sick.

We inched further back, and then my heel hit the small wall at the roof's edge. I jerked to look behind me in fright; the drop loomed and panicked me more. I jolted forward and rebalanced myself.

'There is nowhere to go,' The Hawk mocked in a fake-reassuring tone. 'Lay down and surrender now. Do not try to use one of your abilities. We will take you to a secure facility for processing. There is no need to panic.'

# Chapter 51 - The Roof's Edge

Ed began to crouch. He was obeying them. He was still very pale, but wasn't turning. This was the end of our silly mission; we were just going to have to give up.

I turned back to the edge again, dismay now taking over from panic, searching with last desperate hope for any kind of exit. Maybe it would be better to jump than be captured by them.

As I looked down at the City below, a glint of silvery metal caught my eye. It was one of those helicars.

It was rising quickly towards the roof, the whirr of its four turbines getting louder on its way.

Then, as if competing with it, the buzzing from the advancing drones on the roof grew louder again. I looked back at them. Another two drones had glided in to join the formation above the security guards. The entire City squad started to fan out into a semi-circle enclosing us. Another warning from the hologram, 'Unfortunately, failure to cooperate now will be dealt with severely, by force.' I ignored the threats and squinted back at the rising helicar. Just as I began to recognize the face behind the wheel, a familiar voice shouted to me from it, 'Bill! It's us! You'll have to jump!'

It was Mynos, in the helicar on Max' shoulder with Godfrey driving.

I stepped backward from the edge, eyes wide, and pulled Ed up from his knees,

'Si, everyone, look! It's Godfrey. They're here for us!'

We had a chance.

The others turned incredulously away from our pursuers to see the helicar hovering just below the roofs edge. In that moment, I dropped all the haggling fears and just went for it; our miracle exit. I grabbed Seersha's hand, pulling her into a short run, and we leapt.

Time almost stopped for that second we were in the air; floating against gravity, away from anything, no past and no future, a basketball shot mid-loop.

We hit the padded back seats hard on landing. The helicar bobbed under our weight, its buzz intensified, but we made it.

It was far from over though.

I scrambled on my hands and knees, flipping myself around to face up at the others on the edge.

'Quickly now!' Max barked at them.

Simon went next. We cleared a space for him. He didn't hesitate and launched himself in his chair with a powerful thrust of telekinesis off the roof.

He balanced himself in the air above, before landing on the back seat next to us. Ed and Lorraine now and we were clear.

Lorraine led Ed's hand to the edge but he hesitated, resisting her pull. They checked behind them. The drones were advancing urgently now - realising what we were doing – each with a hologram of The Hawk above it, the tops of the security staff's helmets beneath.

'No, Ed, not now...' I thought.

Lorraine turned to him, grabbed both his hands and kissed him. He suddenly went a shade less pale, snapped out of the freeze, and they jumped together, just as a security guard skidded up to the edge behind them.

They bundled roughly on top of us on landing. They were in, just. The security guard at the ledge raised his weapon and aimed it at us, but just as he did, Simon waved his hand, knocking it out of his grip. It flew off the roof.

Godfrey slammed on the accelerator and we were off.

We were flung backwards against the seat as the helicar shot forward. I twisted around amongst the bodies to see the rest of the guards grouped at the roof's edge. They shot strands of blue electricity at us, but we were now just out of range.

The four drones, however, were chasing us.

We zoomed away from the hospital and down towards the ground, buildings rising up around us. Godfrey was trying to use them as some cover.

'How are we going to shake them?' I shouted, twisting back around to face the onrushing wind and the back of Godfrey's head.

No answer came from him. His focus was on trying to put space between us and them. We silently urged him on while checking behind every few seconds hoping that they hadn't gained on us.

The City wall neared up ahead. We zoomed past an arrowed traffic sign that said, 'No Exceeding Altitude of 6 Meters'

On the ground, in front of the wall entrance-gate, I could see another squad of security specialists facing us. They had two large bipedal robots among them as reinforcements. It was like a scene out of some science fiction movie. The drones were still only seconds behind us in the air.

Fifty metres between us, the squad and the wall ahead. The big robots fired a weaponised ball each of some kind of electrical plasma at the helicar.

Godfrey swerved violently. We just avoided being hit. You could hear the sizzle of the plasma-ball as it shot past. The drones behind dodged them too. We grabbed onto each other and the vehicle's side-walls as it lurched back and forth into balance again.

Almost in the same movement, Godfrey then jerked the steering handles towards him and we tilted upwards sharply to try to make it over the City wall between two palm trees.

I shut my eyes and braced myself. The helicar angled upwards even more in the air, straining under the weight of us all, clearly not designed for this.

A clang shuddered through the floor of it. We clipped the wall, but we were clear.

'Yes, Godfrey, go!' Simon exclaimed.

The open valley plain was ahead of us, but as soon as that bit of delight glimmered, a drone swooped in from the side, close to the back bumper, with its mechanical arms outstretched. It was reaching for the turbine blades to knock us out of control. Max barked in warning.

Simon reacted fast. He slapped the drone backwards with his open-palmed invisible force. The drone spun out of control and crashed into the sandy soil below, but the other three were still chasing and gaining on us. Behind them, another half-dozen streamed out above the City wall to join the chase, along with two manned helicars. There was a swarm now.

'I can't shake them! They're too close and it's too open here!' Godfrey shouted back at us. I checked over the side of the helicar ahead of us, searching for some cover. Lorraine did the same on the other side. What we already knew: scatterings of wiry trees, mounds of rock, a small boarded up building, nothing substantial. Godfrey kept pushing the helicar but the City swarm kept closing.

I looked at the others, hoping someone had an idea. Ed was really pale now, turning transparent.

And then an idea hit me. I knew it was a long-shot but went with it,

'Ed! Can you make us disappear? Now would be a really good time?' He was tightly gripping the back of Godfrey's seat in front of us, his face worried and whitish grey, but he obviously wasn't scared enough.

'I...don't know,' he shouted to the side, hesitantly. 'I've never tried including my surroundings...and I haven't really been very scared since Pleasant Pines.'

'You need to get scared fast, Edgar, and try it!' Simon snapped. 'They're gaining on us and I can't stop them all!'

'Wait,' Seersha said, grabbing Simon's and my shoulders from between us. 'Move!' she ordered Simon. They scrambled in the tight space to switch places, the helicar bobbing and swaying as we flew on.

She sat up on her haunches on the back seat, put both of her hands on Ed's shoulders and closed her eyes.

'Everyone, grab on to each other!' she shouted, the dry air gushing past, blowing her hair back. We didn't question it.

Everyone grabbed each other, as well as Godfrey and the animals in the front.

I glanced behind us again. The nearest drones were now within a few metres, red sensors standing out more against the grey sky, mechanical arms outstretched, reaching.

This *had* to work.

Seersha bowed her head in concentration. Suddenly, Ed's eyes widened fully in terror and the remaining blood drained from his face. At that moment, the entire helicar, and us in it, disappeared.

It was the weirdest sensation, just zooming forward through the air, without a visible body or anything underneath, but incredibly, it worked.

Godfrey jerked the helicar to the left. The drones kept flying ahead.

I turned my invisible neck, still holding onto the others and saw the swarm of drones followed by the security helicars slowing and dithering in the air in confused directions. They had completely lost us.

We zoomed away in our hidden direction through the valley. The Ferfa squad got smaller behind us with the distance and a cautious smile grew in my cheeks. Godfrey laughed at the windscreen in celebration. 'Well done, Seersha and Ed, well done!'

We kept a hold of each other and drifted forward diagonally away from the City towards the valley ridge, still invisible, until the confused Ferfa drones were specks and the City itself was a miniature silhouette behind us.

The mission was accomplished. We got out, with a little help from our friends.

# Chapter 52 - Fly or Die…

The helicar's nose angled upward with the slope at the edge of the valley. We were nearing The Haven again. Relief and triumph started to dawn on me. We let go of each other and the helicar popped back into visibility around us. I could see my own body again and the others', although Ed was still half transparent and shaken.

Godfrey used the rockier terrain to weave in and out of, for cover in case any eyes were on the area.

We were still full of adrenaline, and surprised delight that he had saved us, *again*, but also a little confused and guilty. How did he know?

We levelled out again at the top of the ridge, the canyon a few hundred metres ahead. I replayed the events in my head. It was actually amazing what we had done, if a little lucky. But I guess you need a bit of luck sometimes.

'That was unreal, Seersh!' I said, leaning close to her ear. 'How did you know it would work?'

'I didn't,' she answered. 'I just...hoped, really.'

We smiled.

'I knew I could affect, but that was mainly pure hope,' she continued. 'Turns out, Ed's pret-ty powerful.'

We turned to Ed, still smiling. The colour had returned a bit to his face and his cheeks went a little redder still at Seersha's compliment. But never one for many words, and definitely not one for victory dances, he fixed his trusty headphones over his ears again.

'What time is it?' Simon asked. The message. Seersha checked her watch and answered, 'Ten minutes…'

We were nearly at the canyon's edge.

The helicar dipped and we hovered down into the air above The Haven, the shade surrounding us.
Godfrey began to bank it and we arced around the top of the Spirit Tree before coming to a rough landing between it and the cabin.

'Home, sweet home!' Simon said while levitating himself out onto the ground before the dust had settled or the rotary blades had slowed to a stop.
The rest of us weren't as confident yet and waited for Godfrey to move.

'Get yourselves some water,' he said, opening the helicar door and cocking a leg out.
I couldn't hold in the question, 'Godfrey, how-'
'Have some water first. Don't forget, we'll have to tune in too.'
He sidestepped the question a bit, but seemed to be implying that he was happy, proud even.

We took his advice and all gulped back handfuls of the waterfall. When we turned back around, refreshed, Godfrey was sitting under the Spirit Tree puffing his pipe with Mynos and Max.
'We're in much more danger now that they know us to be an active threat,' he stated, exhaling a plume of smoke as we

joined him.

I glanced at the others, that bit of guilt returning.

'But well done. In the end, it was always the natural evolution of things, this way.'

Another puff. Simon and Ed looked back at me quizzically. Lorraine was kicking a stone lightly on the ground avoiding eye contact. Seersha stared back at Godfrey trying to read him.

'Sorry...for going behind your back, Godfrey,' I offered.

He smiled slightly and looked at the animals on either side of him.

'No. Don't worry, Bill. I had intended it, really. In a way, I did the same.'

'How do you...mean?'

'I knew you would want this. In fact, I was glad you did. Ultimately, young people have to go out and do big things by themselves at some point or other, to really grow. Even if they're risky.'

He watched another small cloud of his drift up into the sky. The others looked surprised at his revelation, which must have been how I looked too, as it was how I felt.

'In the animal kingdom, at the coast, there used to be a bird called the Guillemot. I'm not sure if they're still around. Their growing up process is spectacular.' I started to relax while listening to him. 'When the chicks are ready to leave the nest, the adult leads them to the edge of a cliff near the colony. They then launch themselves off, above the ocean, attempting to fly as far as possible before crash landing on the waves. Some don't make it. They either fly,' He took another puff. 'or die.'

I could feel a soft smile in my cheeks at his words.

'Mynos here kept me up to date with your plan, but I left you to carry it out, up until that particularly tight spot.'

Simon's mouth opened a bit, realising how wrong he had been about Godfrey. We looked at Mynos, he was cleaning his ears, looking busy.

'You could be here practising your hyper abilities for years,' Godfrey continued. 'But it is only when you use them in real, pressure situations, when you have something to lose, when you improvise, that you really learn and mature with them and in yourself.'

'So, that night, when we argued?' I asked, eyes unfocused to the side, remembering. Mynos had finished cleaning and hopped onto a rock closer to Godfrey's knee.

'Yes,' he answered, without me fully finishing the question.

'Of course, I was a little concerned initially, considering how soon you wanted it after arriving here, but most of my anger was more of a test for you.'

I just stared at him with my eyebrows raised for a moment, sniffed a laugh out my nose and then sat down.

'Mynos and I spoke, and decided it would be best to let you do it, without you knowing that we knew.'

'I knew too,' Max added, to me, sitting back on his hind legs, snout high.

'Right...well, that's news,' Simon quipped.

'Speaking of... your message will be going out in...' he checked his watch.

'...six minutes, yes?' Seersha nodded back. 'Well, we can't miss that!'

Godfrey was about to stand, when Seersha blurted, 'Since we're on confessions…'

My heart sank a little, what now?

She turned to me, 'Bill, I should tell you,' Our eyes met. 'I knew about your parents...As well as being able to sense and alter people's emotions, I can see into people's past and future when I touch them.

I stared at her for a moment. 'Whoa,' I mouthed, glad that I was sitting. She continued before the silence got awkward.

'But, I stop myself normally, because it's private obviously, especially with the future, and that's not exactly set in stone anyway.'

The others watched our exchange.

'But when we kissed the first time, that night with the blá, I couldn't stop it and I saw your parents with you, and I knew they were good.'

I gulped. She grabbed my hand.

'I never meddle though, and it seemed private to you, but I knew I could still help you find out for yourself.'

Then I felt a warm feeling in my chest for her; love I suppose it was, maybe, not that I was an expert; and realisation.

'And I just wanted to tell you, all of you, because who need's secrets?' she added.

'You did seem very ok with going through the data-base in the library…' I thought out loud.

'Oh, and I have the digital key to their frequency blocker now too,' she remembered out loud.

Lorraine's eyes widened and she asked,'Does that mean we can broadcast from here?'

Smiles happened on our faces.

'Yup,' Seersha replied, to which Simon said, 'Nice!' and rubbed his hands together.

'Thank you, Seersh…' It was all I could say. It *was* nicer not to have secrets, not anymore. I felt lighter. Hopefully that would be the new normal.

I turned to Godfrey, 'And thank you. Even when we doubted you, Godfrey, you still saved us.' The others agreed and thanked him too. Simon apologised for being so suspicious.

'No worries, Bill, and you all,' he exhaled another ring of smoke and coughed a chuckle. 'It's what needed to be done. And it's understandable, after everything you've been through, that you had doubts. We're all each other has now, and we need to help each other along through the difficult and easy; and most of this world is far from easy.'

He checked his watch again and stood up.

'Best get moving now, don't want to miss it. Seersha, tune us in!'

As we walked together to the cabin, there was movement in the sky. My eyes darted towards it.

A group of birds. It was Ollie.

He swooped down out of their formation and landed in front of us on the edge of the cabin's roof that jutted out from the rock.

'That was a close call back there,' he said to me. 'But *brilliant* to see. Well done, they weren't expecting that.'

'Thanks, Ollie, for the help. It's good to still know you, and

that you're living your best life,' I responded, pointing up.
Godfrey stopped at the door and looked back at me using
my hyper-ability.
'They will be searching for you now, Bill,' Ollie continued.
'Things will be different. We will keep watch up above for you.'
I thanked him again.
'When you see us circling above your tree, that's the signal.'
And he took off again to rejoin the flock.

# Chapter 53 - True News 

We all gathered into the tight Receiver Room and waited eagerly, and slightly nervously, for our broadcast. Seersha clicked and twisted buttons and knobs to tune us in.
'"The State of the Nation"!' Simon dubbed it.
I fidgeted with my hands and looked around the room, from Seersha's posters to my seven friends. And I thought of Ollie again; how amazing it was that his spirit was now as a bird, like he always dreamt of.
After this went out, The Haven might not be our home for much longer; like Ollie said, they *would* start searching for us more intensively. But that was for another day. All that mattered was now; a good rule to live by in general.
Hearing this go out would be a great feeling; knowing that more people's minds would be opened to new possibilities; believing in themselves.

Mynos hopped up onto my lap, both ears pointed forwards at the table-speakers. Godfrey never smoked in the cabin before, but he was now, in celebration I guessed.

'Ok…' Seersha said after she'd finished the set-up. Her hand rested on the laptop-mouse. 'We might have some airtime after the message and the playlist, before they get a handle on the situation and go to dead air. I've patched us into their frequency with the key.'
Godfrey chuckled, 'Very good…'

'So, I was thinking, does anyone want to add another song?' she continued.

'Any requests?'

Ed was first to respond, delighted at the possibility of being a DJ, 'Cool.' he said quietly, sitting forward. 'How about System of a Down? Do we have anything by them?'

'Yup, I have all their albums on here,' Seersha replied and instantly began searching the laptop with the mouse-cursor for them.

'How about, "Toxicity"?' Ed suggested. I knew that track.

'Yeah, good call, Ed!' she commented and clicked. 'Good lyrics...Is that cool with everyone?'

We all agreed. We trusted Ed and Seersha on all things music. Godfrey even resisted a debate on it.

There was about a minute to go until the clock hit the hour. I remembered my Dad, and wondered whether I would ever see him again. But at least I had this gang. We were a nice, weird little family in our own way.

The Aware FM music rumbled into the speakers. I clenched my jaw. Seersha jolted forward to raise the volume on the console. This was it.

'Here we go!' Simon said. Seersha sat back into her chair again and put her hand on mine.

The music ended. There was dead silence from the speakers and ourselves. No Dentridge, nothing.

I felt the tip of an anxiety spike enter my chest.

What if it hadn't worked? But then I heard my voice.

'To the people of Aunn Teer, especially those in the Wellness Centres of the world, my name is Bill.' I sounded a bit nasally. Did I really sound like that? 'Please listen carefully, this is very important and I have to be quick.'
I imagined The Hawk and his staff now scrambling to figure out what was happening, who the rogue voice belonged to and how it got there. The staff in the Wellness Centres probably wouldn't even have noticed it yet. But I reckoned the residents would have.
'I am making this broadcast to tell you that the care you seem to be getting and the news you hear every day is a lie. Not real.
You are prisoners. You have been brainwashed your whole lives, to doubt yourselves, to feel weak and afraid and sick.
But you have special abilities, called hyper-abilities, within, that the medication hides. You have talents and confidence deep inside you. They don't want to see it come out. They want to keep you sick. There is more to this world and life for you.
The truth is, you are unique, gifted and able. Don't be afraid. Believe in your weirdness. Question what they tell you. Don't take their medicine. Don't let them separate us.
I have escaped a Wellness Centre with others, and you can too, just believe in yourselves and not the fear they have created in your heads.
We don't have to let them create a world designed only for and by them.

You can help create your own world.'
Seersha half-smiled at me and squeezed my hand.

'There is only one city. It's called Ferfa, and it is controlled by a man called Elron Hawking Goode and his politics and religion.

They created the so-called Wellness Centres you live in and they create the news media you hear every day, both to imprison and brainwash you without your realising.

All of the deaths and crime in the news aren't true.

If you reject that and accept this real truth that I am telling you, then you will be on the first steps to real freedom and fulfilment.

Don't take the medication if you can, try to really live. There is more out there for you. And you can survive outside of their walls.

When you look up at that grey sky from now on, know that it was once a bright blue, and just over the wall, the sun rises and sets in green and purple every day. Together, we can be stronger as individuals.

Search for your talent. Keep going. This is the real truth.
Mind yourselves.'

On my last word, the opening guitar melody from 'The Day I Tried to Live' by Soundgarden played into every Wellness Centre across Aunn Teer, and it felt like we had done something good.

# The End

Team Phoenix Extraordinary Playlist for Pirate Broadcast:

1: Soundgarden - The Day I Tried to Live
2: The Cure - Friday, I'm in
Love
3: R.E.M. - Radio Free Country
4: Grín Day - Welcome to Paradise
5: Sex Pistols - Anarchy in the City
6: Leonard Cohen - The
Future
7: The Beetles - All You Need is Love

Bonus tracks added by Ed:

• System of a Down - Toxicity
• Susanne Sundfør - Reincarnation

Acknowledgements:

Thanks to everyone who helped me bring this book to life.

To my partner Noelle who always encouraged me to write from an initial idea but then made me work hard for compliments.

My parents, Irene and Dermot, my sister, Leah, for always being there. (Hi, Layla)

Cethan Leahy who helped with editing from an early draft and gave me great encouragement. I highly recommend you check out his excellent YA book 'Tuesdays are Just as Bad'.

My boss, Ray, at MusicZone for giving me a dream job, reading, helping and being a great friend.

Lorraine and Shane for being great friends and inspiration.

Frank for reading and feedback - sound.

Stephen for helping me with cover and other image ideas - sound.

Luke and Adam for curiosity.

Irene for interest, social media info and being a great pen pal.

Kieran for publishing info.

Terry, Sean, Peter, Penel, Rich and Maurice for encouragement.

Cinema Dave for song suggestions and wise words.

Everyone who helped in big or small ways.

My mental health battles.

All things creative.

To anyone with life struggles, I hope you might find some comfort or hope in this book. You will get beyond the tough times.

To those who have fallen, you will always be remembered.